JUSTUS: BLOODWATER

JUSTUS:
BLOODWATER
Geoffrey Sadler

NEW ENGLISH LIBRARY

A New English Library Original Publication, 1982

First NEL Paperback Edition July 1982

NEL Books are published by
New English Library,
Mill Road, Dunton Green,
Sevenoaks, Kent, a division of Hodder and Stoughton Ltd.

Photoset by Parker Typesetting Service, Leicester
Printed in Finland by Finland Printers

British Library C.I.P.

Sadler, Geoffrey

Bloodwater.—(Justus; 2)
I. Title II. Series
823'.914[F]   PR6069.A3/

ISBN 0-450-05440-3

Bloodwater

BEFORE HIM the ground shudders, the high grass cleaving apart to the moving shape in the water. White birds bursting upward in a cloud from the reeds. Clamour of cries and beating wings over-head, blinding and deafening. He sees the spit of land ahead, springs for it in the moment before the gator hits. Mary screams out as the heavy snout slams into the mudbank and slides away. Landing beyond, crouched in the soft, yielding muck, Justus draws the long-barrelled pistol, looking back. Gator snorts, shakes his broad-jawed head. The long shape swings away from the bank, gliding out along the narrow channel between the reeds. One last glimpse of the wet armoured back, gleaming grey-black in the green water, and he's gone. Only arrowing eddies on the surface to mark his passage.

'You okay now, honey?' Justus says.

Mary nods, still pale and tight-lipped from the gator's lunge at the bank. Her own light bow is slung at her back, the arrows, like his, slung from a cord at the neck. She's tied back her white-blonde hair in a horsetail from her face, but the marks of travel show on her plainly: her eyes huge in a face pale and haggard from lack of sleep, the print dress stained with mud and filth, its hem tattered about the knees, bare legs splashed black with that same foul-smelling mud that plasters him from head to foot. Seeing him standing upright and alive across from her, she smiles.

'I'm fine,' Mary says.

Her eyes take in the man before her, the tall, bush-headed height of him, the wide massive set of his shoulders and chest, the body of him black and gleaming, sweat giving the ebony of his skin a smooth, polished sheen. Seeing too his narrow waist, the power of the loins and the straddled legs beneath, Mary's smile brightens, her look becoming almost possessive. This is *her* man, now. He belongs to her, and she to him.

She wouldn't have it any other way.

That same moment, Justus studying her with his own dark eyes, seeing her as if for the first time, whole and entire. Her beauty. Her whiteness. Her selfhood. Spirit. Whatever it is makes her different from any other he has known. Already he knows a closeness with this white woman such as he has never known before. Even Nestor didn't git this close, he figures, wondering a while at the strangeness of it all—that one so unlike himself at first glance should have come to know him so surely in this short time. Knowing all the same that it's the truth.

Wouldn't have promised Sheba like he done Mary, that for sure.

'Good 'nough,' Justus says. He leans over, pushing the gun into his belt and reaching for her with his other hand. The hickory spear hung at the wrist on thong of hide. Free hand coming round to clasp at her waist as he sheathes the pistol. His grip fastens on Mary's wrist, drawing her forward in the moment she leaps. He catches her as she lands, swaying to stand in the ankle-deep mud, spattering them both with a fine black spray. She gasping, breathless as she falls against him, held safe in his black, thick-muscled arms. For a while they stay that way, two figures pressed close together on a narrow spit of reed-grown mud, the only standing shapes to be seen from horizon to horizon.

By now they're a way south, the river itself puttering out to spread in a maze of marshy creeks and inlets. Not a tree to be seen in this brackish wilderness. High coarse-fibred grass and reeds the only vegetation, a tall, green sea reaching to their waists, stretching endlessly on, dimming to merge with the sky on the rim of sight. Hardly a foot of solid earth to be found. Under the grass screen it's most of it water, green again and thickly scummed, a hiding-place for gators and cottonmouths, birds nesting along the mud banks of the inlets. And overhead the immense reach of the sky itself, grey and dark as a gator's hide, telling of storms to come. Thunder rumbling far in the distance as they stand to look, lightning a pale, fitful trembling between earth and heaven at the far lip of the horizon.

A fearful loneliness to this place, where only reptiles and marshbirds exist under the open stare of the sky. Man gits to feelin' stripped naked by it, robbed of the thick cover of the trees and thickets further north.

This a whole different world, an' right now he don't like it none.

'Figger you kin go on a ways?' he asks her, and she nods her fair head, doggedly. Forces a smile as she looks up into his face.

'Got to get there, ain't we?' Mary says. She still holds to his hand, reluctant to part from him even by a touch. 'From the look of it, we got a whole way further to go yet . . .'

'Yeah, that right.' Smiles back at her, his hand squeezing her own. Since they left the shelter and struck southward, Mary has ploughed with him through the worst of the marshy plain. Not a word of complaint. 'Had you figgered for a good one from the first . . .'

Pausing, he gazes out over the arid ocean of green that shivers sidelong to the pull of the wind. Don't do to look too long. Man wouldn't care to take another step.

Justus scowls, flexes his broad shoulders, the old whip-scars itching along his back as midges cluster on him in the sweating heat. Now he remembers Lawrence. His master on Sweet River. The man who put them scars in his back. Took Sheba from him, too, his woman, to be Lawrence's own bed-wench up at the big house. Yeah, an' had Justus hisself fed up like to a stud bull, an' set him to serve them other planters' wenches in the old feed barn, with the bunch of them white bastards lookin' on . . .

He broke from there, been runnin' ever since. Was old Nestor helped him most, he figures. Tole him 'bout how black folks had their own land back in A–frica, set him to head for the big water where he kin maybe git a ship. Nestor taught him to stand up, be a man. How to stay free, not jes' from Lawrence, but in his own mind. That mean a lot to him. He ain't about to forget it.

Don't mean to forget Lawrence, neither. That sonofabitch run him through the bayous, huntin' him like a wild beast long as he could. Maybe he still ain't given up. One day, Justus reckon he go back there. Settle with that one for good an' all.

Not Lawrence only. Jacob too, the black, yellow-eyed driver they got on Sweet River. Was Jacob laid the whip to his back, an' killed his mama too, when she died bearin' a stillborn chile to that bastard, while Justus still nothin' but a baby . . .

Yeah. He got some settlin' up to do, sure enough. Come the time.

Shakes his head fiercely. Coming back sudden to where he stands.

'Let's go,' he tells her.

Thunder mutters afresh in the distance as they start out along the spit of reeds and mud, one behind the other. She letting go his hand as he moves ahead, treading warily on the black, treacherous surface. The far-off sound passes in a moment, an eerie stillness taking over. Force of the abrupt silence is crushing, robbing them somehow of the power to speak. Only the thick squelching of their own footfalls coming back to them as they follow the thin track that leans above the water, as if they walk alone in a land of ghosts.

Under his feet the mud yields suddenly, plunging him ankle-deep in the stagnant water. Justus spreads his arms as he sways to hold his balance, feet splaying, toes digging hard in the black submerged silt below the level of the water. For a second looks like he might go down, but he stands at last, one hand gripping to the reeds beside his head. Mary, who has come cat-footing in behind him the moment the ground gave way, halts above him, smiling. She is already bending to take his arm and help him up, when the look of his hard eyes stays her.

Quiet, that look tells her, though no word is spoken. *Listen*.

Mary listens.

First off she thinks it's the thunder returning. Distant rumble in the dark low-bellied clouds. Then, as no answering strike of lightning comes, she knows it's something else. Another sound, this, from thunder. Deep-toned, throbbing, insistent. And it doesn't end. Its beat like to a heated pulse, hurrying. A dull, pulsating sound that goes on and on, endlessly.

'Drums, somewhere,' Mary says.

In the water below her, Justus makes no move. Stands there, his great body stiffening as his head cocks to the sound, feeling that harsh, insistent pulse beat in the tides of the blood, thudding at his temples and beneath the skin of his wrists. His dark face gone thoughtful, remembering.

You hear a drum beat, you know it, Nestor told him once.

Drums. Threat muttering in the sound as he listens. Now he knows why the masters took them from their black slaves, way back in Nestor's time. These drums ain't like the stuff the white soldiers play. These drums talk. Right now he ain't figured what they sayin', but he don't care for the sound of it overmuch.

Justus shivers, shaking himself clear of the throbbing sound. He's already turned, floundering up the slippery bank, when Mary screams out above him.

'Dear God!' the woman shrieks. She swings away, choking, her hand to her mouth.

Up on the bank, scanning the desert of grass and reeds beyond, Justus sees nothing at first. Then, as his eyes grow accustomed to the play of light and shadow among the green stems, they too find what Mary found.

Near the end of the narrow spit, close to where the mud runs out, a long shape lies wedged in a tangle of reeds: a hollowed-out log canoe, lifting and rolling to the pull of the water. It wasn't at that, though, that Mary screamed.

The nearest of the other shapes floats by him that same moment, bobbing among the weeds and scum at the surface. He sees the outline of a spread, rigid hand in the water, and beyond it the remnant of an arm. White arm, he figures, though by now it hard to tell. Flesh gone foul and ugly-coloured from bein' so long in the water. No fingers to the hand; a row of sockets bared to the bone, and down below, someplace close to the elbow-joint, the flesh took off again, like somethin' sheared it off clean, the way a hacksaw carve through a limb of wood. He sucks in his breath at the sight, feeling the bile rush in his throat. Back of him, Mary kneels over in the mud, harsh animal sounds coming from her as she spews into the green water.

He cain't turn back to look to her. Not now. His glance is fixed on these floating fragments that litter the surface, sound of the drums muttering on and on as he stares at them, his stomach turning. He sees a coiling string of guts that shimmer, rainbow-like,against the weeds and spawn. Cut through again at the edges, cleaner'n a knife. On beyond, another chunk of what was once a man or woman. By now it like to a rotted side of beef, shorn rib-bones gaping through the flesh. White, seething mess of maggots busy in the floating meat. He gags as it washes by him, noting again the sheared-off edge to the carcass, cut down the line of the busted ribs. By now he figures he someplace near knowin' how it come about.

Somethin' with teeth done that, he reckons. Somethin' like he ain't never seen.

Further away, pinned halfway under the upturned log, another shape washes back and forth. Choking already on the vomit in his throat, he takes a forward step. Peers down into the water.

Was a head, once. Man's head. Leastways, still got the beard clinging to the bone of the jaw. Now the long hair is trapped in the splintered wood of the canoe, leaving it to bob helplessly back and forth underwater. Looking down, he meets the stare of empty eyesockets. The nose, too, is gone. And the flesh of the mouth and chin. The stripped skull lifts once more to the eddying movement of the water, showing him the severed bone of the neck. Cut off like to the rest, clean as a whistle.

In the distance the sound of the drums quickens, stuttering to life. Over it, the rumble of thunder returning, louder than before as the dark cloud rushes towards them. In the green shallows by his feet, the moving head grins up to him, sightless now.

He leans, feeling a churning in his gut as it heaves up against his throat. Vomit gushing thick from his open mouth, spattering the unspeakable shapes beneath. Justus shuts his eyes, groaning. Spits, shaking his head against the foul taste in his throat. Behind him, Mary's vomiting gives way to a hoarse retching sound. Her voice through it, whimpering. A child in the dark.

'Oh, God . . . *no* . . . *no* . . . Can't stand no more . . . oh, my Lord . . .'

Shaking her head as he turns, going to her. Shuddering like in a fever as he lifts her up, holding her against him, wiping the last dribbles of bile from her mouth. Stroking her pale, tangled hair until she quiets at last, clinging to him, eyes closed against the things in the water.

12

'Reckon you know who they might be?' he asks at last.

Shuddering still, she shakes her head. 'Cajun folk live out here.' Mary's voice trembling as she speaks. Her eyes open now, but turned from the water beyond. 'Caleb told me how they use them hollow logs—pirogue, they call it . . .' Memory of what she has seen comes back sudden and she flinches, shivering, her hands gripping to him. 'Justus, what you figger did all this? Gators, you reckon?'

Overhead the black bellying clouds sweep closer, a stir of wind lifting the margin of reeds, swaying the tall stems. In his ears the drumming gains speed, pattering like to a fall of rain.

'Ain't gator,' he says, frowning as he shapes his head. 'No gator got teeth for that kinda bite.' He sighs, scanning the vast belt of land that lies shadowed to the coming storm. 'Don't know what in hell it is, honey. Sure hope we don't meet up with it, is all . . .'

The storm is directly above them now. Blue-white sizzling flash as lightning strikes into the reeds. Fierce burst of light mirrored in the water as the world pales and darkens again in a moment. Booming crack of thunder follows close, whip-lashing away across the far reaches of the sky. With the sudden noise Mary cries out, pressing herself to him.

That same instant, the reeds quiver on either side of them, and other dark figures come into sight, rising silent as ghosts from the high green fronds that hid them a moment before.

Reaching for the gun in his belt, Justus finds himself surrounded. Standing shapes in the reeds all about them, their hard eyes upon him, and their weapons levelled. Scanning the ring of ambushers, his gaze is caught and held by the man directly in front. A bent, hump-shouldered figure standing straddle-legged among the reedbeds. Black like himself, the thick curled hair a salty grey. What holds him most for the moment is the heavy shotgun the man has aimed for his chest. At that distance the twin black holes of the barrels are huge, fearsome. Justus clenches his teeth, willing himself to stare back into the bore of the gun. Still he doesn't loose his hold of the long-barrelled pistol. Across from him, the bent man in the reeds smiles. Signs to the others with a shake of the head.

'Go git him,' the man says.

Splash of feet in the muddy shallows as the ring closes on him. Justus holds level on the midriff of the man in front, scanning the advancing faces from the corner of his eye. Closest of them is a slim, smooth-limbed figure whose coppery skin catches the fitful light, gleaming as the bare legs stalk in through the water and reeds. With a sudden shock he sees it's a woman, her loins covered by a breech-clout, her breasts bare. Same glance takes in the features of her face, tawny and smooth-skinned, high in the cheek-bones and with an Indian sharpness to the angle of the jaw. Her nose, though, is broad, almost flat at first sight. The lips, too, are full and thick, like to his own people. For an instant the look of her threatens to daze him—but only for an instant. He has already seen the weapons she holds: in the left hand, a broad-bladed cane knife, in the right, a stone-headed club.

Behind her, shapes of the others, closing in. Not a white face among them, he notices. Every one black or Indian, or like the woman, a mixture of both. On his far side he glimpses a stocky, broad-set Indian whose hair is stuck thick with egret feathers. Glaring on him, hook-nosed behind the levelled bow. Couple of paces along comes a tall thin-limbed black with a hefted fish-spear, stalking the shallows like a hunting bird, covering the ground in long-legged strides. Must be more'n a dozen of 'em, he thinks. And none of 'em armed any better than he is. Best he's seen is an old long-barrelled musket and the shotgun. But against so many he hasn't a hope.

Hiss of lightning sudden at their backs, the world whitening for the instant. The woman stands in the water below him, looking up into his face. Black, intense stare of the eyes goes clear through him, or seems like. Justus takes in the blue-black sheen of the hair she wears braided to the shoulder; the high lifted breasts, so close now he can see the gleam where sweat runs down between. She eyes him a long moment, studying. Same way Lawrence use to eye the black women back on Sweet River. From him her look switches to Mary. She smiles.

'This one for me,' the woman says.

He hears Mary gasp, drawing back against him, the others murmuring round as thunder blasts overhead and the first heavy raindrops start to falling. Below him, the woman lunges, the thick-bladed knife swinging up for a blow. Justus' left arm comes across Mary's body like a bar of black iron, the wrist-hung spear hefting into the palm. Its point holds level on the spot between the woman's lifted breasts.

'No!' His voice low-throated, growling. 'She's mine!' The knife halts in mid-swing. The woman gives back. He can feel her eyes on him still, her glance running over every inch of his body, the smile still at her lips. Justus scowls, uncomfortable even this close to death. This one took a shine to him, that for sure.

That same instant the rain slams down, a drenching sheet, riddling the surface of the shallow water all around. From in front he hears the man with the gun call out.

'Git 'way from him, Jewel!' the bent man says. 'He for the god!'

Abruptly the woman's smile vanishes. Jewel's knife-arm goes down. She steps back into the circle of waiting figures about her. There are other women among them, too, he sees; one black as himself, the other a copper-skinned Indian squaw. Both of them carry long-bladed knives. Up ahead, the man with the gun steps from the reeds, walking the narrow spit towards him.

Justus takes in the humped shape as it comes towards him, bent beneath the thrashing downpour that hits the open land. Close to, he sees one shoulder is humped higher than the other, on a level almost with the head itself. Like those around him, the man is naked to the waist, and his black skin has a faded, grey colouring to it—like Nestor, maybe, or William, he thinks. Through the sheeting rain the face meets him, back of the long gun: a harsh mask, twisted askew, the nose busted, splayed across the cheeks. Over the ridged cheek-bones one eye stares, a blind, milky white. The good eye fixes him, glaring, a strange, startling green in the black of his face.

'Yeah.' The single eye scrutinising him. The thin-lipped mouth wrenches into a grin. 'Yeah, you be good for the god. He like 'em strong . . .'

'What god you talkin' 'bout?' Hardly able to speak now. Rain blinding him, filling his mouth. Streaming in freshets from his shoulders and chest. Abruptly the green eye hoods, the grin fading.

'But one god hereabouts,' the bent man says. 'He call Shango.'

Murmur of assent from the rest, who stand close, their weapons lifted. Beyond them, the thunder rattles, receding as the rain pelts down with redoubled force. Against his back he can feel Mary's moist body, shivering. He too shivers—but not from the cold.

Shango. God of storms an' lightnin's. He out here!

An' they got him picked fer a sacrifice.

Justus bares his teeth, snarling down the shotgun's barrel. His own pistol is inches from the short man's belly.

'You lay a hand to me, you be daid yo' self,' he says.

The expression of the other man doesn't alter. He stays where he is, feet planted in mud, holding the long gun on this huge black man in front of him, ignoring the pistol aimed at his own gut.

Around them the circle wavers. The tall black spearman with the pecking walk makes as if to come in, but a look from the bent one stays him.

'Stay back, Heron,' the one-eyed figure says. 'He cain't take us all, an' he know it.'

Even as he speaks, another man breaks from further along the line, a heavy, wide-shouldered black who nearly matches Justus himself for size. Coming in at a run. Right arm upswung. Justus catches the glint of a lifted blade—cane knife, like the woman Jewel had. The man's left arm hangs useless, withered like a dead tree limb. The hand lacks fingers, bent and twisted to a grotesque hooked shape. From here Justus can see the bared teeth, the eyes rolling in the head. Splashing in through the shallows by his feet, shouting as he comes.

'I take 'em, Soldier!' the big man yells.

'Claw!' Soldier barks at the running figure, his shotgun wavering for the moment. 'Claw, I'm tellin' you . . . stay back!'

His words go unheeded. The man already scrambling up the bank. The others moving in, already too late to halt him. Back of him Mary screams.

Justus catches the moment's flicker of indecision in that one good eye. He goes in fast, swatting the long barrel up and to the side, his own gun barrel prodding hard into the lean ribs near to the heart. Soldier grunts in sudden pain, the gun going off skyward with a shattering blast that outdoes the thunder. Justus grabs the thin neck, swings the smaller man round bodily before

16

the rest can close in. His eyes rake over his shoulder as he moves, looking for Mary as Claw springs up the bank.

'Git back of me!' he shouts.

Too late. Claw is already on them, the heavy knife whistling back for the cut. Halfway blocked from him by Soldier's scrawny body, Justus glimpses again the mad, terrifying stare of the eyes. The yellow teeth, bared like a dog's in the black of the face. Mary is someplace back of him, leaning away from the coming blow. Grappling, holding close to the old man, he swears viciously through his teeth.

At the peak of his swing Claw halts, howling, his eyes rolling back. The rest scramble hastily to land as he stands, yelling, flailing in the water. All eyes on him now, as his shrieks grow louder. Claw drags one leg free of the water, beating at it. Letting go the knife. At once an answering shout goes up from the watchers around him. Each one seeing in that moment the dark lashing shape that clamps itself fast to his lower leg. Suddenly those still in the water are scrambling hurriedly for the nearest muddy ground.

Cottonmouth!

Justus draws a harsh breath, heedless for the moment of the breaking ranks of his ambushers. He lets go Soldier, pitching the short man to the ground, the long-barrelled pistol still levelled as he glances round for Mary. He needn't have worried. The white girl has picked up Soldier's fallen shotgun. Now she stands straddle-legged at his back, hefting the gun like a club, eager for the chance of a blow for Jewel's head, below her in the water. Justus grins savage as a wolf. Looks like they kin put up a fight, between them.

Claw is down in the water, screaming and thrashing, his limbs convulsed. None of the others venture towards him as the snake slips from the body, gliding easy through the green shallows for the bank where the two of them stand. Its head lifting again as it sees them there. On hands and knees alongside him, Soldier pales, his one eye fixed on the wriggling shape in the water.

'The god! The god come!'

The others take up his call, kneeling as Soldier kneels, their heads bowed. Jewel, easing out from the water, sprawls on all

17

fours near Mary's feet, her dark head within reach of the shotgun's butt. As yet, Mary hasn't seen the snake.

Cottonmouth leaves the water, slithering on its belly over the mud. By now its head is inches from his bare straddled feet. Claw still screaming out in the water beyond him. Justus remembers Burns, and swallows, sweating hard despite the hammering fall of rain. At his back he feels her turn, hears the sudden horrified gasp as she sees the creature below them.

'Don't move,' Justus says. He doesn't turn his head, eyes on the snake as it sways close to one itching foot in the mud. 'An' don't call out—he don't like it none.'

Mary stares at him, uncomprehending, wondering if for the moment he's lost his mind. All the same she stays quiet, her blue eyes widening as the cottonmouth edges closer.

Justus still standing, eyeing the flat, levelled head and open mouth and fangs. He could always use the gun, he figures, but ain't no tellin' if he be fast enough. Then, too, he recalls what Nestor tole him 'bout the spirit in a snake. These folk know it too, seems like. He holds where he is, his dark glance fixed on the snake beneath him. Teeth clenched hard, fighting to quell the trembling in his gut.

The snake glides to a hand's breadth of him, swaying its head, uncertain, seeing he makes no move. The thrashing in the water behind distracts it. Abruptly the cottonmouth loses interest. Slides away over the mud and into the shallows, a dark whip-lash shape arrowing through the water, to be lost from sight in the drumming rain.

Justus draws breath, his belly heaving, Mary leaning on him with a shuddering sigh, the heavy gun dropping to the ground. Hearing the thunder and the distant drumbeats clearly now, sensing them as something apart from the thudding pulse in his temples, the hammering of his heart. Around them the ambushers still kneeling. Their eyes on the two standing shapes. Uncertain. Wondering.

'It's a omen, sure,' the woman, Jewel, says. Her eyes on him yet, appraising.

In the green water by his feet Claw flails out wildly, shrieking in agony, the horror of certain death upon him. The withered hand digs mud below him. The half-sunk face upturned, its eyes rolled back, the open mouth gasping for breath. Meeting that terrible stricken look, Justus knows a momentary anger and swings on the kneeling figures hunched beneath the rain, snarling.

'You his friends, goddammit! Ain't you gonna help him none?'

Down beside him, the pistol inches from his head, Soldier glances up. Wary as he is, the one good eye holds a hint of contempt.

'Ain't ours no more,' says the veteran. 'He belong the god. The god took him.'

Justus swears, turning from him, looking again to the bulky yelling shape in the water. Seen close and helpless, Claw is suddenly a pitiable sight. Sure, he left Burns, that other time; but he had to run then, and Burns was white. Somehow, this one ain't the same.

'I sure as hell doin' somethin',' he says.

Gritting his teeth, he lifts the long gun, levels on the spot between those rolling eyes. The shot roars sudden, deafening, the butt thumping into his palm. Above the eyes Claw's head shatters, disappearing. Force of the heavy slug flings him over, rolling a moment before he lies still. Presently he floats face-up in the shallows, his limbs stiffening. Blood and a strange greyish muck spilling from the ruin of his skull, littering the green of the water.

In his nostrils the stink of gun smoke is almost unbearable, setting his eyes to watering. He stands, watching the sprawled body in the inlet. Anger in him still, overriding his fear for the moment: anger at Claw and his so-called friends, who would have left him to die slowly and painfully from the cottonmouth bite, rather than risk themselves.

'Ain't you gonna pick him out of the water, then?' Justus yells.

Around him the others have begun to rise, looking from him uncertainly to Soldier and Jewel, and back again. Weapons still lowered, like they none too sure what they better do. Still crouched by the smoking muzzle of the gun, Soldier nods to them.

'Do like he says,' the one-eyed man tells them. 'The god in him talkin'.'

He sees the other faces: Heron, the hawk-faced Indian with the egret feathers. The dark, admiring gaze of Jewel, held at bay by the shotgun in Mary's hands. Slowly a couple of men venture into the water. Lay hold on the loose-limbed shape, dragging it to land. Thunder rattles briefly, fading. In the far distance the drumming suddenly halts.

Justus sighs, the pistol lowering in his grip. Ain't no use tryin' to hold out agin them all, he knows. Sooner or later, he have to go with them wherever they headed. All at once he's aware of a crushing weight of weariness he'd forgotten before. A burden that falls harder for having slipped his mind. Grunting, he signs to Soldier, and the short man gets awkwardly to his feet. Cautiously, the single green eye studies the black giant who looms over him.

'Okay,' Justus tells the veteran. 'We go with you, no trouble. You try anythin' with either one of us, an' I blow a hole clear through you, old man. You hear me good?'

Soldier looks down the reeking muzzle, his splayed face twisting. The grey head nods, silently. Turning, the old man signs to the rest. They move in warily, drenched still by the bucketing rain, keeping a space between themselves and the two who are now their captives. Justus forces himself to grin. Reaches over to lay a hand gently on the barrel of the shotgun, his eyes and Mary's meeting across the empty gun.

'Best let him have his gun, honey,' the big man says. 'Ain't gonna make no difference now.'

For a while the blue eyes question, then the hardness goes from Mary. She too musters a shaky smile.

'Anythin' you say,' she answers. She looses hold of the gun, letting him hand it back to the waiting Soldier, still keeping Jewel fixed with the corner of her eye.

Justus nods, hoping he looks a whole lot tougher than he feels. He lays his huge black arm across her shoulders, holding her against him, the spear still gripped in one hand, pistol in the other.

Inwardly he hopes they ain't figured how he down to his last shot.

'Lead away, old man,' Justus says. 'We right behind you.'

The rain slackens off as they move, thinning, spattering in the muddy pools. The last of the thunder fades into distance. He and Mary tread mud and water together, following the stooped figure of Soldier through the waist-high reeds. Around and back of them come the rest, keeping maybe ten feet off from them each side. Heron with his hefted spear, Jewel, the Indian; four men struggling to carry the slack-limbed corpse of Claw between them. Thin scatter of moving shapes in the vastness of the landscape, blurred yet by the fall of rain.

Where they headed? he wonders. An' what all this 'bout Shango, an' the god? Don't like none of it, he reckons. Easy enough to figure what they aimed to do first off. An' he don't reckon they like to change their minds even now.

Rain spats heavy on his cheek and he shakes his head against the moisture that mingles with his sweat. But one way to find out now. Holding to Mary, he goes forward through the reeds.

Far in the distance, the drumming sets up again.

'How you come to be out this way?' Justus asks.

He sits back of Mary in the hollowed log canoe, asking his question over her blonde head that leans on his chest, curling a lock of her white-gold hair around his black finger. The pistol sheathed, worse than useless now. In front of him Soldier grunts, back to him as he bends to strike with the short-handled paddle. Behind Justus the woman, Jewel, does the same, and back of her the tall Heron stands upright in the stern, thrusting for the green depths with a long willow pole. At his touch the long boat heaves forward, gliding swiftly through the stagnant water.

Handle good, these pirogues. Look clumsy to first sight, maybe, but ain't nothin' better for this kinda country. Theirs is second in line, as yet. The egret-crested Indian heads the crew in the first, some distance ahead of them, half-hidden in the reeds. Calling out to the others as he leads with the paddle. Further back, behind their own canoe, an older man has charge: grey, broad-set feller in fringed buckskins, his thick hair banded and set in shoulder-length braids, feathered bow slung at his back. Same harsh predatory face as the younger Indian. Same broad-chested build. Same dark intent stare, levelled on their backs from where he leans again for the water. Could be the two of 'em related, someway.

Claw's body back with the old man, in the last of the canoes.

In front of him, Soldier sets on his haunches, glancing one-eyed over the high hump of his shoulder. The paddle laid across his thighs, its blade bright with water as Heron's long pole drives the boat smoothly forward. Seen from behind, the old man's back is a mass of knotted, puckered flesh, the bone of the shoulder horribly disfigured. Studying, Justus wonders how Soldier came by it. Musta been some whuppin', sure.

Catching his look, the veteran grins his mirthless grin. 'We al–ways been out here, boy,' Soldier tells him. 'Our folk lived out in the Choctaw nation one-time, settled down. Once in a while we'd git us trouble from the slavers, but we got by . . . Leastways, till the big war come . . .'

'That when Shango come to us,' Jewel says from behind him.

She leans as she speaks, laying down her paddle. Justus tenses, feeling her warm breasts touch at his back. Fights to disregard the sudden contact of flesh. At the sound of her voice, Soldier frowns, his flattened face harshening. Jewel is quiet.

'Don't do to talk 'bout the god when he ain't here,' Soldier says. 'You know that.'

'He a god, huh, this Shango?' Justus asks.

The one green eye regards him a moment, steadily. Then Soldier turns from him, striking his paddle into the water.

'He the voice,' the old man tells him, not looking back. 'It the same thing, I reckon.'

'Uhuh.' Justus letting it lie. He ain't gonna git no more out of them about this Shango, that for sure. He stays quiet, fondling Mary's pale hair as the pirogues glide on, splitting the dark-scummed surface of the water. Tall banks of reeds rising high and green on every side, screening them from any unseen eyes. By now rain and thunder alike are passed, but the sky still dark, and a dull haze covers the lakes and inlets. The one sound the ripple of water, cleaving to the prow.

'Your folks—they runaways?' Justus asks at last.

'Some, I reckon.' Soldier doesn't turn his head, his stare fixed on the narrow stretch of water between the reeds. 'My old man, he run off when he but a kid . . . but his woman, she

22

black as you or me, an' she livin' free with the Choctaw even then. Yeah, you think on that, boy. Ain't one of us here been a slave since we born.'

'You come by some hard times, seems to me,' Justus says, his eyes on the puckered back, the high hump of the shoulder.

At that Soldier chuckles, grinning as he turns his head. 'Ain't no man whupped me, if that what you thinkin'.' His one-eyed gaze travels on beyond the tall man to where the old Indian in the buckskins squats in the prow of the pirogue. 'See ole 'Gator Head back there? He had a brother once, when we was younger. One time the two of us took a shine fer the same wench—know what I mean?' The thin-lipped grin tight, fierce as he remembers. 'Settled it with war-clubs, Choctaw-fashion. He was good with a club, that boy. He cripped me up a little 'fore I busted his haid . . . Time I got me the girl, wasn't nothin' I could do fer her fer close on a month . . .'

He breaks off, chuckling, the others laughing with him.

Justus eyes the three of them, uncertain. Just how do they stand one with another? he wonders. 'An' 'Gator Head—he didn't do nothin'?'

'No.' Soldier grinning, shaking his salty head. 'Was a clean fight, an' I won it. Kinda thing that happens when two young fellers git their sap runnin' high . . . He was sore fer a while, I guess, but he got over it. We pretty close nowadays, me an' ole 'Gator Head . . . That his boy up front.' Gestures to the squat figure in the pirogue ahead of them. 'Red Wolf, he called. Full-blood Choctaw. But we got us kind of a blood-tie from way back, you might say . . . Yeah, we all of us close, come to think.'

'Look like you got a roughed-up back, yo'self,' Jewel says from behind him.

He feels a light, feathering touch on him as the words are spoken, her fingers following the thick, ridged scars of the whip. Justus draws his breath, scowling. In front of him, Mary senses the sudden change and turns, her blue eyes questioning, suspicious of what they cannot see. Meeting her gaze, he shakes his head. Touches her face gently. Mary nods, sober-faced. She turns back, lying against him as the boat slides through the reeds.'

'Yeah, they laid a whip to me once.' Frowning still at the

23

memory. Even now the thought of Lawrence stings him keener than the lash itself. 'On a sugar plantation north a ways from here—an' only once. I got clear one night, been runnin' ever since . . .'

'That so?' Soldier smiles amiably back over his shoulder, paddling as the canoe takes a swift turn through the reedbeds ahead. 'You done well to git this far, boy . . . They come after you, huh? Try to bring you back where you run from?'

'One of 'em died tryin',' Justus tells him. Then, questioning, 'How come you found us back there? You come lookin' too?'

Back of him he hears the low-throated chuckling of Jewel and Heron, laughing together. Strange, he thinks, how alike their voices sound. Then again, maybe it ain't so strange a–tall.

Soldier leans back from his stroke, his green-eyed glance raking the man behind him. 'Could say that, I reckon,' the old man answers. He doesn't smile. 'Storm-time, that the time to feed the god . . . When the thunder come, we git to go out lookin' . . .' The one eye fixes on him, studying. 'Out in this country, ain't hard to see folk a–comin'. Specially when they got a white wench with 'em, huh?'

Justus doesn't answer, letting the jibe pass for the moment. So far, he figures, their captors are friendly enough; Claw's death, and the snake, saw to that. All the same, from what he has heard of their talk of Shango, he senses big trouble to come. Better not push them too far. Not yet.

'Ain't no friend to white folks, is you, honey?' Jewel asks, her breath warming his back.

'It white folks you set out to kill, that right?'

In his mind recalling the hideous floating shards in the water. Against him Mary shudders, drawing a quick breath as she too remembers. In front of them both, Soldier nods his head.

'Few Cajuns hereabouts, trappers an' fishermen an' suchlike . . . We git to find 'em, they feed the god, right 'nough.'

'We sacrificed 'fore we come out this time,' Heron says from behind them.

'Uhuh.' That explains the fragments in the water, he guesses. 'An' your people, they all black like us, or Choctaw. That right?'

'Near 'nough.' Soldier still not turning. 'Few Cricks an'

24

Cherokee throwed in, I guess. An' some of us ain't none too sure who we is—that right, Jewel?'

Justus catches the sting in his voice. Senses too the sudden tensing of the girl who crouches at his back.

'Take it easy, Soldier, you hear?' Heron says.

'Jes' jokin', boy.' The grey head swings, its mirthless grin returning, glancing again to the silent figure of Justus. 'They brother an' sister, see? Git kinda close at times, even if they did have 'em different mothers.'

'We had us the same father.' Heron's voice is curt, the old man's jibe rousing the anger in him. Now he glares at the big bush-haired man seated in front of him.

'You ain't answered my sister yet,' Heron says. 'You a friend to white folks?'

Justus scowls at the words, feeling his great fists clench. Since Sweet River, ain't no-one talked to him that way an' come off alive.

'They ain't no friends of mine,' he says, not troubling to look round as he speaks. But his hand still in Mary's hair, stroking the softness of it with calloused fingers.

'How about her?' Jewel asks. The dislike is plain in her voice.

'Mary different,' Justus tells them, putting his arms around her as he speaks, as if to shield her from them. His eyes hard, glaring. Ready for the first hint of a fight. 'She my woman. Anyone else lay a hand to her, he gonna git hurt bad, you hear?' For a fleeting instant Mary smiles, takes his hands to lay them over her breasts, covering his hands with her own. More than ever, she's thankful to have him by her. Knowing herself alone but for him among these blacks and Indians with their strange animal scent and hostile glances. The looks of the men, wanting her. The women, wanting to cut her to pieces. Good to know that Justus will defend her. Not that she ever doubted it. She'd do the same for him among her own people.

Scary, all the same, being the one white woman alive in miles. And all the other white folks no more 'n bodies in the water. She flinches at the memory, shuddering, clasping more tightly to the black hands at her breasts.

'Best tell that to Shango, come the time,' Heron mutters sourly behind them, digging his pole deep in the green floating water. None of the others speak.

On either side the land firming, low slopes and hummocks rising from the mud, making small islands among the reeds. Bushes and thickets growing on them above the level of the water. Here and there he catches sight of a lone stunted tree. Far ahead, a dim looming shape outlined through the haze, like land rising clear out the water. Suddenly, unexpectedly, the clamour of drums breaks out afresh, louder and more fearful than before.

'So Shango brung you outa the Choctaw nation, huh?' Justus fights to quell the tremor in his voice. Sound of the drums brings back those mangled limbs and the marks of the teeth that killed them. The questions in his mind still unanswered. Who this Shango anyhow? And what in hell is the thing they bein' fed to? As if sensing his unease, Soldier glances back to him and grins.

'That's right. He give the word, an' we go with him.' Soldier pauses. The one green eye measuring him carefully. 'You see him, you know why.'

'What do you aim to do?' Mary, speaking for the first time, her voice ringing strange in their ears after a long silence. As she speaks, she is aware of Jewel's hostile stare.

'That for the god to say,' Heron says back of them. 'You see him soon enough.'

In front the last line of reeds give way, and the hollowed log glides into a lagoon that stretches almost as far as the eye can see. Pale light filtering through the clouds overhead, raising an eerie gleam from the flat surface of the water. Out beyond, the looming outline takes shape. An island in the lagoon, covered over, screened from sight by thick bush and trees. At its centre, a log stockade.

'Looks like we home,' Jewel says.

Up ahead the men in Red Wolf's pirogue lift their arms, yelling. Pointing to a litter of fragments in the water. Shouting out to Soldier as the scraps come floating down towards them. The one-eyed veteran nods, grunting. His paddle across his knees.

'Looks like they fed him good today,' Soldier says.

Justus sees the mauled remnants as they float alongside.

26

Clenches his teeth to look away. Abruptly Mary leans over the side and is horribly sick.

'Yeah,' Heron says behind them both. 'Look like we home all right.'

He sinks his pole, the long boat skimming over the open water.

Sound of drums on the island yonder, meeting them as the pirogues cross the still waters of the lagoon. Seeming to beat on beneath the surface of the lake itself as the long prows slice through the scum and weeds, sending greenish-brown waves curling away, creaming to white ripples in their wake. To Justus, holding Mary as the humped shape of the island nears, their sound is like many voices, calling together. And back of the drums themselves come other noises: shriek of bone whistles, and a rhythmic regular chanting. The force of the sound is overwhelming. Justus trembles, feeling its pulse invade the body itself, thudding with the beat of his blood.

The island rears up ahead of them, green of trees and bushes momentarily blocking their view of the stockade. Soldier and Jewel dip their paddles, their boat following Red Wolf around the curving fringe of the land. Gliding by leafy branches hung with vines, roots trailing down into the water. Overhead, the huge moss-covered trunks go climbing skyward, their upper boughs lost to sight. Glancing up as they glide past, he sees that some of them have steps cut into the boles and are fitted with wooden platforms higher up: lookout posts. The fleeting glimpse immediately cut short as a fresh surge of green crowds the waterline. Justus turns, swallowing, feeling the beat of the drums grow stronger.

Ahead of them the shrubbery parts, opening on to a narrow inlet. Heron ducks his head as the canoe moves in beneath a tunnel of branches, a faint greenish light spilling on to them through the leaves. The noise of the drums and the chanting swelling all the time, echoing against the water and the trees. Mary turns her head towards him, her features strange, fearful in the green light, her eyes questioning. Justus meets her gaze in silence, unable to give her any answer. Mary's head sinks at the look. She buries her face against his chest, her slender body trembling.

After a while the level of water sinks, exposing the muddy bed of the inlet. Where the land begins to slope upward, they leave the boat, dragging it to shelter among the bushes beside the water. The five of them going uphill in single file, Red Wolf's party already walking on ahead. Further back, 'Gator Head and his men beach their pirogue, bending to lift the inert body of Claw from the boat.

Away from the water, a trodden path leads upward through the thickets. Justus follows it, hardly aware of the raking thorns, Mary close behind, stumbling over the uneven ground. Black and copper of naked bodies in front and behind them, penning them from any hope of flight. The huge black man snags his toe in a jutting root, smothers a curse. By now, he knows, he's helpless: cut off by water and by land. The place is a natural fortress, ringed by the open lagoon, thickly screened by its bushes and trees. Ain't no way they gonna git outa here, unless this god of theirs give the word.

Shango. That name still sticks in his throat. Could it be, he wonders, he really about to meet a god?

Breaking from the last of the thickets, they find themselves in open ground, the bushes cut back to make a clearing, maybe thirty or forty yards all round. Only a scatter of the tall trees left, their notched trunks towering into the clouds. Darker shapes of men in the platforms overhead. Silent. Watching them come.

Now he sees the stockade.

High wall of rough-hewn logs, set one into the other, rearing high almost as the trees themselves. A muddy ditch surrounds it, running downhill at one point to join the stream they rode in on a while before. Somethin' down there, low in the wall; look like a iron grille of some kind. What in hell that for?

Bark and moss on the outer wall of logs. Here and there the branches left on, giving a further screen to the place. Cresting the line of the rampart, a row of sharpened stakes. Gazing, he sees that each stake is set with a shrivelled head. Seems like they nod as he approaches, the empty eyes staring down on him. Some of

28

them skulls already; others with the flesh puckered and dried like withered fruit, wisps of hair clinging in places to the dead flesh and bone. Justus stares back at them silently. Back of him he hears Mary's indrawn breath.

From the stockade itself come the noise of drums and chanting, loud enough now to smother the other sounds. He can feel it taking him over, its hot magic entering him, giving his throat the salt taste of blood. In front of them a slat bridge leads over the murky water. Red Wolf's group are already crossing over, Soldier glancing back one-eyed over his bent shoulder, signing them to follow. He steps on to the flat strips of wood, Mary staying close at his back as the others come after.

Underfoot, the slat bridge shakes, swaying from side to side. They grip to a vine rope laid alongside to keep from falling in the ditch. Close to, he sees it deeper than he thought. Deep enough for a man to drown, no trouble a–tall.

Above him the shrunken heads grin and stare, nodding on their sharpened spikes. Justus sucks in his breath, puckers to spit in the sluggish flow of water beneath. His eyes drawn again to that metal grille, low in the wall. From here he sees that water flows into it, going underground, inside the stockade itself. Nearside the ditch, the ground parcelled out in what look from here like garden patches. He sees corn growing: collard, okra, goobers. He clings to the humming rope and stares, uncomprehending.

Up ahead, a heavy log gate swings open, its front nailed white with skulls. Making for that gap in the wall, he feels the ground shudder underfoot. The chanting and the hammering drums meeting him like a blow.

'SHAN–GO! SHAN–GO! SHAN–GO!'

Inside the walled stockade, the ranked heads closing in around them.

The open space shudders with noise. The air awash with the sound of drumming, chanting, squealing of voices and bone flutes, the rhythmic beating of hands. The ground underfoot trembling to the pounding of naked feet. Justus sees a huge compound with sod-roofed huts ranked in straight lines, close against the walls. In the centre, a great tree looms towards the sky, lopped of all its branches, its gnarled bole nailed and hung with clusters of skulls.

29

Further off, on a raised mound beyond, a massive log building stands apart from the rest, its doors shut.

In the open stretch by the tree, a swaying mass of people.

Packed surge of sweating bodies stamping and whirling, leaping in the air with upflung arms. He sees lithe black girls in coloured headties and stained deerhide skirts, sweat running from their bared breasts as they crouch and weave, heads flung back to call on the god. Feathered Indians in breech-clouts, black men in frayed breeches; others whose looks mix both races: dark skins with Choctaw features, broad Negroid faces with the bronzed skin of Indians, some of them naked. Gleam of black and red bodies, sheathed in their sweat. Under their feet a pall of dust boils upward, coating men and women alike.

Nearest him, a long, thin-bodied man whose face recalls the skulls on their spikes overhead, standing, beating the drum slung at his neck. Beyond him, a line of figures crouching low on the ground, long-fingered hands at work on the drums before them. The roar of interlocking sound coming to him like the crying of many voices. Justus stares, the blood-beat shaking him to his toes. Ain't never seen drums like this, he reckons: the shape of them long and thin, like to an hourglass; hide thongs up the side; the beaters hitting the stretched skin of the drumhead with a hooked stick, drawing with the free hand at the thongs along the side. Justus trembles to the sound. Not the tight, voiceless rattle of the drums the whitefolk soldiers use. The noises alter with each move of the hand, like speech. Somethin' strange about it, scarin' to hear. Like the drum has a spirit that talks when it touched. Like he listenin' to the voices of ghosts.

At the outer rim of the circle, other figures cluster: naked bodies of children, dust-covered, clapping and stamping in imitation of the men and women in the circle itself. Older men and women, white-haired, bent, crouched on the ground, their scrawny shoulders hunched, the dust sifting down to clothe them. Out beyond he sees pigs and chickens runnin' loose; thin-bellied dogs whose ribs show through their mangy fur, their cries adding to the clamour all around.

In front, the ring of dancers withdraw, and he sees Shango.

Tall man, towering high over all about him. Tall and thin as a spirit. Long, lean reach of outspread legs and arms as he spins and stamps in a smother of dust, chanting in time to the hurrying voice of the drums, blowing a strident blast at the bone whistle that hangs from his neck. The gaunt body is hung with skins, flying out from him as he moves: plated tree-bark look of stripped gator hide; thin, smooth sheen of snakeskins dangling from his waist. About his neck the bone whistle, a necklace of claws and fangs, a round, smooth stone, fitted by a hide thong. On his arms other dark shapes, twining. With a sudden shock he knows them to be snakes. *Living*, gliding over the flesh, moving as he moves.

'Dear God,' Mary breathes from beside him.

'SHAN–GO! SHAN–GO!'

Beneath its covering his flesh is smooth, its colour black, deeper than night. Blacker than ebony under its coating of grey dust. Sight of him fearful, the grim, feather-crested head thrown back as the drumming stutters at speed. The crowd of dancers spinning, swaying, falling. Shango yells, leaps in the air. From a clay jar he drinks, spraying the liquid from his mouth on the circle of worshippers, spattering them. The colour of it red as blood. Justus swallows, feeling Mary shudder, gripping to his arm.

Yeah, the big man thinks. This one a god all right.

Shango flings up his hands, calling out, the clay jar smashing to fragments against the ground. Abruptly the drumming stills. The dancers fall silent. The crowd hold their breath, turning slow to look towards those by the open gate.

Justus stands, hearing his own breath echo in the sudden stillness, feeling the force of their eyes upon him. Mary still holding to his arm, her fingers gripping his black flesh. With the stilling of the drums, something of his own power returns. He pulls the gun at his waist, thumb curling in readiness at the spike of the hammer. About him the others falling back, giving the god in him room. Red Wolf and 'Gator Head, Jewel and Heron: all of them watching him, waiting. Back of him they lay down Claw's body in the dust.

Soldier apart from the rest, cradling the empty shotgun. His one eye fixed on Shango as the huge man turns, stepping slowly towards them with his long arms outstretched, the live snakes rippling against the flesh.

'The god comin'.' Heron's voice behind him, muttering.

He senses the movement around him as they bow their heads together. Stays as he is, fixing his own gaze hard on the tall, oncoming figure, feeling the first moisture prickle on his brow as the heartbeat trips against his ribs, his palm sweaty around the pistol butt.

Four or five paces from him Shango halts, lowering his snake-clad arms. Justus meets his fierce look, clenching his teeth. The face of Shango is gaunt, hollow-cheeked, patterned with spiralling marks cut into the flesh, the bared teeth filed to glinting points. In the darkness of his face his eyes show huge and staring, black stones, threaded with blood at the whites, drilling through him where he stands. Justus holds the stare, snarling inwardly against the fear that trembles low in his belly. He can sense the power of those eyes coming out the body to meet him, pushin' at him, the way the twister pushed at the live-oaks in the bayou.

Justus stands, glowering. He ain't about to fall. Once he go down, he know, he gonna be finished.

Hint of a frown, crossing the scarred features of the god like a passing cloud. For an instant that terrible gaze falters, puzzling, trying to search beyond the eyes of the heavy-set man in front of him. Failing.

Justus holds with the look, glaring. His own will hardening at the momentary sign of weakness. Shango cain't figure how he walked in here armed, with the others backing off from him and a white woman by his side. Somehow Justus senses that Shango has never had to face a man in this place who wouldn't give way. That he too feels the possibility of fear. Sensing this sure as the scent of blood as he stares back into those bloodshot eyes, Justus feels the worst of his own fear leave him.

Shango strong—stronger than any man he met. But he a man, after all.

The clouding look passes in an instant, Shango's eyes slitting as the coiled snakes hiss along his arm.

'Soldier.' The voice low, edged with menace. Shango standing motionless, his stony glance still on Justus as he speaks. 'Soldier, I want to know how come this man here right now, an' how he still got his gun. You hear me?'

32

Across from them, the veteran swallows, not daring to lift his head. Licking his thin lips, Soldier makes a jerky nod.

'Tell it,' Shango says.

Soldier tells him.

Shango hears out the story in silence, frowning, his harsh, penetrating glance shifting swiftly from Justus to Mary, from the white woman to the prone shape of Claw, and back again. His stare is with Justus as Soldier bows, halting for breath.

'So the cottonmouth killed Claw, huh?' Shango murmurs, his dark face brooding.

'Just when he was about to cut 'em down,' Soldier says hurriedly, eager to be finished. The sooner this over, the better for him. 'We—we figured—musta been the god took him . . .'

'That so?' the tall man leers, baring his sharpened teeth, one hand gesturing carelessly to the giant who stands before him. 'An' this one, you figured he got a piece of the god in him, that right?'

Soldier draws a careful breath. His head bent so as not to meet those eyes.

'Snake turn back from him,' the veteran says. 'That sure the way it look, back there . . .'

'He's a good trade fer Claw,' the woman, Jewel, mutters from back of them.

The circle of listeners freezes the moment she speaks. Shango's look touches on her and the woman is quiet, bowing over with the rest.

'Heron.' Shango doesn't raise his voice, but there is venom in his speech. 'Ain't no-one ask your sister to say nothin' yet. Tell her from me she keep quiet when the god talkin', or maybe we go talk someplace else. You hear?' He jerks his head, indicating the big log house on its mound beyond them.

Heron frowns at his sister, nodding slowly. 'We hear you, lord,' Heron says. 'Me an' her both.'

'Good.' The sound almost purring, deep in the throat. The gaunt man turns again to Justus, his stony eyes probing, searching someplace for a weak, unguarded spot. 'So you a god too, huh?'

Justus stands, meeting the glare of the eyes. He doesn't answer. At once the dark stare hoods, narrowing. Shango's mouth closes over the filed teeth, setting to a hard, grim line.

'This a god you lookin' at, boy,' the tall man says, the words coming tight through his teeth, hissing. 'My name Shango, you hear? I rule storms an' lightnin's. Rule snakes, too. Ever–thin' that moves, I the god. Back there,' one hand points sidelong to the log structure, 'that my place. That where we sacrifice, come the time . . .' He smiles suddenly, the points of his teeth showing. 'Now boy, you gonna give me yo' name?'

'Justus.' He grits back the word, hand closed on the pistol, the long barrel trained on the lean gut of the man in front of him. 'I a man, an' you don't scare me none.'

Beside him he can hear Mary's shuddering breath. The white girl standing braced, her feet spread flat to the ground, ready to spring, to fight in spite of her fear. All around them the waiting faces, spattered from Shango's bloody blessing a moment earlier, eager for the slightest move. In his ears the stillness pulses, throbbing like a beaten drum.

Shango laughs, throwing back his head. He lifts his arms where the thin snakes twine, his hands gripping them at the neck. Holds them out ahead of him. Justus hears Mary's sharp, instinctive cry as the flat heads lunge close to their faces, hissing, mouths open to bare the poison fangs. Cottonmouths, both of them, like the one that took Claw and Burns.

Justus looks back into the tall man's eyes, holding the gun level on that thin gut.

'Boy, you dumb,' Shango crows. 'You figure I kin be hurt? This a god you seein' . . . Take a look!' He extends his arms, smiling. Justus takes in the scars of puncture-marks in the black flesh and feels his gut flutter at the sight. He seen snake-bites before, but never so many. An' never on a man who stood up alive, talkin' to him, like now.

At the look on his face, Shango grins broader, teeth glistening.

'Yeah, boy. Reckon you know it.' One hand moving for the barrel of the .44, gripping the neck of the hissing snake as it comes. 'You figure you kin hurt me with a gun, huh?'

Within himself Justus fights a fresh onset of fear. Looking into the hard eyes of Shango, he feels the hair prickle along his neck. Can the tall man read his mind? Does he know, by

34

whatever power is his, that Justus down to his last shot? The big man grits his teeth snarling. His finger slippery at the trigger.

'Try me,' Justus says.

He watches the face of Shango as he speaks, seeing the knife-toothed leer fade, and a swift flicker of expressions succeed it. Thwarted anger first, then a hint of fear. His own expression doesn't change, his gaze never leaving the gaunt face in front of him. The tall man frowns, thoughtful, scanning him sidelong, his eyes narrowed.

'Could be Heron right,' Shango mutters. 'You a good trade fer Claw, at that . . .'

Same moment he speaks he swings around. Arms held out as he looks toward Mary, who shrinks back from him with an instinctive cry of fear.

'*She* come with me,' Shango says, his voice low so none of the others hear, or seems like.

'All women git to lie with the god . . .'

But at sight of the black muzzle aimed at his belly he checks, looking back.

'You try it, an' I blow yo' haid off,' Justus tells him.

For a while he feels the tension like a noose at his neck, throttling him. In front of him, Shango glowers, a vein pulsing in his thin neck, his broad chest heaving. Justus still tryin' to figure what comin' next, when the tall man puckers and spits like a snake. Justus stands, teeth bared as the warm spittle hits him full in the face, watching as Shango crows and leaps, flinging up his snake-clad arms. Behind him the crowd of onlookers cries out.

'God touch him!' Shango yells. 'He spared!'

He turns, moving with measured steps through the dust, thin shoulders drooping, head sunk, as if the force of the encounter has drained his powers for the moment. Halfway from them he whirls around, pointing with one long finger to the inert shape of the dead man in the dust.

'Bring him up to the long house,' Shango says. 'He feed the god.'

He stands watching as a group of men take up Claw's heavy,

hanging body. As they move, stumbling towards him, the gaunt man's glance shifts to the hump-shouldered figure of the veteran, who stands with his head bowed.

'Soldier.' Shango's look is on the old man, hard and merciless. 'These two come in with you. It for you to see they don't run. You hear me good?'

'I hear you, lord.' Soldier keeps his head down, one eye looking to the ground.

Shango's long head nods. For an instant his stare comes back to Justus, hard and penetrating. Standing quietly, the spittle running down across his cheek, Justus reads the hatred there and knows himself afraid. Abruptly the tall man turns, arms spread as he calls out to the watching crowd.

'The god tired!' Shango calls. 'He go rest, now!'

The tall figure starts away from them, stalking silent through the dust that rises about his long legs, the skins and ornaments swinging and clashing as he moves, the snakes still writhing against his arms. In front the crowd part, letting him through. From close to the rank of drummers a seated woman rises awkwardly to her feet. Broad-set, heavy-bodied woman, skin gleaming black and smooth as velvet, naked to the waist, the thick flesh hanging in glistening rolls. Between her massive breasts a gleaming metal object, a crescent moon, hung from her neck by a chain. Rolling as she moves, waddling to join the taller figure of the man, the two of them making for the raised temple on the mound. Behind them the men with Claw's body.

Back in the circle a bone whistle blasts, and the drums set up again.

'Put the goddam gun away.' Soldier's voice, muttering from alongside him as the people lift their heads. 'You safe fer now, boy. An' don't move to wipe that spit from yo' face.'

Justus obeys, breathing hard, looking to Mary's white shocked face as the relief courses through them both. Neither one of them moving. Standing as all the others stand, like they still waiting for something to happen.

Shango and the woman lost to sight now inside the log temple. Claw gone with them, the men who carried him already turning back, the great doors closing behind them.

For a time the many-voiced pounding of the drums is the only sound, while the people stand and wait. Abruptly, the silence is broken. Close to the open gate, a man yells, pointing. A single cry goes up in answer from the sweating ranks beyond: a high, wavering shriek. The sound of it freezes the blood in Justus' veins. Beside him, Mary clenches her hands to stop them trembling.

'Take a look outside,' Soldier tells them.

Others in front of them as they move, streaming towards the gate. Blocked as he is by arms and faces, Justus sees enough.

Down by the iron grille outside a stain of blood is spreading, darkening the muddy waters of the ditch to an ugly red, fanning like smoke as it washes outward. Among the reeking stains, other objects float. Gobbets of chewed flesh. Fragments of bone.

Claw has gone to feed the god.

Turning back, retching at the taste of bile in his throat, he meets Mary's gaze. She barred by his great back, unseeing. But knowing all the same. Now she holds to him as the crowd mill at the waterside, yelling as the drums quicken, clinging to him as to life itself.

'Don't leave me, Justus,' Mary says.

Over her head he meets the one-eyed gaze of Soldier. The veteran frowning, already impatient to be gone.

'You best come with me,' Soldier tells him. 'The two of you be sleepin' in my hut tonight. After that, ain't no tellin', I reckon.' He signs to them, moving away, the heavy shotgun cradled in his arms.

For a moment Justus stands, deaf to the drumming and the outcry by the water's edge, holding her slender body against him as if to shield it with his own from the dangers all around. In his mind a turmoil of thought. Of Claw, the black man he killed out of mercy, back there in the marshes. Now vanished. Torn to fragments by the teeth of the god.

What they got in there? Shango know how to use it, that for sure. An' he ain't done yet. When he gonna make his next move?

Justus shrugs off the troubling thoughts, scowling, Mary's hand in his as the two of them turn to face the veteran.

'We're comin', old man,' Justus says, frowning as the two of them follow the short, humped figure across the compound, where figures weave and stamp in the thickening spray of dust. Thinking.

When he first lit out into the wilderness with the dogs back of him, he figured he was free. Now it looks like he found his own kind, an' he back in chains agin.

'You a fool to go up agin Shango,' Soldier says. 'That one cain't be hurt.'

Inside the sod-roofed hut it's already dark, a shadowed gloom enclosing the three of them together. Their nostrils filled with the rich scent of earth and foliage, mixed in with the stagnant reek of the water beyond the stockade. Squatting on the dirt floor, his back to the wall, he doesn't answer at once. Looks to where Soldier sits hunched in the open doorway, hands on his knees, eyeing the thick, moist slab of sky that fills the space between. A soft, untouched reach of darkness, overset by the black frame of the door. The heavier play of shadows inside. Back of him in the gloom, Mary shifts slightly on the reed mat that serves for a bed and Justus turns, smiling in reassurance, laying his hand over hers where it rests on the ground.

'How long you known him?' Justus asks.

The man by the door grunts. Shrugs his thin misshapen shoulders, not troubling to look back to Justus by the wall.

'Cain't tell fer sure. Ten year, maybe.' He scratches at his flattened nose, frowning into the night. 'Guess he allus kind of strange, even when he a kid. Could set down an' be someplace else in his haid. Talkin' with the spirits an' all. Know what I mean?'

'Uhuh.' Justus figures he kin understand it, at that.

Across from him the veteran talks on, not turning.

'Brung us outen the Choctaw nation when the big war started,' Soldier says. 'Claim the god come into him that time. Tole him we got to git clear, go someplace else.' He pauses, twisting to glance back swiftly over the hump of his shoulder. 'Way he sees it, we be safer out here in the wilderness. Look like he right, don't it?'

'Guess so,' Justus answers levelly. His shoulders fitted against the wall, bracing himself with the hut as a man might test the bars of his prison, checking it for strength. Another image in his mind as he moves: of the woman who went with Shango into the long house—the fat, black woman with the moon-symbol at her breast.

'Who the woman with him?' he asks. 'One with that moon-thing hung on her neck?'

'That Mama Odu.' Soldier's voice comes back to him, low-pitched, almost fearful. 'You watch out fer her, boy. She a goddess, kin call on the moon an' the tides . . . Come to us coupla years back, from a plantation we burned. Now she sleep along of Shango in the long house.'

He falls quiet, his one eye probing warily at the shadows all around as if afraid of some unseen thing nearby that listens to his every word.

'Yeah, that long house—' Justus leans forward, his eyes glinting in the shadowed dark. 'How 'bout that place, Soldier? You know what they got in there?'

'Don't ask!' The other's voice grown hoarse, terrified. Soldier licks at his lips, half-turning to glance at the dark outside. 'Sides him an' the goddess, ain't no-one come outa there alive. You got any sense, boy, you keep away from there, you hear?'

Beside him in the gloom, her hand grasps his more tightly. The words getting to her. Justus too hears, hardens his face against it, his own speech stony as he questions.

'Sound to me like you *know* what in there,' Justus says.

'Ain't sayin' nothin'!' Soldier's splayed features setting in harsh, rigid lines as he speaks. Swings round on his heels to face them, his one good eye glittering strange in the dark of his face. Right now, he looking at Mary, huddled up by the wall with her chin rested on her knees. His words, though, for Justus as that one eye fixes its gaze upon her.

'That one only gonna bring you trouble,' Soldier tells him. He lifts a long-fingered hand, pointing to the pale-skinned figure by the wall. 'She unlucky, boy. Out here, every woman gits to lie with the god—an' what that Shango want, he gonna take.' Pausing, the gleam of that one eye shifting over to the tall man across from him. 'Sooner or later, he gonna take her too.'

'He better not try,' Justus says. Staying where he is as he speaks, shoulders wedged against the wall of the hut, his eyes hard on Soldier across the darkened space. The words coming from him cool and threatening, feeling her hand flinch as it grips at his own, knowing in that moment her fear. And his.

Shango still in his mind, like some tall tree in a man's path, blocking out the light. Ain't met nothin' like him before, he knows. 'Cept back on Sweet River, Lawrence had the same kinda power, maybe—like he could do what he wanted with any of the slaves, like he did with Sheba, and himself. The big man grits his teeth, remembering.

But then, Lawrence strong because he backed up by a whole lot of other whites—the soldiers an' their guns, that kinda thing. Himself, he ain't as strong as most of the niggers in the plough an' hoe gangs. Justus took Lawrence one time. He could do it agin.

Shango ain't the same a-tall.

What power Shango got come from in him. From the spirit. The god inside him. It a way more 'n anythin' Lawrence had. An' he strong-lookin', too. The thin build don't fool him none. Justus seen nigras built that way could dig ditches fer a week. Come to a fight, that one gonna be harder'n any man he known. Justus grates his teeth together, scowling in the darkness.

Across from them, by the open door, Soldier turns his back again.

Justus lets out his breath in a harsh sigh. the sound hissing through his teeth. Still holding to Mary's hand, he turns his back on the man by the door and lays himself down on the mat of reeds. Mary moves with him, lying down beside him. For a while they stay that way, each looking into the other's face, feeling the weight of the dark and silence pressing on them both. Justus lifts a hand to her face, stroking the tangled, blonde hair drawn back into its horsetail knot. His fingers sliding gently over the smoothness of her cheek, touching the one shallow graze of the scar beneath the eye. Her look searching on him. Justus smiles. 'You pay him no mind now, you hear?' he says.

Mary turns her face against the stroking hand. Brushes it with her lips. 'Long as you by me, he ain't gonna worry me,' she tells him.

Presently he dozes, his hand at her face as his own eyes close. The two of them ate some kinda corn mush with Soldier about a coupla hours back, and warmth and weariness combine to over-power him. Justus lets his head sink to the ground, his mind drifting loose from the hut, from Mary. Shango. The stockade. The blur of thoughts running together. Streaming out to a gathering swell of darkness . . .

Touch of her hands upon him brings him awake, his eyes opening to find her close against him, her breath warm at his ear, her white arm locked at his neck. The slim length of her body pressed to his, moving against him, gently insistent. Justus looks back into those wide eyes, questioning. Mary meets the look, her smile uncertain. She doesn't speak.

Reading the expression of the face, he nods, knowing that she has not slept. That the fear is still on her. That this is her one way of forgetting.

Her face leaning above him now, the eyes half-closed. Justus feels her body quiver against him. He reaches one hand into the thick richness of her hair, brings her face down to meet him. Her mouth covering his, opening hotly as their tongues probe together, her left hand gliding down to caress the bulge at his groin.

Warm smoothness of her belly as it slides against his own. Justus reaches for her. Finds the calico dress pulled up by her breasts. Beyond the belly's white mound his hand meets the soft, downy growth of her loins.

'Already shucked my drawers,' Mary whispers.

Her thighs open as she speaks. His fingers enter her, fondling, stroking at the tiny bud of flesh within until it trembles and grows hard to the touch. Mary moving against his hand, her eyes closing, her own hand urgent upon him, unbuttoning his pants to ease the throbbing manhood loose. Stroking him along his length, cupping the smooth flesh of the head and squeezing gently. Justus catches his breath, lets it out slow. He rolls over on to his back, lifting her across him.

Mary straddles over him, kneeling. Raising herself above the stiffly risen rod that strains towards her, throbbing, bursting with his sap. Taking his hand from her, she comes down: a white body, gleaming pale above the darkness of his, her whiteness holding a black moisture at its core. For a moment she moves herself gently

41

on him, her soft inner flesh brushing the tip of his manhood. Justus groans under her, shuddering. He about to go crazy pretty soon.

Mary's breath leaves her in a harsh, gasping sound. She opens, lowering herself on to the swollen force of him, taking him to her, guiding his black maleness deep into her body.

Over by the doorway Soldier sleeps, leaning against the wall, unseeing as the bodies lock and fuse one with the other. Unaware of the writhing pulse of limbs that touch and cling, the heaving struggle against the ground. Unaware too, of the last, fierce spasm that holds them fast together. Two shapes become one as they shudder and cry out. The black into the white, the white on the black. Warm and content, moist with the sweat of their loving, they hold to one shape, letting the slow tide of pleasure ebb, taking them in its wake.

The hell with Shango, Justus thinks from someplace far in the back of his mind.

He clings to Mary, smiling. The two of them sleeping as the blackness slowly turns to grey in the open doorway beyond.

'*LAFAYETTE HERALD*', *AUGUST 3rd, 1865.*
Trapper's body discovered.
Grave opened in wilderness.

CAJUN TRAPPERS SETTING SNARES IN THE BITTER CREEK REGION FOUND THE BODY OF MR CALEB KIMBALL, BURIED IN A SHALLOW GRAVE, WRITES OUR REPORTER. MR KIMBALL, FORMERLY A SCHOOLTEACHER IN BUFORD, TEXAS, HAD NOT BEEN HEARD OF SINCE HE AND HIS WIFE WENT UPRIVER INTO THE WILDERNESS TO TRAP FURS MORE THAN A YEAR AGO.

THE BODY WAS UNEARTHED FROM ITS RESTING PLACE BY MR ALPHONSE JOURDAN AND HIS COMPANION MR LOUIS VERNET, WHO DISCOVERED A MOUND OF FRESHLY TURNED SOIL IN A CLEARING RECENTLY DEVASTATED BY A TORNADO. ALTHOUGH PARTIALLY DECOMPOSED, IT WAS IDENTIFIED AS THAT OF MR KIMBALL BY CITIZENS OF PALMETTO, HIS LAST STOP UPRIVER LAST YEAR. FROM WOUNDS VISIBLE ON THE BODY, AND FROM ADHESIONS OF BLOOD AND FLESH TO THE WOOD OF A FALLEN TREE NEARBY, MR JOURDAN AND HIS FRIEND CONCLUDED THAT DEATH HAD RESULTED FROM CRUSHING BENEATH IT. HOW THE TREE HAD BEEN REMOVED FROM THE BODY, AND HOW MR KIMBALL CAME TO BE BURIED, REMAINS A MYSTERY. THE GRAVE WAS MARKED WITH AN UPRIGHT WOODEN POST.

NO SIGN WAS FOUND OF MRS MARY KIMBALL, THE DEAD MAN'S WIFE. THE TWO TRAPPERS DISCOVERED TRACKS IN THE SOFT GROUND NEARBY, BUT THESE WERE SOON LOST IN THE SURROUNDING WOODS AND THICKETS. ALL THE SAME, IT MAY WELL PROVE TO BE A SINISTER DISCOVERY. THE TRACKS WERE THOSE OF A WOMAN AND AN UNSHOD MAN. FROM THE DESCRIPTION, IT IS THOUGHT THEY MAY WELL MATCH THOSE OF THE RUNAWAY NIGGER JUSTUS, LAST HEARD OF ARMED IN THE WILDERNESS FOLLOWING THE DEATH OF MR ISAAC BURNS. THE THOUGHT OF A HELPLESS WHITE WOMAN, ABDUCTED AND AT THE MERCY OF THIS VIOLENT BLACK SAVAGE, IS TOO TERRIBLE TO CONTEMPLATE.

IT IS THE HOPE OF THIS PAPER THAT OUR FEARS FOR MRS KIMBALL ARE ALREADY TOO LATE. PERHAPS THE UNFORTUNATE WOMAN HAS FOUND SOME MEANS OF RIDDING HERSELF OF THE BURDEN OF HER BEREAVED LIFE, THEREBY SURELY SAVING HERSELF FROM A WORSE FATE THAN DEATH.

Pale light at the curtained windows, seeping through, pushing back the shadows to the far corners of the room. Halfway to morning already. Out in the yard by the quarters, a cock sets up to crowing.

Lawrence lets the sound pass, his mind elsewhere. He lies on the bed, the thin white limbs asprawl on the thick spread of the quilt beneath, watching Sheba's bowed head and the smooth brown of her shoulders as she goes slowly down on him, her warm tongue flickering over his belly, down to where his standing pole rears up from its bush of hair. Sheba gives a sly grin, looking up to him. Ducks her head again to take him in her mouth. Lawrence makes a low, cat-like purring sound deep in his throat and lies back, hands behind his head, his eyes closing as the slow torment of his pleasure begins.

Soft, liquid lapping of her tongue at his flesh the one sound in the shadowed room. Lawrence smiles, his breath coming short as the warmth of her inner lips enfolds him, sucking, squeezing, drawing the flow of his hot juice up along that pulsing root, whose head beats urgently against the enclosing lips. Her tongue touching on the drop of moisture that swells at his manhood's throbbing tip. Lawrence gasps. Groans aloud. Lies back again.

Ain't nothing he can teach this one, he reckons. She knows all the tricks. Times, he gets the feeling she enjoys it even more 'n he does himself.

Sheba turns, moving lengthways on against him. Crouches, offering her sleek haunches to his face, bringing her own warm zone within reach of his lips and tongue. Lawrence slides beneath her. Burying himself in the moist furred warmth of her. Down beyond, her own mouth works on, bringing him in a rush to the peak of his climax . . .

At the door, a sudden frantic knocking.

Abruptly her mouth leaves him. The surge of pleasure checked suddenly, at the rim of fulfilment. Lawrence curses, coming out from under, rearing up angrily on the far side of the bed.

'What in the hell . . .' he mutters.

'Missa Lawrence? That you?' Hagar's voice at the door, questioning.

Lawrence grits his teeth at the sound, his hands clenching.

Nosey old bitch! She knows damn' well he's in here, and who he got with him. Cursing again, he slides from the bed and on to his feet. Reaching for his pants from across the nearby chair.

'Yeah, Hagar. What is it?' In his mind wishing the old bat in hell. Have to get rid of her soon, he figures. She's forever poking her nose in where she ain't wanted.

'Massa Lawrence, come quick. They's a bunch of Yankee soljers on the road, headin' towards the house!'

For once, a note of panic in the voice. Buttoning his breeches, Lawrence scowls. Yankee soldiers, huh? Had to come sooner or later, he guesses. The old man warned him a while back, 'fore he died. And lately he's heard tell of other plantations being visited. No need to ask why they're comin', the blue-bellied bastards!

All the same, he'll be ready for them. They ain't gonna catch *him* out!

Pulling the shirt on over his head, Lawrence twists his mouth in a vicious thin-lipped smile.

'Have Jacob blow the horn, an' git the nigras called in,' he calls to the old woman outside. 'Tell their officer I'll be out in a while.'

'Sure thing, Massa Lawrence.' Hagar turns in the doorway awkwardly, grunting with effort. Hearing her shufffle down the passage, Lawrence smiles again.

'An' make sure they stow the whips someplace first!' he shouts.

Sheba's still there as he turns, buttoning the front of his shirt. The smooth brownskin girl kneels on the bed, her palms stroking the silky surface of the quilt, the small pert face lifted to him, her dark eyes sly as a cat. Lawrence eyes the damp furred space between her thighs. Smothers a curse as he recalls what he just missed.

'Sheba.' His voice curt as he moves for the door. 'You stay here, wait for me. We ain't through yet, you hear?'

'I hears you real good, Massa Lawrence,' Sheba says.

She eyes the closing door, smiles, running her tongue over her lips, remembering the taste of his white flesh. Hugging her breasts, Sheba purrs in her throat, contented, guessing what's still to come.

Things a whole lot better'n with Justus. She's the master's woman, now. Kin look anyone in the eye. An' while she up here with him in the big house, ain't a thing they cain't do!

Outside, the line of blue-uniformed riders draws up front of the porch.

Sitting astride his horse, Maitland frowns, watching as the big, husky black sends out a ringing blast on the horn and the rest of the slaves gather in from the nearby fields. Sun's coming up already, and his mount flicks its ears at the flies. Maitland swats at a buzzing shape close to his head, feeling the slippery warmth of sweat pin the blouse to him at his armpits. Inwardly he wonders what misguided sense of duty brought him out here to this godforsaken country, when he could just as easily have taken a desk job in the city. He sighs, thinking back with regret to the clean, sweet air and rolling farmlands of his native Indiana. Should have stayed there—he knows that now. Out here, the air's so hot and wet, you start to sweating at first light. And the stink off the bayou tops is enough to turn a man's stomach.

Behind him the uniformed horsemen fidget, hard-faced and impatient, stretching their legs in the stirrups. Sergeant Elliott; Corporal Rose; Troopers Taggart, Johnson, Moody, Craig . . . They've all been with him a while; the bunch of them fought together at Atlanta, and a number of other places—unnamed, forgotten skirmishes for a stretch of woodland or the crossing to a creek. Not Gettysburg or Bull Run, maybe, but fights all the same. Kill men just as dead. In affairs of that kind, a man soon gets to know who his friends are.

Maitland eyes the house in front of him, his lip curling. The big house—that's what they call it out here. Some house, he thinks. See one and you've seen them all. Clapboard and shingles for the most part, the porch with its fake Grecian pillars. Painted wood trying to masquerade as stone. He's seen farms in his own state a way better than this.

Still, looking over to the slave quarters, he can see why it looks so big to them. Those wretched little cabins, wouldn't house beasts in them back home.

46

In front of him the crowd of blacks, gathering at the call, the bunch of them standing resignedly in front of the house, heads down, not daring to look him in the eye, seems like. Scanning one face after another, Maitland frowns harder than before. These blacks are a sorry lot, he thinks. Must have had the spirit beat from them long ago—if they had any in the first place. Maybe he shouldn't think it, seeing he's here to set them free, but all the same it's what comes to mind. Most of them have this gutless hang-dog look they put on as soon as a white man comes by. He's seen it plenty of times. Then again, it could be pretence; a sort of animal cunning, perhaps. Maitland's glance pauses at the figure of the frail old black man who stands stoop-shouldered slightly apart from the crowd. For a moment he could have sworn he saw something flicker in those eyes, averted from his own. Then the moment passes, and he shakes his head. Nothing there, after all.

Glancing back, he catches Elliott's eye, and the thick-set sergeant grins.

'Kinda sheepish-lookin' bunch, ain't they, sir?' he says.

'Yet look at them, Sergeant,' Maitland gestures towards the silent ranks of the waiting slaves, bewilderment in his voice as he speaks. Studying the powerful build of the men and women alike, the heavy shoulders and broad chests, thick with muscle from hard labour on the land. 'The way these people are built, they ought to be able to take on the world. And here they stand like children, waiting on the word of a single white man in that house yonder.' He shakes his head, sighing. 'Sometimes, Sergeant, I wonder what this war was all about.'

'Don't trouble on that, sir.' Elliott grins again, scratches an itch in the greying stubble of his jaw. 'Ain't seen a nigger yet could stand and fight. As for the waitin',' the grin narrows, turning sly, 'Guess you could say we're in the same boat, right now.'

Maitland scowls at that. The sergeant's joke has touched a raw nerve.

'She told me he'd be out in a while,' the captain says. His grip clenches on the reins in his hand. 'He better not keep us waiting much longer.'

He glares at the closed door as he speaks. All the same, these two-bit plantation owners. Power over the blacks has gone to their heads. Set out here in the back of beyond, they have nothing to compare themselves with. Pretty soon, every last one of them thinks he's something special.

Maybe this Lawrence won't be so high and mighty once he finds out why they're here. He's still sitting his horse and frowning as the door opens.

Lawrence comes out on to the front porch as the sun flares above the horizon, dressed for the occasion in his dove-grey coat and breeches, black string tie over the white ruffed shirt, his head crowned with a wide-brimmed planter's hat. For a second or two he stands, looking around him, sipping at the mint julep he has in his hand.

'Mister Lawrence?' Maitland's voice cutting sudden in the silence, sharp and impatient. At the sound Lawrence looks up, smiling, as if seeing the slim, fair man in the blue cavalry blouse and yellow-striped breeches for the first time.

'I have that honour.' Stepping off the porch as he speaks, drink in hand. 'Don't believe I caught your name, sir?'

'Captain James A. Maitland, United States Army.' The officer salutes briefly, ignoring the other man's proffered hand. 'We are here to perform a duty, Mr Lawrence. It is possible you may find it an unpleasant one.'

'That so?' Lawrence smiles, leans back on one of the painted pillars, sipping at his drink.

'You best git on an' perform it, I reckon.'

Looking into that smiling face, Maitland checks a sudden surge of anger. This fellow is beginning to annoy him, standing there as if he couldn't care less. The captain frowns, tight-lipped, gazing frostily on the man across from him.

We'll see how much you care, all right. *Mister* Lawrence!

'As no doubt you are aware,' the words coming from him harder than he would have liked, the irritation plain in his voice. 'As you must know, Mister Lawrence, following the victory of the Union forces, all slaves in the United States have been pronounced free.' He pauses, fixing the plantation owner with a stare of undisguised hostility. 'I am here to tell your workers that they are no longer bound to you. That they are no longer required to work for you, or for anyone, without

48

payment for their labour. Do you understand me, Mister Lawrence?'

Lawrence tastes the julep as it slides down his throat: sharp, burning sweetness of whisky and sugar blended together, the neat tang of the mint underlying them both. Lawrence savours the warm afterglow. Nods to the captain, still smiling.

'Reckon I git your meanin',' Lawrence says. His glance shifts to the blacks, waiting in silence, all of them looking towards him, ignoring the blue-clad horsemen in front of the porch. 'You best tell them, I reckon.'

At his answer Maitland frowns again, uncomprehending. Turns to the sergeant alongside. Elliott shakes his head, uncertain. Abruptly the captain draws himself upright in the saddle, shifting about to face the silent, stooping crowd of blacks, trying in vain to fix on one who will look him in the eye.

'You hear me?' Maitland calls out to a point above their bowed heads. Angry as he speaks, sensing the hopelessness of it all, feeling the clammy hug of sweat at his armpits and chest as the sun lifts higher. 'From now on you people have no master. You're free, all of you! If you want, you can leave this place now. No-one has the right to stop you from going!'

No answer from the bunched mass of slaves in front of him. Maitland eyes the stooping, half-naked figures with distaste. Back home, where he hardly ever saw a nigger, he was all for abolition. Close to, he finds them ugly and strange. Something in the broad, flat noses and thick lips, the long, dangling arms, that repels him. Most of all that dumb-dog beaten look they've got. More like animals than people. And by now the stink of their sweat is getting to him. Even the smell of them different, like some alien beast. Maitland bites on his lip. All at once he wishes he was miles away from here.

'Did you hear what I just said?' His voice ringing harsh in the new-fallen quiet. 'You're free!'

For a while no-one answers. Then the tall, reddish-skinned one at the front glances up warily, licking at his lips.

'Where else we gonna go, Captain?' Mede asks.

Meeting the sullen features of the tall man, Maitland finds himself lost for words. The look of this one throws him altogether:

thick, wavy hair with reddish lights in it—his eyes too pale for a black man, too. The soldier doesn't have to think too hard to guess at the kind of thing that's been going on here. His face flinches at the thought.

Like bedding down with an animal, he thinks.

Back of Mede, other voices can be heard.

'That's right, Cap–ten. Ain't noplace else fer us, fer sure.'

'Massa already tole us we free,' one of the women says.

At that, Maitland holds up a white-gloved hand for silence. Slowly he turns in the saddle, looking to where Lawrence leans by the pillar, smiling, finishing his drink. 'Is this true, Mr Lawrence?' Maitland asks, knowing from the look in those narrowed eyes that he's been caught, outsmarted by this backwoods planter.

'Sure is, Captain,' Lawrence grins, toying with the stem of his glass. He lifts his head, squinting in the harsh sunlight. 'Way I see it, you come too late. I already freed 'em, like Ruby told you just now.'

'May I ask what wages have been agreed?' By now he can no longer keep the malice from his tone. Useless to show it. He senses that Lawrence must already have thought of that too.

'Cain't pay no wages, Captain,' the planter tells him, smiling yet as he sets down the empty glass on the porch stoop. Signs to the old house servant, who bends with an effort to gather it up. 'I ain't none too rich at present, with the war an' all. Know what I mean? No, what we settled on is a share of the crop, see? They help me git the cane harvested next season, they kin take their cut. Share an' share alike, is how I see it.'

'I see,' Maitland answers dully. He's lost here, and he knows it.

'Course,' Lawrence is saying pleasantly, the smile at his lips, 'There'll be other matters to consider, come the time. Like the food an' shelter I provide fer my workers, the tools I give 'em fer the job, that kind of stuff. They got no way of payin' fer that, right now, Captain. Reckon that'll have to be deducted from their share of the crop, huh?'

'I reckon so,' Maitland murmurs. The disgust that thickens in his throat bids fair to choke him. 'And I don't suppose you could let them loose, to find work elsewhere?' he asks.

'Hell no, Captain.' Lawrence shakes his head. The look on his

50

face is almost hurt. 'We're close, me an' these people of mine. I cain't stand to see 'em trampin' the roads beggin' for somethin' to keep 'em from starvin', thievin' maybe . . . See, it's my duty to make sure they git food an' someplace to sleep. Work's gonna be here for 'em, long as they care to take it.'

Maitland glowers into that smiling face. Turns again towards the waiting blacks, their covert glances meeting him. Sullen, defeated looks from every one he seeks out. They know the way things are. Now, maybe he does too.

The hell with them, he thinks. Not one of them worth it.

'Yes,' Maitland says at last, defeat in his voice now as he speaks. 'I think we understand each other, Mister Lawrence.'

'Sure glad to hear you say that, sir.' Lawrence grins, leaning lazily against the porch pillar. 'A pleasure to know the two of us kin see eye to eye after this tragic conflict 'tween the states . . . Then agin, we both of us Americans, ain't that right?' He half-turns, glancing back to where the servant carries his glass away. Grins, with more than a touch of malice this time. 'Sure you won't stay an' take a drink with me, Captain? Julep sure is good . . .'

'Thank you, Mister Lawrence. I have duties to perform elsewhere.' The officer swings his fretting mount, swatting at the flies as he turns. Signs to the riders at his back. 'You need no further advice from us, that much is plain.'

'Just as you wish, Captain.' Lawrence chuckles behind his hand. 'Good day to you, sir.'

'Good day, Mister Lawrence.' The last words spat back over the shoulder.

The line of horsemen heads back along the narrow dirt road, sound of the animals' hooves falling hard on the rutted earth. Pretty soon only a cloud of dust can be seen. Lawrence sets his back to the pillar, eyes half-closed.

Sure was too smart for you, Mister Yankee Yellow-britches.

'Okay.' His voice brings all their heads around. His eyes open, touching keen as the cut of a whip on each sullen face in turn. 'You heard. You know how it is. Now git on back to work, you hear me?'

He stands watching them as they drift back out to the fields. The sun getting up higher, beating down on their half-naked black bodies. The bowed heads asnd slumped shoulders tell him the whole story. All of them beaten. They know it made no difference —the war, freedom, whatever. Noplace else for them to go. An' while they're on Sweet River, they better do like he tells them.

Nestor is last to go, the old man standing with his grey, salty head lowered, eyeing the white boss cautiously, sidelong. Ain't no surprise to Nestor. He seen it comin'. The war a white folks' thing anyhow. Noway they gonna git offen this plantation, less they run.

So far, Justus the only one made it by runnin'.

Remembering that, Nestor smiles. That boy smart, all right. He gonna git loose. Maybe git clear away over the big water, like he never did himself. Long as one man loose, he figures they's some hope fer the rest.

He stops smiling, aware once more of where he is, and of Lawrence's keen stare upon him.

'You too, Nestor,' Lawrence says. 'Man works fer me, he ain't got no time to stand around.'

'Yassuh, boss.' The old man grins, bowing at the word. 'I goin' right 'way, boss.'

He turns, a frail, stooped figure in the sun-drenched landscape, shuffling away real slow after the rest.

One day, maybe, the old man thinks, stumbling over hummocks in the roughly sloping ground. *One day.* But it sure as hell ain't now.

Lawrence watches him go, frowning for the first time since he came out on the porch. Never did care much for Nestor. Always figured he was someplace at the back of Justus breakin' out from Sweet River, though he never could prove anything. Now he eyes that thin back, smiling meanly. Once he's sure he has these blue-bellies off his back, he kin settle with Nestor.

Sweet warmth of the liquor in his gut sets his thoughts back inside the house, and Sheba waiting for him there. Lawrence nods, his cold eyes hooding. He'd all but forgot her for the moment. Now the growing bulge in his breeches is starting to remind him.

Lawrence goes back up the porch steps, stalks along the passage at a hurrying stride, throwing open the door of the room. He leaves the door open as he goes in.

Over in the middle of the curtained room, Sheba slides from the bed, quiet as a ghost, moving cat-like over the floor to meet him. Sunlight that blasts in at the window barring the sleek brown of her skin with deeper shadows.

'Sure has seemed like a long time, waitin' here for you,' Sheba murmurs.

Lawrence laughs. Pitches his hat across the room. Peels off his coat, letting it drop to the floor. She leans towards him, his mouth seizing fiercely on her own. Lawrence tearing at the black necktie as Sheba hurriedly unbuttons the front of his breeches.

'Don' worry, Massa Lawrence,' Sheba tells him. 'I'm gonna make it worth your while, jes' you wait an' see . . .'

He doesn't answer for a moment. His breath coming short and harsh in the quiet of the room. Watching her as she lays hold on his straining organ, stroking him to hardness. Sheba grins, her own eyes half-closing. Sinking to her knees, she draws his manhood to the smooth space between her breasts, cradling him there. Smooth touch of her skin tormenting him as the throbbing head of his penis nestles at her throat. Lawrence sighs, shivering. This time, he knows he ain't gonna be long.

'That's my girl,' he murmurs, looking down on her in the moment before the surge of feeling takes him over.

He doesn't bother turning to shut the door behind him. If Hagar ain't learned to keep her eyes to herself, he sure gonna give her somethin' worth watchin'.

A mile or so away, on the road towards Palmetto, Maitland reins in his horse. Sweat beading his brow, his face hot and red in the harsh Louisiana light, he turns to the grey-stubbled figure of Elliott beside him.

'Just what in hell did we fight this war for, Sergeant?' the captain asks.

Elliott grins, shrugs his heavy shoulders in their stained blue covering. 'Can't tell, sir. Beat folks like him, maybe.' He eyes the fair man, thin lips puckered. 'What's wrong, sir? Ain't you glad we won?'

'The hell we won,' Maitland says.

He touches his heels to the flanks of the animal under him, and the horse starts forward, the line of riders following the dirt road over the hill crest, heading for Palmetto as the sun comes higher over the flatlands and bayous of Lafayette County.

Sound of one drum beating from the compound beyond the open doorway, its solitary voice carrying to him where he lies on his mat of reeds. The sound low-toned, reverberating in the eerie stillness of the morning.

Justus rolls up on one elbow, coming awake, his hand closing on the butt of the pistol as his eyes accustom themselves to the changed light. The darkness rolled back now, the light in the doorway blue and bright. The air already hot and moist, making him sweat at the armpits.

Another day beginnin', sure enough.

Over by the door, the figure of Soldier leans upright, the long-barrelled shotgun gripped in both hands. Turning, stooped under the low roof of the hut, his one eye fixes on the prone shapes by the wall. The thin-lipped mouth wrenches in a grin. 'The god callin',' Soldier says. 'Come on outen there, you hear?'

Back of him Mary shifts and stretches, yawning awake. The warmth of her still close against him as he moves to hands and knees, checking the weapons laid out beside him. The bow and sheaf of palmetto arrows, the hoop-iron headed spear, the pistol, the long-helved woodman's axe. Slowly, carefully, Justus gathers them up. Slings the bow. Thrusts the gun into his fastened-up breeches. Getting to his feet, he sees Mary rise in turn, picking up her own light bow. Justus meets her eye, forces himself to smile.

No sense in goin' out there lookin' to be killed, he figures.

He follows Soldier's stooping shape out by the open door. Harsh light spearing in his eyes as he leaves the shadowed hut. Squinting against the sun's drizzling fire, he draws himself up to his full height; feeling the trodden earth of the compound under his feet. A tall, wide-shouldered black, bush-haired, hung with weapons. The spear in one hand. The other clasped in readiness on the butt of the belted pistol. At his back, Mary lays an arrow to the string of her bow.

In front of them the stripped tree bole casts a thin, grey shadow across the ground, its nailed white skulls grinning in the windless heat. Caught in that bar of shade, the drummer crouches, his lean back bent as he strikes, the hooked stick tapping as his free hand flexes the thongs. The pitch of the ghost-voice altering to his movements, rising and falling strangely, moment by moment. About him other figures gather, squatting in the dust, a silent circle of onlookers whose unclothed backs gleam black or red in sunlight: men, women and children alike sitting wordless, waiting as the sound goes on.

Justus' stare cuts over the open ground. Scans the high wall of the stockade that pens them in on every side. Somethin', too, he ain't noticed before: hewed tree forks, set into the ground, over-looking the ramparts. Maybe a half-dozen of them altogether, he figures at first glance, the upper forks lashed with hide ropes and what looks like a wadded pouch. Some kinda giant slingshot, from the look of it. Fixed in the ground back of them, he sees the low handled outline of winding gear. Justus nods, frowning in thought. Close to, these things could do some hurt, he reckons.

In answer to the call of the drum, other figures drifting over from the huts surrounding the inner wall of the stockade as he stands and watches. Their half-clad bodies black and copper in the morning light, carrying long-barrelled guns, and belted knives; horn-tipped Choctaw bows; arrowshafts headed with edged obsidian or flint or bone; long-shafted spears; cane knives and clubs. Justus studies them as they draw in towards the circle of watchers in the tree's shade. Beside the white patrols or the soldiers on the Lafayette road, he reckons they ain't too well armed. He seen nothin' here that shoots more'n once without reloadin'. Old single-shot muskets, shotguns loaded up with nails and scrap. Here an' there a single-shot pistol. Still, fixed as he is, he don't aim to treat 'em light. For what he seen, they close to a hundred in this place, an' the women armed same as the men.

In front of him Soldier turning, his broken face hard and impatient, the one green eye slitted against the sun.

'Stay close,' the veteran mutters.

Justus falls into step as Soldier heads for the squatting circle beyond, following that twisted shoulder, dipping and lifting as it weaves a way through the crowd. Treading where Soldier treads, his bare feet find space between the limbs of the seated watchers all around. Mary stepping close at his back, holding to the bow and its notched arrow, head held up, meeting the dark, hostile eyes about her with a level stare. The drum still beating as they step together, footfalls smothered in the soft, rising dust.

Up ahead, they reach the edge of the circle. Soldier squats, facing the drummer, laying the shotgun over his knee. Justus moves aside, settling on his heels. Bedding the shaft of the hickory spear in the dirt, balanced against his palm. Drawing the pistol so that it rests on his thigh, his hand covering the grips. Mary follows, crouching to his left, half-leaning against him as if to draw strength from his more powerful frame. Her arrow still fitted to the string.

Scanning, his look takes in a tight ring of faces: Red Wolf with his dark, hooked features, broad hands spread on his naked thighs, the black penetrating eyes staring intently. Beside him, the figure of old 'Gator Head, white, thick hair in a snowfall almost hiding his face. His eyes, too, dark and glittering against the yellowing, withered skin. On the far side comes Soldier and beyond him, Heron sprawling long-limbed in sunlight. At his shoulder the bronzed glister of Jewel's smooth body, her head turned towards Justus, its dark, deep eyes on him, searching. Out by her he glimpses a second slim form, its hue the same deep bronze as Jewel herself. The face that meets him is so like Jewel's a man cain't hardly tell them apart. For an instant he finds himself staring, unwilling to believe.

'That Diamond, her twin sister,' Soldier murmurs from alongside him.

Justus ducks his head in answer, turns from the probing eyes to face the drummer. The rest of them with him, looking out across the compound to where the long house rears up on its mound. Their faces intent, watchful. Waiting.

Abruptly the sound of the lone drum stutters, falls silent. Over at the long house, the doors swing open.

Shango stands in the open space, his long hands lifted. Black tall height of him towering against the risen light, rimmed suddenly in red fire. Taller than a ghost, tall as the trees around. At his side, the squat figure of Mama Odu, black of her flesh gleaming to match his own, the curved moon symbol throwing back fire at her breast.

Around him the sound of breath drawn sharply inward. Justus feels his body clench, steeling himself for what may lie ahead, his hands gripping the weapons.

Up by the long house, Shango lowers his arms. He turns, pushing the great doors shut. The drum sets up again as he turns once more, stepping towards the circle of watchers. Mama Odu alongside as he moves at a slow, measured walk, raising a spurt of dust with every step. The drum in time with him as he walks, the beat falling as the foot comes down. When at last he stands at the innermost ring of onlookers, the drum whirs briefly, and is still.

'The god come,' Shango intones from high above their heads, filed teeth bared as the lips draw back. His eyes fixed, staring at some point in the air beyond. As he speaks, the seated people sway. Bowing forward against the ground.

'SHANGO!' All of them shouting together, the sound fearful in the morning quiet.

Still squatting upright with Mary beside him, Justus senses that fierce stare coming his way. Meets it, the hairs prickling at his neck, once more feeling the awesome power of those piercing eyes. Mary, stricken by that look in her turn, steels herself to face it wide-eyed. Shango's keen gaze spanning her from head to foot. The look of him terrible, felt surely as a touch on flesh. Mary grits her teeth at the sensation, her face growing hot. Narrow-eyed above her, Shango snarls.

'The god sent us word,' the tall man says. The rest of them look up as he speaks, their eyes intent upon him. His eyes, though, on the bushy-headed man by his feet and the slim, fair-haired woman beside him. 'This one come to us with piece of the god in him, brung a white wench taggin' 'long after.' He pauses, one long finger lifting. His thin face unsmiling now as his glance cuts from one to the other. 'That a sign to us, ain't that right, Mama Odu?'

'That right, Shango.' The fat black woman at his side grins, her face rippling as the flesh creases. 'It a sign, sure 'nough.'

Justus, listening, swallows a thickening lump in his throat. Right now he don't know what Shango dreamed up, but he sure he ain't gonna like it one bit. Across from him, Mary pales, her glance wavers, her white face uncertain. Above her, Shango points suddenly to the seated figure of Justus.

'This boy show us how it gonna be,' Shango calls out, his voice ringing harsh in the open space. 'We gonna take our boats out to the white folks' places, an' lead 'em taggin' long after, like he done. White folk gonna be our slaves . . . Better yet, we gonna kill every last one. Give them to the god!'

As he speaks he's smiling, licking his lips, the points of his teeth showing wet, the black, harsh eyes lidded over. Down beside Justus, the white woman shudders, gulping for breath, her face pasty in sudden terror.

Around her the others nod, murmuring assent.

'That right! We take 'em!' Soldier breathes, his fierce face mask-like, staring.

On the haft of the spear his grip tightens, clenching. Justus feels fear like a sudden jagged flickering along his nerves, the sweat pricking out on his brow and the palms of his hands.

'The time right,' Shango breathes in answer. He stands tall above the seated crowd, teeth bared, grinning, spreading his long, dark hands. 'White folk fightin' one with another still; they ain't gonna look for us comin' to 'em from the swamps. We hit their plantations, chop 'em good, we git everythin' we want . . . more fighters, more women—sacrifices for the god . . .'

He breaks off, his breath coming harsh, the broad chest heaving, the eyes glassy, staring out ahead. At his side Mama Odu howls, her head flung back, her massive black body jerking, out of control.

'*Yeah, that right!*'

Shouts going up all around him where the others squat, swaying now, their eyes shut, sweat of them reeking in the packed space.

Beside him, Mary ducks, hiding her face. Justus clenches his teeth, hearing the breath hiss from back of his throat, the salt taste of blood in his mouth, the frenzy of gasps and cries taking him, as the pulse of drums threatened to do before.

'Nothin' gonna stop us, you hear?' Shango yells shrilly, his arms lifting. 'The god in us, an' he strong . . . *strong* . . .'

He repeats the word, intoning it as a sound, eyes shut as the

58

sweat gathers on his lean face and the veins thicken and pulse in his neck. Mama Odu gives a high-pitched cry, falls to her knees in the dirt, her great belly arching as she leans backwards, thrusting in spasmodic movement with her huge thighs spreading open.

Shango whirling as the rush of sound grows louder, sweat spraying off him, his finger on Heron, pointing.

'You, Heron! You the scout.' He gasps for breath, the slitted eyes questioning. 'Which the white folk plantation nearest? Tell it!'

'Blackwater.' Heron's face holds a stunned look, his eyes on Shango as he breathes the word. 'West a ways. No more'n a night's journey, lord . . .'

'That the place!' Shango grins, throws back his feathered head and stamps in the dust. 'Come nightfall, we go Blackwater! Hit the place 'fore sun-up!'

His sharp glance switches, fixing again on Justus, who squats dry-mouthed, watching him warily, like a a cornered jackrabbit might look on a snake. Blackwater. That Devereaux's place, he thinks.

'You boy!' Shango breathing above him, beads of sweat spattering him as he moves. 'You brung us the sign . . . You come with us to Blackwater, boy . . . an' bring her after. You both there, ain't no way we kin go wrong . . .'

The words end. Only the harsh, shivering sound of his breath before the lone drum hammers into life once more and the squatting folk give out a shrilling cry. Shango turns, looming tall as a spectre against the sun, looking to where Mama Odu thrashes on the dusty ground, her eyes shut, grunting beast-like as the spasms take her over.

'The god give strength!' Shango calls.

He stands, stripping away the belt of skins to stand naked before them all, his gaunt body heaving and shaking in the force of the blood-frenzy he has whipped up. He kneels, hands on the fat spread thighs of Mama Odu. Enters her, crying out.

Justus hears Mary's retching cry, reaches to hold her to him, covering her face. Grim-faced, he forces himself to watch as the thing is done: the body of god and goddess enmeshed in a tangle of limbs, coupled, each fusing into the other with their terrible power.

Around him the upsurge of voices rises to a deafening climax and the rhythmic pulsing of the drum drowns out all other sounds.

Over their heads a night-owl sweeps, calling. He glances up to the sudden beat of wings, the low, hooting cry. Watching as the feathered shape skims by, vanishing into darkness. Justus licks his lips, swallowing. Still don't care fer night birds, even now. He turns, settling himself as the prow of the long pirogue cuts through the water ahead, the black surface smooth and gleaming, yielding with hardly a ripple to the long boat's passing. Crouched in front, Soldier turns, his paddle dipping, the one eye fixing on him over the high, humped shoulder.

'Not far, now,' the veteran tells him, the mask of a face grim against the dark. 'Heron know his way, I reckon.'

Justus makes no answer, watching as the paddle strikes and the boat slides on through the lilies and the thick carpet of weed. The night air heavy and close upon him, the reeking scent of flowers and mud overpowering in his nostrils. He wipes a wet palm on his breeches, feeling his belly pulse uneasily as he moves. Pretty soon, he knows, they gonna be killin'.

Ain't that what you was always after, Justus boy? Kill you some whites?

Pirogues in the water on either side, front and back of him: low, gliding shapes that glisten as their paddles cut the water, sending up a strange silver light. He ain't got round to countin' 'em yet. Must be a dozen, at the least, halfway empty, most of them. Shango countin' on company when they turn home. He scowls, his glance shifting from one boat to another, checking for familiar faces. Heron is way ahead of them, upright in the stern of the leading boat as he thrusts on the pole. Jewel in that boat with him, and Diamond her sister. Back of them, it's Red Wolf an' a coupla Choctaw bucks. Tracking across, his gaze halts at Shango, his gaunt, long-limbed shape leaning erect in the bow of the pirogue, feathered and hung with his array of skins, the bone whistle at his neck. Mama Odu's squat, ebony bulk huge at his back and behind

60

them the steersman—Indian name of Crow Feather, stocky and bow-legged, his arms unusually long for so short a man. Shango catches the look, turns to meet it, smiling, showing the points of his teeth. His huge eyes staring. A stray shaft of moonlight strikes fire from the thick-bladed cutlass lying in his lap.

Justus breathes hard, looking away, forcing himself to fix his gaze on the humped back of Soldier as the one-eyed veteran bends to his work. Up ahead, the tall, fronded reedbeds fall away. Trees thickening at the waterside: live-oak, cypress, cottonwood, leaning over the water, their low boughs overhanging them as the boat glides beneath, long twigs trailing in the dark of the water.

'Justus.' His name a faint whisper in the rippling stillness. Half-turning to the sound, he finds her white, scared face. Her wide eyes upon him. Justus doesn't speak. Lays a hand on her pale arm that trembles at his touch.

'Justus.' Her look on him, begging. 'I can't go through with this. I've never seen these people before. I can't just go out and kill them like animals or something . . .' Her eyes welling suddenly, reflecting the moonlight. 'Justus, I ain't never hurt no-one in my life . . .'

He eyes her in silence, knowing there are no words. They goin' to kill *her* people, an' she got to be there. There no other way it kin be. Leave her back there at the stockade, an' one of them would sure as hell try for her. 'Sides, Shango decided she part of his sign. Ain't no goin' agin that, fixed as he is.

'Just stick by me, huh?' Justus tells her. His hand strokes her bare arm, soothing, his voice husky, soft and tender. 'It goin' to be all right, girl. You hear me?'

But he knows as he speaks there nothin' he kin do. He as helpless as she is.

Didn't oughta be this way, he thinks. Wasn't countin' on him meetin' no black folks out here; but iffen he had, he'd of thought it might be better'n this. Here it like Sweet River almost, with Shango the boss. An' Shango one hell of a lot harder to git free from.

'Yeah.' Mary's voice subdued, scarcely to be heard. She looks down, brushing at her wet face. 'It'll be all right, I guess, Justus.'

He watches her a while, then turns again to face forward, scowling into the dark.

Back of them, Cedar stands to drive his long pole into the water. Tall man, Cedar, like his name. High, hawkish features like to an Indian's, with a black gleam of hair and dark, piercing eyes. His skin deeper than any Choctaw's, though—dark brown, almost black. Nigger's skin. One ear hung with a thick loop of bone. He eyes Justus in silence, stonily. Strikes again with the pole to send the boat surging forward under the trees.

Overhead, the boughs part suddenly and the moon shines full upon them. Blaze of silver light over dark sweating backs and lifted faces. Ripple of shining phosphorescent fire on the black, scummed surface of the water. As the light falls Mama Odu calls out from the pirogue across from them, arms and face raised to the ghostly brilliance of the moon. From the boats all around comes an answering chant.

'Odu! Odu! The god come!'

'Good sign, boy,' Soldier says, looking back to him. 'Goddess raise the moon. Gonna be good huntin' come mornin'.'

He doesn't answer, looking to where the fat black woman still calls out, her face and breasts and upraised arms bathed in the fall of light, silvery fire glinting from the metal crescent hung between her breasts. Justus eyes those gross, ecstatic features, remembering. Swallows.

'What in hell this all about, Soldier?' he asks the humped high-shouldered back that bends in front of him. Speech comes awkward, thick in his throat, trapped by the war of feelings inside him. 'They white folks, sure, but they ain't done nothin' to us. Why we gotta kill 'em?'

'God give the word.' Soldier doesn't turn his head, coming upright as the paddle trails water on its blade. ''Sides, they own slaves, don' they?'

'Still ain't harmed us none.' He knows he oughta shut his mouth, but the feeling inside won't let him. It got to be talked out, he figures. 'You live free all yo' life, Soldier. How come you gotta kill these folks, huh?'

'We lucky, boy.' Soldier gives him a raking glance, his green eye burning fierce as he speaks. 'That don' pardon them for what they

62

done to our people. We hittin' them 'fore they think to hit us, you hear?'

'I guess so,' Justus murmurs, his head sunk, the wash of feelings churning in his stomach.

'Trouble with you,' Soldier tells him, 'you lost yo' haid over that white piece back yonder. You want to be smart, you better not ask no more questions like that. Specially with the god close. He don' miss nothin'.'

Justus nods, silenced by Soldier's warning. Soldier is right. He should have kept his mouth shut after all.

Up ahead of them, Heron calls out, lifting his pole from the water. The long pirogue runs up against the bank, hiding itself in the high grass and reeds. Heron, long-limbed and slender in moonlight, lays down the pole as Jewel and Diamond spring ashore, their smooth bodies dappled silver-black under the trees. The heavy cane knives gleaming in their hands. Around them the other crews ship paddles, making for the bank.

'Blackwater!' Heron sings. He darts ashore after the other two, hefting the spear as he moves. Further along the bank, Red Wolf leads his Indians into a bed of reeds. Across from them he sees Shango's boat as it turns, heading towards them, the gaunt figure standing, looking shoreward. In the dazzle of moonlight the fixed stare of his eyes is hard to bear. Justus looks away, his hands sweating.

Back of them, Cedar lifts his pole, their prow beaching in the thick mud. Soldier crouches, leaps over the side, holding the shotgun in the crook of his arm. Justus goes after him, landing ankle-deep in the mud and reeds. Holds out a hand to Mary as she jumps in turn. She lands, thudding hard against him, gasping for breath a moment. In that moment Justus pulls the Colt from his waist, thrusts the weapon into her hand.

'Take it,' he tells her, his dark eyes locking with hers. 'One of 'em lays a hand to you, use it. An' don't miss. You got but one chance.'

Mary bears with his gaze for the instant, her look searching, questioning, her hair washed silver in the strange light. Face and body gleaming pale against the dark, moving shapes all around. slowly she nods, taking the gun from his hand.

Cedar comes leaping ashore after them, long-handled axe gripped in one hand, in the other, a pitch-coated wood knot. Several of the others carry them too, he notices. Gonna be burnin' as well as killin', come the time.

Beyond them both, Shango springs to the land. A shout goes up as he crouches there, arms upraised, looking about him. Light on the glittering cutlass, the puckered bites on the arms, flickering over the gaunt skull-face with its carved patterns, the staring eyes, the pointed glint of bared teeth. Back of him Mama Odu waddles through the shallows, a heavy-bladed knife held crossways in her hand, its edge sending back a white curve of fire.

At the top of the bank they muster, standing ranked together in the waist-high grass. All eyes on Shango as he moves to the head of the column; Heron beside him, the spear back at his shoulder; Crow Feather standing stump-legged to his back. Justus scans the mass of eager faces. More'n thirty of 'em, he reckons. An' close to half of 'em women. Jewel catches his eye and smiles. A cruel smile, like to a cat, dark eyes half-lidded. The light spilling on her bare, lifted breasts. Justus meets the look for a moment, then she turns away.

Yeah, he figures. Women git to like it as much as the men, give 'em the chance.

Shango signs with the cutlass in his hand and they go forward, threading in silence through the high grass and the clumps of live-oaks that cover the slope ahead. Justus sticks close to Soldier, following as the humped figure moves swiftly uphill in front of him. Mary at his back, hurrying to keep pace, stumbling from time to time as her bare feet slip in the sodden grass.

Tall fronds of grass whispering, stroking at his body as he pushes through. Up in the live-oaks an owl hoots, and he sucks in his breath at the sudden sound, sweat breaking from every pore of his skin. In front of him, Soldier breaks into a loping run, headed for the crest. Justus follows, aware of other moving shapes in the grasses on either side. Gleam of weapons and glancing eyes. Beyond him the ground levels out suddenly. He tops the rise, reaching back to haul Mary up after him.

'We here,' Soldier says, halting in front of him, looking to his gun.

In front of them a high spreading forest of cane. Field after field, stretching far as the eye can see. Dark ocean of moving stems under the moonlit dark of sky. Cane growing way above a man's haid. Stems thick as two, three fingers set together. Dirt roads between the fields leading to a huddle of cabins further off. Over beyond them he sees the looming shape that has to be the sugar-house; the white-painted building with its pillared porch, set apart from the rest. White folk's house. Justus scowls, his lips setting to a narrow bitter line. He unslings the bow from his back. Remembering Lawrence. Sheba. That time in the sugar-house on Sweet River. And the other times in the feed barn. With the wenches.

Soldier right. They all bastards the same. Kill' em boy, while you got the chance.

Glancing back to where Mary stands, both hands gripping the long-barrelled pistol, he frowns again, confused by the look in her eyes. Turns away again. Suddenly, he don't feel easy in his mind.

Up ahead, Heron and Shango standing close together, talking in low voices.

'They got dogs,' he hears the tall youth say. 'Gotta take 'em out, 'fore we go in.'

Shango nods, signs to Red Wolf. The heavy-set Choctaw bends to shake out a hide noose from his belt. Somethin' else hangin' there, too, that looks like a chunk of meat—rabbit leg, maybe. Red Wolf grins, turning to push a way by him, and he sucks in his breath sharp as the scent hits his nostrils. Swamp rabbit—an' stinkin' pretty high. They thought of the dogs all right.

Red Wolf and the two Choctaw bucks are already gone, taking the dirt road beyond at a silent rapid lope. Blending with the darkness, their shapes lost to sight. In front of him Shango swings around suddenly, his long arms spread. Light glinting keen on the whistle and claws at his neck, the white glare of teeth and eyes.

'You, boy!' Shango tells him. 'You go with Heron. I want that sugar-house fired, an' quick. Cedar,' his look shifting to the tall man further back, 'bust in them quarters, git the slaves loosed, you hear me?' He touches the bone whistle at his throat. 'We take the big house from the front. By then, these fields should be afire, too. Now, git goin'.' His eyes on Justus again as the last words come from him, hissing through his teeth.

Justus stands, saying nothing as the gaunt figure heads off to the left, following another narrow track that curves round to take the big house from another side. Mama Odu's bulky shape follows him, and Crow Feather with his stone-headed club. Other outlines of women and men, bent over in darkness, moving out after him without a sound. Soon they too are gone, their bodies swallowed by dark and the thickly spreading canefields all around. Justus looks to Mary beside him, from her to the others who stand, waiting, weapons in their hands: one-eyed Soldier with his shotgun; Cedar, shouldering his long axe; Jewel and Diamond with wood knots and their heavy-bladed knives. Up front of them, Heron turns his head.

'Let's be goin',' the slim spearman tells him.

The path winds out between the high walls of cane, the thick stems growing tight and close together, all but shutting out the light overhead. No way through, there, they got to follow the road. The party moves at a loping stride, footfalls and breathing the only noises in the fresh-fallen stillness. Heron in front with his pecking walk, long legs raking over the hard-trodden earth, spear back at his shoulder. Out to the side of him, Soldier goes on at a shuffling run, careful to keep his long-barrelled gun from hitting on the canes. Justus licks at drying lips, lets fall his hand to touch the hoop-iron knife at his belt. Ain't brought the spear along, this time; man kin only carry so much, he figures.

Back of him Mary, running barefoot, stubs her toe on a hummock in the ground, bites down on the grunt of pain. Jewel chuckles softly from beside him, dark eyes aglint in a scatter of moonlight as she looks his way, smiling, moving a shade closer to brush him with her warm flank as she runs. Justus sets his teeth at the touch of her flesh, scowling as she moves out ahead.

Sooner or later, that girl gonna be trouble for him.

Seems like miles before the dirt road turns at last, angling back of the canefields towards the quarters and the sugar-house. Away on their right the cane falls back, leaving open space where the light falls in thick, silvery bars across the ground. At Heron's lifted hand the bunch of them halts, crouched in cane shadow, looking out ahead.

Down by the quarters other dark shapes move: Red Wolf and his Choctaws. Against the line of buildings, Justus sees the hounds as they spring up on their feet: two big mastiffs, like the ones they run him with a while back, standing huge in moonlight, the hair bristling on their bodies, starting to growl from deep in their throats as the smell of intruders comes wafting over to them from the cane. Even as he watches the meat hunk lands in the dirt, close by their feet, and the two dogs start in for it together. Same instant Red Wolf and his Choctaws are out from the shadows and on to them. Justus sees Red Wolf noose the nearest, slipping the hide thong over the head as the animal's jaws close on the rotten meat, dragging back to throttle it taut about the neck. The second hound has swung away when the others hit, and the noose clamps over its muzzle. The Indian leaps, dodging the huge head whose jaws spatter him with foam. He hangs to the muzzle, lying across its neck as the other man draws his knife and sinks it low into the flank, under the ribs. Stricken, the big hound grunts and keels over, the pair of them hanging to it as the long knife strikes again.

Red Wolf still grappling with the hound he has snared as the other lies quiet. The squat Indian drags the beast upright, hauling it on to the hind legs as the noose bites through the fur. Sight of the creature's head flung back, the eyes staring wide-open, frantic, desperate. Red Wolf snarls, the muscles bunching along his arms. Growl of the dog choking off with its breath. All at once the great head lolls aside, the legs giving way. The Indian lets it fall, loosing hold of the snare. From beside him the other two men get up, the nearer of them wiping his blood-stained knife.

'Time to go,' Soldier mutters.

Heron lets out his breath with a hissing sound, then leads them off at a run for the huts beyond. Cedar pushing forward, hefting the long-handled axe. Justus runs with the rest, holding to his bow. Mary reaches to him, stumbling, and he takes her hand in his, loosening his grip on the hoop-iron knife. Up ahead, the quarters loom silent against the dark, their doors barred from the outside. Cedar draws breath, his hard eyes narrowed. He darts forward from the rest. Swings with his axe at the nearest of the doors. Planks give way to the blow, splintering inward. From inside the building, a woman screams.

Justus whirls towards the sound, distracted for the moment. Almost as he moves, he senses a darker shadow that looms abruptly in his path. A big, heavy-muscled black man, coming at a run from around the corner of the nearby cabin, the whip raised and curling above his head.

Driver man!

Justus slewing around on his heels as the whip comes over, too late to fit an arrow into his bow. His left arm up to shield his eyes. Justus feels the blacksnake strike, winces as the lash bites and pulls away, slicing into the flesh. For a frozen instant he meets the driver's thick-lipped furious face, breathing harshly a few paces from his own. The whip going back again as the blood starts to pour from his torn arm . . .

Same instant, blast of a heavy gun.

Mary's shot smashes into the driver at close range, blowing a bloody fist-sized hole through the middle of the body, slamming him into the cabin wall. He chokes and lets fall the whip, his thick lips spilling blood over his chin, echoes of the gunshot battering back as he heels away and hits the dirt headlong and lies still.

Turning, he sees her standing there, the gun held out in her grasp, trailing smoke. Justus swallows, eyeing the white, stunned face, the trembling of her body, heedless for the moment of the blood that trickles from him to the ground. Right now, ain't a thing he kin say.

Further back comes a roaring gush of flame and the sound of men shouting. Looking, he sees the far canefield ablaze, the close-set stems flaring up together as Shango's men pitch in their torches. From the dirt road comes a rush of dark figures, weapons gleaming in the light of the flames. The foremost of them tall, feather-crowned, hefting a cutlass. Shango lifts the bone whistle to his lips. The shrill blast saws on the nerves.

'Kill! Kill for the god!' Shango yells. He heads his men in a charge for the big house, long legs driving under him. Mama Odu rolling at his back, moonlight glinting on the thick-bladed knife in her hand.

More shrieking from the cabins as Cedar's axe goes in, smashing the door, beating it loose from its wooden pins. Heron rounds on them as the whistle blasts, breathing hard, his face like to a young boy's, eager and excited at the thing to come.

'Git to the sugar-house!' Heron shouts. Jewel and Diamond lighting their torches as he speaks, the wood knots blazing up sudden against the dark. The bunch of them break into a run for the bulking shape of the sugar-house beyond the quarters, as Cedar's axe busts another door and lets out a fresh group of terrified slaves. Justus and Mary running with them. Not speaking. Helpless.

The thing started now, an' ain't no way they kin go back.

Up at the sugar-house, the doors open on to the hot night. Inside of it stacked with the cut stems of cane. Diamond lunges past him, whooping, pitching her torch in a flaring arc towards the heaped sugar. The torch thuds into the cut stems, the flame wavering once but blazing up again as the sugar takes. Jewel comes in behind her sister, flings her own torch in. After her, one of the others . Flames start to lapping up the cane, roaring as they reach the walls. The sugar-house begins to blaze.

Jewel turning to him, grinning, the harsh light beating orange on her face.

'Yeah, kill for the god!' Jewel says.

Back of the sugar-house, a fresh crackling as fire catches in the canefields further on. Heron lopes towards the big house, where the doors slam back and dark, uncertain figures are stumbling out on to the porch, guns in their hands. Shango's party rushing them from the other side. Soldier frowns. Leans to cock the double hammers of his gun, his glance darting to touch once on Justus, who stands fitting an arrow to his bow, the blood trickling still from his wounded arm. Soldier smiles, his dark face twisting.

'Let's go, boy,' the veteran says.

At the quarters, slaves are pouring out as Cedar smashes down one door after the other. Some of the women are still yelling out, but there are men among them, and some are looking around for weapons: rocks, stray cane stems—anything, their eyes already wild and staring in the fanning light of the flames. A second driver, pounding up towards the quarters, is washed down beneath a tide of black, thrashing bodies. Justus catches a glimpse of rocks and jagged sticks hitting at somethin' on the ground. Hears the terrible high-pitched scream as they smash the life out of him.

'Yeah, that right! Kill that sonofabitch driver good!'

'Kill! Kill for the god!' Heron yells from in front of him, rushing the porch with his long spear lifted. Justus following, and Mary, the pair of them caught up by the sudden, headlong surge of the packed bodies behind them.

Flamelight shivers on the front of the big house, catching the figures on the porch in a lurid glare, their features etched in the light of the fire. Justus sees Devereaux, balding and heavy—paunched, struggling to bring up the long gun in the grip of his hands, shirt open over his chest, pants sagging, braces hanging loose. Other shapes back of him, slimmer, younger. His sons maybe. One don't look no more'n a boy from here. From inside the house, he reckons he kin hear women screamin'.

The long gun levels, blasting into the onrush of black bodies. Out by Shango a running figure shrieks, spins round and falls. Other shots racketing from either side as his sons open up in turn. Justus ducks, feeling the hot wind of the slug as it buzzes past above his head. Up ahead of him, Soldier triggers off both barrels together, the boom of the shotgun echoing huge in the open space. The big white man yells, hammered against the doorpost by the force of the blast, the heavy charge of nails and metal slugs all but ripping him apart at the middle. He clutches his belly, spilling down, the long gun rattling out across the porch.

Crackle and splutter of burning canefields all around. The high screams of women, and the frenzied shouts of the attackers. On the far side, a full-toned roaring from the blazing sugar-house. Justus fits a palmetto shaft to the bow-string, his fingers hurrying, deaf to the sobbing cries of Mary as she tugs at his arm. Shakes her loose as a gun cracks from the porch and a dark shape carrying a torch goes sprawling down, the wood knot guttering out against the ground. His own arrow whips loose, the sound coming back to him as the white man leans and sags by the wall, his gun sinking as he plucks at the feathers in his side. Justus stands a moment, watching him, feeling the saliva thicken in his throat until he figures he goin' to choke.

Ain't this what you always wanted, Justus boy? Kill you some whites?

'Kill! Kill for the god!'

Shango gains the porch, the cutlass lifted. Red flamelight like blood along the blade. He's at the sagging white man before he can turn, swings back-handed to chop him across the neck. The man chokes as the blow hits. His head lolling stupidly sideways on the hacked neck. Blood sprays from the gaping wound as he goes down, spattering Shango's chest. The tall man shrieks, brandishing his bloody knife.

The young kid at the back drops his smoking gun to the ground. Turns to run back inside. Lurid light falls on his terror-stricken face, the blond tangle of his hair. Heron comes in like lightning, the long spear dipping as it strikes. The iron spearhead whistles through the thin back and breaks out at the chest, the kid yelling once as the spear ploughs through him. Justus hears the dull thump as the point hits on the doorpost at the far side. Heron shakes the thrashing body loose from the blade, darts in over the threshold, the others pouring after him, treading the sprawled limbs underfoot.

Down by his feet Devereaux groans, trying to lift himself on his hands out of a spreading pool of blood. Justus sees the lifted face, the mouth dribbling dark at the corners. The stump-legged figure of Crow Feather leaps in by him. Swings the stone-headed club down. The skull gives way with an ugly crunching sound. Devereaux goes down again, his head vanishing under the blow. Back of him he hears Shango's frenzied shouting.

'They women in there! Bring 'em out, you hear me?'

Shango grins, standing blood-spattered in the leaping light of the flames, the long blade dripping in his hand. Justus meets the mad stare of those eyes and turns away, feeling a tight knot of sickness bind his gut together.

In front the wave of bodies parts. Mama Odu bulks in the doorway, dragging a struggling white woman after her along the ground, the woman screaming like a rabbit in a snare: older woman, greying hair shaken loose over her fear-struck face. Behind her, two Choctaw bucks have hold of a young girl, gripping her fast between them, the gown ripped to show the white

71

gleam of her bosom through the cloth, the young girl whimpering, frantic in terror, her eyes wide and staring, but seeing nothing. Mama Odu drags the older one to her knees on the wood of the porch, one black hand fastened in the greying hair. The licking glare of flame touches on the broad-bladed knife she holds.

'This one for Odu!' the black woman calls out.

The woman screams out again in the moment before the blade slashes her across the throat. The cry gives way to a thick, gurgling sound, her eyes rolling back. A bright spray of blood fountains out from the severed neck, falling in thick drops on the earth beyond the porch. Mama Odu stands back, her knife running dark and shiny in the strange light, watching as the woman slumps down among the other bodies, jerking like a wry-necked chicken in its death throes. Mama Odu smiles.

'No! Oh, dear God!' Mary cries out back of him, her voice choking in her throat.

Shango stands over the whimpering girl as his men pin her down, holding her spreadeagled on the floor of the porch. Their hands ripping away the cloth so that her breasts fall free, throwing back the skirts from her spread thighs. Watching, Justus sees the pale sheen of her naked body in the light of the flames, the dark nipples taut and erect in terror, almost black against the white of the skin. The smooth mound of the belly. The reddish tufted patch that covers her between the thighs. Shango leaning above her, letting fall the skins from his waist. The thick, pulsing stand of his member, jutting huge and dark from the gaunt line of his body. The girl looks up into his smiling face and screams.

'To the god!' Shango cries.

He lets fall the cutlass and lowers himself on the girl's outspread body.

Her first scream stills as his manhood forces its way into her. Shango's hard hands at her breasts, crushing them. Thrusting his body brutally into hers, bucking and levering back and forth in a savage, urgent rhythm. The girl moans softly, whimpering. Her head fallen sideways against the ground, her eyes staring wide into the glare of flame as the canefields blaze all around. Shango sweating, gripping at her, eyes shut, teeth grinding as the moment comes fast upon him. Abruptly he shudders, breath leaving him in a harsh, snarling sound, jerking as he shoots into the whiteness of her body. Shango grunts, pulling out. Sits a moment, breathing hard. Then he grins. Signs to Soldier. The one-eyed veteran shucks his pants. Climbs on to the whimpering girl, grunting like an animal as he pushes his way inside.

He hears Mary's retching cry from behind him. Turns about to look. The white woman leans on one of the porch pillars, hanging over as she vomits on to the ground, the empty gun trailing useless in her grasp. Her body shaking, helpless in revulsion. Justus spits away from him, his face flinching. All at once, he feels like throwing up too.

Stepping over the ruck of bodies in the doorway, he takes a look inside. One look is enough. His glance takes in a group of screaming black house niggers, stumbling in their heavy skirts to escape the knives and clubs of their attackers. He sees a slim brown-skin housemaid overtaken and thrown to the ground, her dress dragged up over her head as the men hold her down. Heron on his knees, entering her, his back to Justus as he bucks and moans. Beyond them, a fat grey-haired man-servant cowers in a corner of the room, his hands clasped to his loins, gibbering and mewing in terror. From the dark spreading pool under him, it's plain he's already wet himself. Diamond stalks in towards him, her face hard-eyed, merciless. The old servant squawks, ducking his head as the blow comes down. Diamond chopping on the back of his neck, hacking at him again and again as his bulky figure collapses to the floor.

From the nearby passage a screaming housemaid comes rushing in, slamming into him as he stands, barring the door. Close behind her the lithe shape of Jewel, the cane knife lifted and ready in her hand. At sight of her the maid spins round, ducking away from Justus in an effort to escape. The movement takes her out of his sight, down by the inner wall. Jewel comes by him, breathing hard, the heavy knife poised for the blow.

'Kill for the god!' Jewel gasps, eyeing him sidelong as she strikes down.

'Oh, my Lawd!' He hears the crouched woman squeal once, then the sound cut off by the ugly chopping fall of the knife.

Jewel steps back in the doorway, breathing hard, smiling, the cane knife dripping dark along its blade.

Somethin' in her look sets his gut to lurching. Justus staggers out, bile at his lips as his feet tread soft, white corpses, sprawled one on top of another in the porch. He finds he's sliding in a pool of blood. Out on the porch Soldier is through, and the white girl has a third man on her, face clenched, breath hissing, rutting her like a beast. Justus glances but once, then turns from them. Could be Crow Feather, he cain't be sure. Under him, the girl has done screaming and crying. Now she begins to chuckle softly. A mad, hair-prickling sound, low in her throat.

A deep, wrenching roar as the sugar-house blows its roof, the whole building bursting outward as the sugar goes up to the flame. The blast showering blazing fragments everywhere, spattering into the canes where the thick sap bubbles, burning. Chunks of flaring wood and jagged cane stalks whining as they lash the open space. Justus hears the screaming of slaves in the quarters. Sees men and women hit by the flying shards, going down, the fire spreading swiftly to the roofs of the nearby huts. From the closest of them a lone figure rushes out in flame, shrieking, rolling, beating itself against the ground.

Oh, my God! Shaking his head. Eyes brimming as the sickness wells up inside him, wondering how in hell he keeps from throwing up.

The canefields are a surging mass of flames now, cane stalks crackling and spitting in the heat of the blaze, sap bubbling in the scorched stems. Back of him someone tosses a torch into the big house and flames lick up at the curtains in the window. From inside comes the beginnings of a scream that is suddenly, brutally cut off.

The housemaid they had down, he thinks. And then: God help us all!

'C'mon! Git goin'!' Shango on his feet and clothed, brandishing the bloody knife, his eyes moving fast from one to the next, stopping where the last man grunts, pulling out from the white girl's quivering body.

'Yeah,' Shango says. 'Bring her 'long. She for the god.'

His glance shifts as they drag her away, still chuckling to herself.

Locks sudden on Justus. The big man meets those fierce, staring eyes, bloodshot and glinting in the light of the flames, seemingly themselves ablaze.

'You okay, boy?' the tall man asks.

'I reckon.' Justus forces himself to hold that fixed stare, unsmiling, a dull pain still in the arm where the whip struck him. 'God in me tired, I guess.'

For a moment Shango frowns, his eyes hooding over. Then the tall man throws back his hollow-cheeked head and laughs, baring his long teeth, light flaring on the sticky stain of blood that covers his chest and arms.

'Yeah, reckon you right at that.' Shango grins, his harsh stare still probing at the man in front of him. Finding a solid wall back of the big man's eyes. Abruptly he turns from Justus, calling out to the others on the porch. 'Let's go, you hear me?'

He blasts on the bone whistle, and the bunch of raiders starts down off the porch, still holding to their fouled knives and clubs, Jewel and Diamond going by him at a run, their lithe bodies sleek with sweat and spattered with blood at the breasts and thighs. Justus feels his gut clench like a giant hand. He gets a hold on Mary's waist as fire blossoms from the open doorway of the house, drawing her away from where she clings by the pillar.

'C'mon, honey,' he tells her, his voice hoarse and shaky. 'We gotta be goin' . . .'

Mary has done vomiting now. Her face still pale, ugly for a moment in shock and pain. She shakes her head dazedly, eyes wide, a wet trail of saliva at her open mouth. Justus recalls the white girl and shudders. He gets a grip on her arm, pulling hard as she fights him, dragging her from the pillar. Down the steps, one by one.

'C'mon, Mary.' His voice pleading as his grasp subdues her. 'You all right with me . . .'

Mary gasps. Relaxes in his hold, her white face stricken, the eyes almost mistrustful on him. For a while he wonders if all this has sent her crazy, too.

Slowly, Mary draws breath. 'I hear you Justus,' she says. It seems that her voice comes to him from a world away.

Through the blazing canefields, stumbling along the dirt road as the scorching flames fan them from either side. Soldier in front of them, struggling to fasten his pants as he runs; Mama Odu, the knife still running blood on to her heavy hide skirt; tall outline of Shango loping ahead, blasting on the whistle as he goes. The night paling now to the sound of screams and bellowings of pain, the dull rumble of buildings that burn and collapse, the crackle of spreading flame . . .

At the far end of the dirt road from Blackwater, a yelling mob of fugitives run into them, slaves from the quarters, men and women. Some kids there, too, looking scared to death. Some armed like Shango's men, others wailing helpless, knowing they alone now with no-one to look out for them. He sees Red Wolf grab at a shrieking black woman, sees the thin black man who reaches to thrust him back.

'You leave go my woman, you hear?' the man shouts.

One of the other Choctaws grabs him by the hair. Sinks a stained knife hard under the ribs. The man hits the dirt, coughing blood as he writhes on the ground. The woman screaming out as Red Wolf drags her away through the trees.

Justus follows them, numbed beyond feeling at what he seen, holding to Mary's white arm as if it the last thing he got in all the world.

Blackwater blazing behind them, lighting up the sky as they gain the pirogues along the bank. One-eyed Soldier already seated there, looking back for him. Justus springs for the boat. Lifts Mary in after him. Back of them Cedar comes lunging out of the flamelit dark, dragging a young girl in a headtie who sobs against his clutching hand, her eyes pouring wet, her bared breasts shuddering uncontrollably. Cedar pitches her into the boat, climbs for the stern, her sobbing the one sound as he lifts his pole.

Crow Feather already pushing Shango and Mama Odu out over the water, firelight snaking bright over the surface as they move. Heron back, too, and his sisters. Right now, Justus cain't bear to look at any one of them. Heedless even of the pain in his arm, he looks for Mary's face in the gloom, trying to reach her, sensing her suddenly cold, remote from him.

You done it, he thinks, as a far crash and a gush of sheeting flame tells of the big house falling. You sure as hell did it. Kilt you some whites, sure 'nough.

Ain't that what you always wanted?

'No.' He breathes the word fiercely into the darkness, the pirogue sliding out from the bank as those slaves left behind line the water's edge, yelling and pleading to be taken along.

'No! Didn't never want nothin' like this! I swear to God!'

No-one to answer as the long boat starts upriver, fierce light throbbing above the trees as they move. Justus sits quiet, Mary's silent empty look meeting his as they turn for home. Only fire and death left behind them.

An' in front, ain't no way of tellin'.

Nowadays Nestor have trouble sleepin', so he still wakeful come the time that light start to shakin' in by the window an' along his cabin wall. He watch that thing for a while, tryin' to work out how come. Then he slide his old legs out from the crib, pullin' on his frayed kersey breeches. He figure he gonna find out where that light comin' from.

Jacob leaves all them doors unbarred now. Nights, he busy with that gal Esther he got in the quarters. 'Sides, he knows they ain't bout to run nowhere. His old face puckers into hard, bitter lines. Noplace fer an ole buck like him, that fer sure. Nestor shrugs, easin' the door open. Steps outside cat-footed, lookin' about him.

Needn't have worried none. They all out there lookin'. Mede standin' there with Chloe, an' Little Lucas by him. Ruby an' her boy Nathan. Glory an' William. Cato. Most all of 'em he knows, they there. An' all of 'em lookin' out to the one place. Where the light comin'.

Nestor look with them. Way south on the skyline the edge of the land afire. Bright yellow-orange light, kinda pulsin' an' throbbin' 'tween the earth an' the sky, settin' 'em both afire, seemingly. From here ain't no sound—it a way too far off. All the same, kin only be but one thing.

'Somebody sure as hell got a fire on their hands,' black Cato says.

'Oh, ma Lawd!' That Ruby agin. she always set up to wailin'

77

'fore long. Turnin' her chile so he hide his face in her dress. 'Somethin' terrible goin' on, I just knows it . . . Lawd save us, Nathan honey . . . it wickedness, sure 'nough . . .'

'What you figure, Nestor?' That Mede askin' him. Echoes of the light on him as he looks around. Got his arm about Chloe like he aim to keep her from hurt. She hangin' on to young Lucas where he stood in front of 'em. Nestor watch how the light catch on them, strikin' on Mede's red back, on the sharp, black face an' high shoulders of Chloe. An' on Lucas, who take from his mother in looks an' colourin'.

'You reckon they set fire to the woods out there, maybe?'

Nestor a long while answerin', his face all hard an' puckered up like he ain't any too sure.

'Cain't tell,' the old man says after a while, still lookin' on the throbbin' light as it flickers over his face. 'Way I see it, there ain't nothin' much in the way of woods out south. An' ain't no swamp gonna catch light like that . . .' Pauses, his old eyes narrow and keen. 'Looks to me like somebody's place afire there. Ain't sure what, but it goin' up, all right.'

At his words they all fall quiet, lookin' out to the bright glare on the horizon.

'No sign of Jacob yet,' Glory says, grinning. He and William stood with their arms about each other, away from the rest. 'Reckon that Esther keep him busy, sure 'nough.'

'Yeah,' Cato chuckles. Looks over to the one cabin with its door still shut. 'He got him somethin' better to do, I reckon.'

Lawrence, too, the old man thinks, his look shiftin' on towards the big house yonder, lit now an' then by the distant flames. He got Sheba up there. Ain't nothin' gonna bother him tonight.

'They's smoke comin' up outen there, pa!' Lucas calls out, his voice ringing out in the darkness.

Over beyond them, the cabin door bursts open and Jacob comes boilin' out. Looks like he hauled on his pants in a hurry, an' his belt ain't fastened up, but he got a hold on that big blacksnake whip. The look of him mean an' tough, as always. Seeing him, some of the niggers start to drift quietly back to their own cabins.

'What in hell y'all doin' out here?' Jacob shouts. He licks at his lips nervously like a dog before it springs, yellow-green eyes cuttin' from one to another, the long whip startin' to slither out 'long the ground as he flicks it in his hand. 'Git back in them cabins, an' fast, 'fore I strips yo' backs clean!'

His look stops at Nestor. The old man not fixin' to move a–tall. That crooked grin at his face as he looks up to Jacob slow, steady-like.

'Ain't you heard, Jacob?' Nestor says and touches the rabbit foot at his neck. 'We free now, ain't none of us a slave no more. Massa tell you that, huh?'

Jacob scowls an' holds off, studyin', way a dog might after someone cracks him on the nose. He know Nestor a long time, an' he know he got to be careful. This one got power in him.

The big driver stands and scowls. Right now he ain't got a thing to say.

Back of him Esther in the cabin doorway, fightin' to pull up the shoulder of her dress where it fall off from her tits, reachin' out after him, callin'.

'Hey, Jacob honey. Come on back to bed, you hear?'

The rest of them bustin' to laugh at that. Men an' women alike grinnin' an' chucklin'.

'Yeah, that right,' Glory calls out from back of the others. 'You go light another fire, Jacob. Look to me like she hot fer you, sho' 'nough!'

Jacob swings for the voice, his broad face hard and savage as a dog's. Cain't see who it was. They all there laughin' now, an' ain't nothin' he kin do. Come mornin', though, he make 'em sorry. Jacob looks once to the glare in the distance and turns away. Ain't none of his business. Starts back for the cabin, lookin' mean at them over his shoulder.

'Yeah, man! Go give it to her, Jacob honey!'

'Crack that whip, you hear?'

'I figger he gonna strip her clean, jes' like he said!'

The driver glances Nestor's way. Ducks his head, givin' in.

'Jes' git in them cabins,' Jacob says.

He goes in, the door closing. After a while the laughter dies down again.

'Reckon we better do like he says,' Mede tells the others.

Nestor nods, his withered old face gone sober. Ain't gonna

make no difference. They know it, him an' Jacob both. They still slaves, either way. He watches as the other men and women file past him, headed back for their own cabins. Lucas lookin' back once before he follows his ma an' pa.

'Sure would like to git to see that place,' the boy says.

Mede gets a hand to his shoulder, pushin' him for the cabin door.

'I figger it best we don't know, maybe,' he says.

Nestor stays on after the rest. Lookin' out south to the glare of light.

Justus out there someplace, the old man thinks. Wonder how that boy makin' out. Could be he got somethin' to do with that fire out there, maybe? For some reason the thought troubles him. Nestor frowns, shrugs his shoulders like he shakin' off a bad spirit from him.

Don't pay to think too long on it. Boy might even be daid by now.

He turns. Bent-backed old man with wrinkled skin and salty hair, shufflin' towards the cabin door as the sky pales out an' that fire burns away on the rim further south.

It gettin' on towards morning, the dark greying out on the water, letting in a feeble, ghostly light that glimmers in among the ripples and the weed. Justus shivers as the long pirogue parts the matted growth ahead, feeling the moist air clammy on his skin. Trees giving out to long, reedy mudbanks on either side as they gain the marshes. Grey-backed gators flat-bellied on the mud, their jaws opened wide, peering at them yellow-eyed as the packed fleet of boats glides past.

Mary beyond him in the middle of the boat, the useless gun in her hand, staring down at the hollowed log under her feet and the slow, stagnant heave of water to the prow. Her face washed empty of all feeling. He eyes her for a moment, and looks away to the reedbeds yonder. Right now, she a way off from him.

Soldier in front of him, leaning easy into the stroke, the harsh features placid, sated. Justus studies the twisted back without emotion, feeling numb and drained. Back of him the girl sobs on in the bed of the canoe, and a stone-faced Cedar sinks his pole deep in the water. The blood on his arm turned sticky and hard now. The bleeding stopped, only a numb pain left behind. He feels the itch of the blood as it dries. Grimaces, hitting at the flies that hover above the surface of the water, his glance taking in the pirogues all around. Shango and Mama Odu and Crow Feather, Red Wolf's Choctaws, Heron and his sisters. His eye measuring them coldly, remembering.

They got the white girl from the plantation in one of the other boats out in front a ways, steering close to the bank. She sits there upright in the middle of the boat, hands clasped in front of her like she don't seem to notice the dress tore clear off her to the waist, showing her white body naked to them all. The pale flesh bruised here and there from their hands. She turns even as he looks, glancing back to him over her shoulder. He sees the hair tugged and wrenched loose about her face, her mouth bruised dark like somebody hit her . . . the wide stare of the eyes goes clean through him, seeing nothing. Justus thinks again of her crazy laughter and bites hard into his lower lip.

'Mama,' the girl says, her voice quiet as she calls, the sound carrying over the water. She looks towards the thick reeds on the spit of land to their left, starting to smile.

'Over here, Mama . . . I'm over here . . .'

Same moment she flings up her hands and sways outward, plunging into the water.

Justus hears their sudden frantic shouts as the girl flounders, arms flailing, legs thrashing. The ripped dress comes away, her body gleaming pale among the weeds.

'Git to her!' Shango yells out, standing in the hollowed bed of the pirogue, his thin face twisting in thwarted fury.

Not a man among them moves as the girl thrashes around in the water. She's still calling out, something they can't hear. From the reeds a grey scaly shape goes slithering for the water, log-like as it breaks the surface, the ripples smoothing back from its heavy, thrusting snout.

'*Gator! Gator in the water!*' Heron calling out from beyond them, his voice shrill. In the boats to either side men fumble for their weapons, hurriedly.

Justus doesn't move, his eyes still on the floundering girl as the big gator comes in to hit from below, slamming like a powered sledge into her lower body, the white shape lost amid the churning water. The surface seethes, boiling as the pair of them go under. The gator's tail flicking up once, lashing as it breaks surface. A string of bubbles burst in the weed, slowly, one after the other. Thin thread of blood curling out, red against the stagnant green. At once the surface settles.

Shango across from him, looking out over the water, his harsh face unsmiling. The tall man spreads his arms. Gives out with a high, wavering cry.

'God took her!' Shango calls.

In the pirogues, the captured slave-women scream like to startled birds. Back of him the one Cedar brought along leans to spew over the side, the puke splashing from her mouth into the water. Justus looks on at the point where the ripples settle, fanning out. Numbed, his face bare of all expression.

Mary didn't turn when the gator struck. All the same, when the noise came in the water, her body shook. Now one slow tear runs from the corner of her eye and out along her scarred cheek, the trail of it shining in the grey, unearthly light.

'I'm here, Mary,' Justus says.

He covers her hand with his own, seeking reassurance in the warmth of flesh. But Mary's hand is cold to the touch. She makes no answering move, neither to shake him off or to respond. Like he ain't even there a–tall.

Blast on the bone whistle. Back of them the long pole strikes home. The men turning back to their paddles as the long-prowed boats sweep on through the mat of weeds and water-lilies coating the surface of the water.

Back at the stockade the gates are open, drums beating as they enter. 'Gator Head and the others who stayed behind sending up a deafening shout at sight of the captives and the bloody knives. Shango grinning, exultant, as he welcomed by his people.

'The god drunk well, this time,' the tall man calls out, holding up the fouled blade of his cutlass above his head. 'We go out agin, come the day!'

Stutter of drums in answer. The fierce, throbbing chant:

'SHAN–GO! SHAN–GO! SHAN–GO!'

Shango bows his feathered head like a restive stallion at the sound. Leans to squat down in the shadow of the tree with its load of skulls. Around him the lithe bodies leap and turn, sound of their footfalls hard against the trodden ground.

Justus slumps in the doorway of the hut, his breath coming hard, eyes dull, uncaring as he watches Shango and the swarm of dancing figures around him. Mary and Soldier sinking to the ground beside him, looking out ahead, none of them speaking. From out of a knot of dark, swaying bodies, Jewel moves towards him, kneels to set down a skin water-bag by his feet. Blood-flecks still at her breasts and thighs as she bends to lay her hands on him. Justus makes no move, scarcely feeling the gentle touch of her as she cleans the dried blood from his ripped arm and binds it up, winding the limb in a thick, grey layer of moss.

'Spanish moss,' Jewel says, her dark eyes warm upon him. 'Take out the hurt, sure 'nough.'

He doesn't answer, not troubling to look, only Mary in his mind this moment. The white woman sitting empty-faced beside him, her hands clasped before her, close by him, yet a world away.

Jewel nods, her dark face unchanging. Gets to her feet, stalking like a deer across the compound where the other bodies whirl and bend. After a while Justus struggles up against the wall of the hut. Reaches to grasp the wrist of the woman beyond him.

'Let's go, honey,' he says.

Mary gets to her feet unresisting, not looking him in the face. From across the open ground, Shango's keen eye fixes them as they move for the doorway.

'Where you haided, boy?' the tall man asks.

Turning in the open doorway, meeting the hard stare of those eyes, Justus feels the onset of a terrible weariness.

'Spirit in me need to rest,' the big man says, forcing himself to stare back into those huge, bloodshot eyes. 'Go sleep now . . .'

'Uhuh.' Shango smiling meanly, lips peeled from the points of his teeth. 'How 'bout her?'

Seeing the look of those eyes touch on her, Justus remembers the girl they spread for Shango on the porch of the burning house—the one who laughed, and went to the gator on the way back. Knowing Shango has the same thing in mind for Mary right now, he stills the growing anger. Fights down the urge to fly at the tall figure and smash out its life against the ground. Bitterly, Justus smiles in answer.

'Remember the sign,' he tells him. 'She come after, I reckon.'

He turns then, forcing himself not to look behind him, going on into the welcome dark of the hut as the drums pound on and the swell of voices rises to meet the sound.

Mary coming in after him as he hits the ground, his eyes half-closed. He watches as she lays herself down across from him in the far corner of the hut, lying silent, open-eyed to the gloom. Her stare striking on him, through him, but telling him nothing.

Nothin' he kin say. She saved his life, he knows. Another time, he might thank her for it. He could maybe take hold of her now, comfort her. But inside he knows it ain't the time. She seen too much on that plantation to think straight fer a while yet. Come to think, he ain't too sure he gonna forget it himself.

Justus looks towards her once, but only the blind stare meets him. The big man sighs, his face clenched into hard, sober lines. He rolls on his side, his back to her as his eyes close.

One last thought in his mind before he sleeps. The long house, an' that thing they call the god—the thing with teeth. Somehow, he gotta find out just what it is they hidin' there.

Quiet inside the dark of the thatched hut. The two of them lying there, still, without sound. The black man, the white woman, lying apart. Neither one makes a move. Neither speaks.

They do not make love.

Wakes as the pale light of early morning spreads over the compound, the night shadows retreating. In the hut doorway the light beckons him, dull and greyish-coloured, halfway between night and morning. Justus sits up slow, rubbing at his eyes. Across from him on the dirt floor Mary lies quiet, sleeping at last. For a while he stays motionless, looking on the white woman's outflung body that was denied to him the night before, the pale, heavy tresses that fall to cover her face from him. Recalling the time at Blackwater, he shivers, a sour taste hitting the back of his throat.

Gets to his feet, stooping under the low roof. Heads silent for the open doorway.

Soldier already awake and sitting with his back to the far wall. He don't move, his one good eye following the big man as he goes, pushing out to the light. Justus don't heed that look. Right now, he don't care to look any one of them in the eye.

Outside it's still quiet. Dead, grey halflight over the compound and the huddled huts. Over by the gate a lone dog runs, limping, tracking through the dust. Up on the walls the wizened heads stare down, grinning on him. Feels the foul taste threaten again. Puckers to spit in the dirt. After a while his mouth feels clean, but the aftertaste lingers someplace in his mind.

He's made it halfway to the stockade wall when the voice stays him, coming from one of the huts to his right.

'Oh yeah, little sister,' Jewel says.

Hears the hunger in that voice. It speaks to him, matching his own unslaked need. He halts a moment, feeling his groin stir alive. For a while, there's no other sound.

Moves to the shadow. Hoping he ain't been seen.

Now he sees them.

Grey light in the entrance of the hut outlines them. Jewel and Diamond together. Gleam of their bared limbs as they kneel face to face, holding, touching. As he looks on their mouths meet, open, tongues twined in a long, drawn kiss. Each girl reaching to cup and stroke at the other's breasts.

God damn, the big man thinks. Ain't never seen this before.

Sure, back on Sweet River there been Glory an' William, but they men; it different somehow. Women, it a whole way different. An' knowin' how Jewel come after him, he knows it ain't the only thing for her. Jewel kin take on a man, too, sure enough.

An' given the chance, he the man she'd choose.

Thought dies, pushed someplace back of his mind. Justus stands frozen by the wall of the hut, watching as the two women smooth and fondle at each other's bodies. Jewel throwing back her head sudden, gasping, her eyes half-shut as the nipples come up hard in Diamond's hands.

'Yeah, sister. You do that to me now . . .' Jewel says.

Diamond don't say nothin'. Lowers her dark head to take the nearest nipple into her mouth. Crouches a while, sucking on it real slow, her hands slithering down between her sister's thighs. Jewel moans out, her breath fluttering. Eases over, lying flat to the ground.

Sisters, the thought goes through him. Strange. From a far distance, seems like, Justus watches as Diamond parts the other woman's legs, ducks her black-haired head to go down. Her long hair falls, blue-black and gleaming, over Jewel's thighs. For a while the lapping sounds of her tongue and lips and Jewel's moaning are all that he hears.

A shiver takes the tawny body, running up from the loins to the dark crown of the head. Jewel yells out, her hand clenched in the thick hair of the woman beneath her, grunting at the first foretaste of pleasure. Abruptly she slides her slender body round, Diamond rolling on her side as Jewel brings her mouth to her in turn.

Watches the joined bodies as they twist and writhe, the shuddering spasms that already begin to shake them both. Strange feelin' to it, somehow, they bein' sisters, and all. Still, after what he seen at Blackwater, it could be a whole lot worse.

Ain't nothin' wrong with it, Nestor said once. Maybe he right here, too.

Hears the moaning of two voices together, the locked, tawny shapes lashing and heaving as the twin ecstasy takes them both. Coming, Jewel and Diamond lift half from the ground, calling out high and loud, then sinking back heavily to earth, pearled with sweat, slowly unjoining one from the other.

Seems like the beat of his heart on his ribs loud enough to rouse the whole camp. Down at the root of him the fierce need takes his flesh, swelling up stiff and hard against the cloth of his breeches.

He oughta git from here, he knows, but seems like there no way he kin move.

Across from him in the doorway, Jewel opens her eyes. Seeing him there, standing back in shadow. The woman smiles, a knowing look to her face. From here, he guesses, she kin see the way it takin' him, too. All at once he swallows, uneasy, almost afraid.

He seen somethin' he didn't ought to see.

'I see you, Justus,' Jewel says.

Stretches out lazy as a cat, showing him the tawny, sweat-smooth body bared all its length. For a time he holds with it. Takes in the tautly lifted breasts, the glisten of wetness that speckles the hair at her woman's core. Now Diamond too turns her head, her dark features sullen and watchful as before. Her sloe-black eyes, like those of her sister, devour him, inch by slow inch.

'Like what you see, huh?' Jewel asks. Strokes down a hand for her pleasured loins, as if she guidin' him to the place.

'I reckon,' the big man says. Swallows again. Forcing a smile, wishing himself away from here and back in the hut with Mary.

'You want to come over?' she asks.

Catches the sly mockery in her voice. Shakes his head, the spell broken.

'Reckon not.' Hears his own voice come harsh. Turns to go, already angered at his body's betrayal. 'I best be goin' back . . .'

Jewel's dark, probing stare holds him for a moment. Then the woman nods, smiling again.

'Another time, Justus,' Jewel says.

Turns from her without a word, headed back across the compound, tryin' to slow his step so it don't look like he runnin' from them. Back of him, though, he hears their laughter.

Ain't no foolin' them. They know.

Sun starting to rise above the reeking swamplands in the east. Justus feels the first of its heat as he gains the welcome entrance of the hut. Halts to wipe the sweat from his face—sweat that has nothing to do with the heat from the sun.

Best he stays clear from Jewel, he figures. That one trouble, sure enough.

He ducks his head, pushing back inside the hut as sunlight blasts the compound beyond.

'PALMETTO CHRONICLE', SEPTEMBER 4th, 1865.
Plantation massacre!
Twenty believed dead in outrage at
Blackwater.

BLACKWATER, PLANTATION HOME OF THE DEVEREAUX FAMILY, HAS BEEN DESTROYED BY FIRE AND ITS INHABITANTS MASSACRED IN A BRUTAL ATTACK BY NIGGER RENEGADES. PLANTERS AND OTHER CITIZENS FROM THE PALMETTO REGION, ALERTED BY THE SIGHT OF FLAMES, RODE OUT TO FIND THE PLACE A GUTTED RUIN, WITH THE CANEFIELDS FIRED AND THE BIG HOUSE AND OUTBUILDINGS BURNED. MR FRANCIS DEVEREAUX, THE PLANTATION'S OWNER, WAS FOUND MURDERED, TOGETHER WITH HIS WIFE LOUISE AND HIS TWO YOUNG SONS MARTIN AND THOMAS. THEIR BODIES AND THOSE OF THEIR BUTCHERED HOUSE SERVANTS, WERE DISCOVERED IN AND AROUND THE WRECKAGE OF THE HOUSE ITSELF. A NUMBER OF FIELD HANDS WERE ALSO KILLED.

FROM THOSE FIELD HANDS WHO SURVIVED THE ATTACK, COUNTY SHERIFF WHITESIDE LEARNED THAT THE ATTACK WAS MADE BY A BAND OF ARMED BLACKS AND REDSKINS, WHO SLEW INDISCRIMINATELY AND WITHOUT MERCY AFTER FIRING THE OUTBUILDINGS AND FIELDS. THE KILLERS FLED THE SCENE OF THEIR CRIMES BY BOAT TO SOME UNKNOWN HIDING-PLACE IN THE MARSHES, TAKING WITH THEM SOME DISAFFECTED FIELD HANDS. AMONG THEIR LEADERS WERE A TALL BLACK OF UNUSUAL SIZE AND SAVAGE APPEARANCE, HIS CHEEKS TATTOOED AND TEETH FILED IN A BARBAROUS MANNER, AND A SECOND BLACK OF POWERFUL PHYSIQUE, ACCOMPANIED BY A WHITE WOMAN. THIS LAST DESCRIPTION SUGGESTS THE RUNAWAY DESPERADO JUSTUS, AND IT IS POSSIBLE THAT THE WOMAN IS MRS MARY KIMBALL, REPORTED MISSING A SHORT TIME AGO FOLLOWING THE DEATH OF HER HUSBAND. WHETHER THE LADY IS A CAPTIVE OF THE AFORESAID JUSTUS OR AN ACCOMPLICE IS NOT YET CERTAIN. ONE WORKER'S CLAIM THAT SHE SHOT A NEGRO FOREMAN WITH A PISTOL HAS YET TO BE ESTABLISHED.

THE FATE OF THE DEVEREAUX THEMSELVES WAS SHOCKING BEYOND BELIEF. MR DEVEREAUX FELL TO A CHARGE FROM A SHOTGUN, AND HIS SKULL WAS SHATTERED BY A CLUB. HIS WIFE

HAD HER THROAT CUT BY A FEMALE SAVAGE, AND THEIR SONS WERE DONE TO DEATH IN A SIMILAR BLOODY FASHION. EMILY, THE YOUNG DAUGHTER OF THE COUPLE, WAS OPENLY VIOLATED ON THE PORCH OF THEIR HOME, AND HAS SINCE DISAPPEARED. ONE CAN ONLY HOPE THE UNFORTUNATE GIRL HAS BEEN SPARED FROM FURTHER SUFFERING.

RESPONDING TO THIS DREADFUL OUTRAGE, SHERIFF WHITESIDE AND MR JOHN LAWRENCE OF SWEET RIVER PLANTATION ARE AT PRESENT ENLISTING VOLUNTEERS FROM LOCAL CITIZENS IN THE HOPE OF BRINGING THE PERPETRATORS OF THE ACT TO JUSTICE. MR LAWRENCE FEELS HIS RESPONSIBILITY IN THE MATTER KEENLY, AS JUSTUS WAS FORMERLY HIS PROPERTY, HAVING ESCAPED SOME MONTHS AGO FROM SWEET RIVER. IT IS THE HOPE OF THIS PAPER THAT NO ABLE-BODIED MAN IN PALMETTO SHALL SHRINK FROM ENLISTMENT. DEFEATED WE MAY BE, BUT THERE ARE LIMITS TO WHAT MEN WILL ENDURE.

MEANTIME, IT MAY BE THAT THIS SHOCKING ACT OF VIOLENCE WILL BRING HOME TO THE UNION AUTHORITIES THE FEARFUL DANGERS OF PREMATURE ENFRANCHISEMENT FOR OUR BLACKS. CLEARLY, THE KILLERS OF BLACKWATER HAVE SHOWN THEMSELVES BEYOND CONSIDERATION AS HUMAN BEINGS, AND MAY NOT HOPE FOR LONG TO ESCAPE THEIR RIGHTFUL PUNISHMENT. WE OF THE 'PALMETTO CHRONICLE' DEMAND IMMEDIATE AND MERCILESS ACTION AGAINST THESE MURDERERS BY THE MILITARY. FAILING THIS, OUR NEW MASTERS MAY YET FIND THAT WE OF THE SOUTH ARE STILL ABLE TO STRIKE BACK ON OUR OWN BEHALF.

'He be back in a while, I reckon,' Soldier says.

No-one answers him. He goes quiet, bent over with one twisted shoulder up high as he swabs his gun with an oiled rag. Stare of his one green eye on the barrel as it catches the light. Back of him and overhead, above the level of the stockade, the sun starting to break through the mists that lie thick over the marsh and lagoons all around.

Justus sees the compound stretch all but empty in the dead grey light. Thin scatter of figures walking the open space from one hut to the next. Old folk stay crouched in the doorways, heads sunk forward on their chests. Here and there a kid or a stray dog runs loose in the dust, noise of their hollerings falling loud against the morning stillness. He stays where he is, his back up by the wall of the hut, watching the slim black girl who crosses the open ground. Stepping loose-limbed and easy, her long-fingered hands way down by her sides. The gourd with its fresh water balanced atop her head, swaying a little with her as she moves.

Mary on his near side, standing upright in the doorway, raking the compound with a listless gaze, the white-blonde hair tied back from the pale, unsmiling face. She still ain't said hardly a word.

The figure of the walking girl passes beneath the stripped tree-bole with its freight of skulls, black of her gleaming body greyed and barred with shadow as she goes by, dust puffing up silently around her feet. Some distance on, in front of one of the huts, a heavy-limbed negress leans over on her knees, pounding grain with a wooden pestle; seems like the blows falling in time with the young girl as she crosses the compound to the shade beyond.

Like one of them villages Nestor tole him. Back in A–frica.

An' no way he gettin' loose from it that he kin see.

He shakes off the thought almost in anger, frowning. Staring over towards the girl across the half-empty compound, he finds his gaze caught suddenly, held by the dark gaze of Jewel who squats on her haunches over by Soldier, facing him, eyeing him narrowly and smiling.

'Any day now, god have his festival,' Jewel say, black glint of her eyes upon him, one with a smile as she fondles the haft of the cane knife lying naked on her bare brown thigh. "Fore the autumn rains come. You hear 'bout that yet, Justus?'

'Guess not.' Frowning still, he holds with her stare, catching a glimpse as he does so of Soldier's crooked grin as the veteran squints up from the barrel of his gun. 'You tryin' to tell me somethin', woman? That it, huh?'

Jewel stays smiling, watching him. From what he seen, anybody else who talk to her that way like to get a knife pulled on him. With Justus though, this one always smiles, like she kin go back of his eyes an' inside, see him seein' her body in front of him, all brown an' smooth an' firm, with its clean, close womansmell. Knowin' it there for him any time he care to make a move.

'Festival of the god, it our time,' Jewel tells him. Leans closer, her full lips parted, touching herself lightly in the space between her breasts. 'It the one time us women git to choose us a man for ourselves . . . That day, we take any man we please, an' he got to go along . . .'

'That's right,' Soldier grins.

Over beyond them, her brother and sister, Heron and Diamond, wait in silence, the lean, young black crouching in the grey dust, his spear laid back to his shoulder, his gaze on Justus, hard and unsmiling. Back of him Diamond stands, shifting her weight uneasily from one foot to the other, swatting at the early flies with the heavy-bladed cane knife, her dark, lithe shape so like Jewel it hard to tell them apart. Diamond, though, got a quieter, sullen look to her. Ain't no time for words, seem like. Right now, she tired of waitin' around for Shango to get back.

Caught in the snare of those dark, slitted eyes, Justus runs out of words, feeling her look like a warm touch on his flesh, disturbing him, getting him restless.

'Jes' think on it, Justus,' Jewel nods, her smile grown sharper. ''Cause come the time, I be thinkin' 'bout you, sure enough.'

Justus swallows, made uneasy by her words and her mocking smile. He about to make some kind of answer when a hand comes down soft on his shoulder and Mary speaks from above him.

'He has him a woman already,' Mary says.

At her touch the big man turns to glance upward, starting to smile in his turn. A while back, he was wonderin' if she'd get around to talkin' at all. Now, watching her gaze and Jewel's lock together, he gets the feelin' that Mary come back from wherever it is she been.

'That right?' Jewel still holds to her edged smile, dark eyes raking the figure of the white woman across from her, going up and down slowly from head to foot. 'An' you gonna keep him, huh?' Jewel says.

At once, the grip on his shoulder tightens. 'Maybe I am,' the white girl murmurs, her eyes still hard on Jewel.

Around them he can glimpse other watching faces, sly smiles and narrowed eyes. All of them eager, intent, waiting for something to happen. Justus scans the hard, clenched features of Heron, catches the slight tremor of Jewel's hand on the knife-haft. He reaches up, smiling, to lay his own dark palm over the hand on his shoulder.

'Could be she right, I reckon,' Justus says.

Feeling her hold relax in the instant he speaks. Mary, too, sensing that she ain't alone.

Sight of his smiling face sets Jewel frowning suddenly, her dark eyes downcast to where she draws lines in the dust with her knifeblade. Mary she might have taken on her own. But not the huge bush-haired black man whose hand covers hers right now.

'You heard the man.' Soldier still grinning crookedly where he leans back of his long gun. 'Best you let it lie, huh?'

Jewel doesn't answer him, her dark features sullen as she glowers at the ground by her feet. Back of her Diamond shifts her weight again from one foot to the other, ready to be gone.

'Yeah, we heard.' Heron's voice coming tight through his teeth. His look goes through Justus like his spear went through the body of the white kid at Blackwater. For a while the big man finds it hard to meet those darkly slitted eyes. 'You comin', Jewel?'

Getting to his feet, coming smoothly upright behind the long spear he carries. At a sign from him, the dark girl rises, wiping the knifeblade on her breech-clout hem. as she stands as if in thought, her look still for Justus.

'Come the time, you for me,' Jewel tells him.

Heron says nothing. His harsh stare says all he needs. Justus meets the levelled eyes. Watches in silence as they turn away, moving across the open compound, the thin, erect figure of the spearman, his lithe sisters beside him as they stalk cat-like through the rising dust. Justus breathes out, slowly. Smiles.

'Guess you kin set down now, honey,' the big man says.

Mary's breath comes out in a sigh of relief. The white woman lets go her hold on him, sinks down by his side, squatting on her haunches in the open doorway. Looking to him, she too smiles.

'Guess you come outen that pretty good,' Soldier tells him, chuckling as he lays down the gun in his lap. All the same his one eye fixes keenly on the bigger man across from him, not troubling yet to spare a look for Mary, who still doesn't speak.

'All the same, she right, that Jewel. Come the festival, she be seekin' you out, an' you better go 'long—Heron git mighty mean when a man tell her no, you hear me?' His lean lips twist into a grin, but the one green eye holds level and hard. 'Was I you, boy, I'd do like she say. Jewel some wench, sure 'nough. Some fellers in this place be rippin' yo' arm off jes' to be where you is, right now. . .'

Justus scarcely hears the words, his thoughts with Mary as he turns, letting one hand rest at the nape of her neck, touching the warm flesh gently through the soft, blonde hair. She turning to him as the hand touches, her face lifting to his. Justus reads the look of recognition in her wide, blue eyes, the parted lips: like she comin' back to him from cross the far side of the world. Looking for her, he feels the quickening pulse-beat of his blood that tells of those nights of unquenched need, lying apart without speech or sign, waiting for her to come back. That same need now, fierce in him, clawing his throat until the water threatens back of his eyes. And with it another feeling: tenderness thickening in him at the marks of suffering in her pale, haggard face. Justus lifts his free hand, his fingers touching softly, following the furrow of the scar beneath her eye, feeling her tremble at the unexpected gentleness of his hand upon her. She raises her lips to him, and his mouth comes down softly to cover her own. For a while they stay that way, each taking in the other's warmth and sweetness. Then, slowly, their lips draw apart.

'You see my woman,' the big man says at last, feeling the strength flow in him as he shifts about to meet that one green eye. Sureness in the dark lines of his face and body as he speaks. 'She give me everythin' I need.'

'Uhuh,' Soldier shrugs, one high shoulder lifting. His look goes on beyond Justus to the white woman. Her blue-eyed stare meets him levelly. Pride in her eyes now, where a moment back there was emptiness. At that look, the grey-haired veteran pouts, his thin lip curling. Turns from her slowly, looking down.

'Have it your way, boy,' Soldier says, touching his gun as if to reassure himself. His leathern features creased into a frown now, as he shakes his grizzled head. 'One thing sure. You gonna be sorry, come the time . . .'

Justus about to talk back at that, but no words come. All at once his look shifts to the looming walls of the long house on its mound. At sight of those closed doors he no longer smiles, the frown returning. For a while, he come near to forgettin' . . .

Shango took off at first light with the raiding-party, crossing the lagoon in their narrow pirogues. The place he makin' for, Willow Bend, further off than Blackwater, but Shango ain't worried none. He aimin' to hit the plantation in plain daylight, while the hands in the field. Either way, he got the white folks outnumbered. Must've taken half the fightin' men an' women out the stockade with him this time—fifty, maybe sixty armed raiders. Mama Odu went in his pirogue, an' other leaders in the boats. Most of the Choctaws went along too: Red Wolf, Crow Feather, old 'Gator Head . . .

Knowin' what like to happen there, he sure glad they ain't took Mary nor hisself along. Another time like the last, an' he figures he couldn't keep from spewin'. He hates to think what it might do to Mary. One sign of weakness, an' they gonna be on to him—an' Shango more'n the rest. Got to be thankful he ain't gonna see what they do at Willow Bend.

All the same, ain't no way he foolin' hisself 'bout the way it is back here. He an' Mary both of 'em prisoners in this place, as sure as if they tied. The one reason they alive is that snake, the cottonmouth that bit Claw an' let him be. While they reckon he got somethin' of the god in him, they ain't gonna dare hurt him none. Soldier, he figures, gettin' to like him more'n a little by now—an' Jewel, she took a shine from the first. Heron, too, while he don't care to see his sister turned down to his face, ain't likely to go up agin Justus yet awhile. Come to think, they most of 'em ain't so bad. But for the killin' at Blackwater that he seen, ain't too much difference 'tween them an' some of the nigras back on Sweet River. Give Mede or Cato chance, they might take to killin' white folks, too.

Shango the whole trouble here. Him an' Mama Odu.

At that he scowls, the lines in his broad face deepening. Shango there agin, a tall shape across the sun, blockin' him off from all hope of the big water. More'n the others, Shango knows. Snake or not, he know fer sure that Justus a man, not a god. Knows Justus know he ain't a god neither. Out here, Shango an' the goddess been runnin' the roost, but now they seein' the one man big enough to stand in their way. Sooner or later, Justus know that Shango gonna try to kill him. In this place, they room fer only one god.

An' maybe they hit at Mary the first. Git to him that way.

Snarls at the thought, his great fist clenching, teeth grinding hard one against the other. Come the time, he might just rip out the big son's heart, if he git the chance.

Eyeing the shut doors of the long house, he sobers, fingers unfolding as he frowns in thought. Just what they got in mind for him? he wonders. An' what that thing with the teeth they got hid in that place, behind them doors? Sooner he git to know, the better.

Yawp–ing noise from up on the rampart brings his head around. Others gittin' up to look as he turns. Sees Cedar up on the wall above them, blowing into the hollow bull-horn that hangs by the sharpened stakes.

'God comin'!' Cedar calls. Sets his mouth to the horn again. A low, moaning blast echoes over the island slopes. Out across the lagoon, from beneath them in the distance, he hears an answering shout.

Over by the far row of huts, the thin-bodied figure of the drummer takes his stand, the speech-like patterns of sound coming abruptly to life as he wields his hooked stick on the stretched frame of hide. From the huts themselves other figures come tumbling out, making for the sound: shapes of men and women and children, dogs and pigs mixed in among them as they run and call one to another, most of them with their weapons ready to hand. Heaving upright by the hut wall, Mary beside him, Justus scowls deeper than before. He been expectin' Shango back fer long enough. All the same, it come too soon.

He follows Soldier hastily up the makeshift ladder that leads up to the rampart, Mary back of him as he moves, slithering and gasping as she clings to the rungs. Up above them, Cedar stands looking by one of the huge catapults, a growing crowd about him. Justus gains the head of the ladder as Soldier leans by the stake wall, breathing hard, the gun in the crook of his arm. He clambers up on to the rampart, reaching back to draw Mary after him, still holding to her as they reach the edge of the stockade and look down.

Mist so thick out there today they don't see Shango comin' till he nearly on them. Now his pirogue heads the rest, breaking the fog-bank halfway across the lagoon, prow carving through the black water as other boats ease from the murk further back. Justus takes in the tall, upright shape, squatting like a black feather-crested shadow in the bed of the canoe, Mama Odu a shorter, bulkier outline behind him. By now they all of them gettin' closer, poles hefted as the narrow log-boats skim the surface of the water. Justus sees Red Wolf and the white-haired figure of 'Gator Head; Crow Feather, too, in Shango's pirogue, long-armed and stump-legged as before, half-standing to hold up something in either hand for those on the walls to see. Something that drips into the dark water, held by its hair. Up alongside him, Mary turns back with a gagging sound, her face paling at what she sees.

'Easy, honey,' Justus murmurs, his hand closing over hers in the same moment. At the touch Mary turns, swallowing back the vile taste in her mouth as she looks into his face. Her eyes on his, she nods, not speaking. She, too, knows better than to break down right now.

They stand, watching the line of boats pass from sight under the green curve of land below. In the compound more drums set up to beat, and a gathering crowd takes up the chant.

'SHAN–GO! SHAN–GO! THE GOD COME!'

'He be a while gittin' up here,' Soldier mutters from beside them, looking down over the wall with his one good eye to where mist wreathes over the thickets and trees of the slope. His voice comes back to Justus over the raised hump of his shoulder with its grey, knitted scars. 'We got time to git off the wall, I reckon.'

The big man nods his agreement. He's about to turn back when Mary grips at his arm, drawing him to the wall again. At the look of fear in her face he stands quiet.

'Justus.' Her voice no more than a hoarse whisper, so that he strains to catch the words. 'Justus, I reckon I saw a man tied in one of the boats. A white man . . .'

He lays a finger to her lips and at once her voice stills. But for all that, the fear stays, plain to see in the pale stare of her eyes. Justus hopes his own unease don't show in his face. He makes for the ladder, going first down the rungs as the beat of drums throbs on from below. Eyes on her bare, white legs as she too descends. Feet on the ground at last, he reaches to lift her down. Mary holds a while to him, suddenly aware once more of the dark, hostile faces all around, the harsh, pulsating chant, the eerie heart-cry of the drums.

Justus scowls, aware at this moment of her body pressing warm against his, and with it the threatening surge of his flesh after long denial. The big man draws breath slowly, eases Mary from him to look her in the eye, forcing himself to smile.

'Jes' hold up, huh?' Justus tells her. 'We git by all right.'

Pale as she is, Mary makes an effort to smile in answer.

'Count on me, Justus,' the white woman says.

Back of them both, Soldier comes down the quaking ladder, hunched like a spider, swinging one-handed from one rung to the next. Lowering himself awkwardly to earth, his body twisted over, he lands on his feet. His one eye regards them levelly, and in silence.

Turning from him, Justus finds the compound thronged with a mass of jostling shapes: blacks and Choctaws and mixed bloods; grey-headed oldsters and pot-bellied children; young girls, half-naked men with their old guns, cane knives and spears—all of them moving to the insistent voice of the drums, leaping, stamping, shrilling, chanting, the noise growing ever louder in his ears. Facing them, Justus sets his teeth hard, shutting his mind to the clamour, fighting to hold his thoughts on Shango, and the coming meeting. Up overhead he hears Cedar sing out again.

'The god come!' Cedar yells.

He says nothing, watching as the gates swing back and the pulsing chant quickens.

Shango stalks in by the open gate, tall and thin as a ghost from the old country. The cutlass bare in his hand, fouled dark and wet with blood, his black flesh spattered with thick splotches of red, harsh features breaking into a grin that bares his jagged teeth. At sight of him the shout goes up with redoubled force.

'SHAN–GO! SHAN–GO! THE GOD COME!'

Shango grins again. Lifts his arms in acceptance, shuffling a little on his toes. Back of him Mama Odu comes waddling, sweating hard, her body splashed with blood, her skirt drenched with a dark, ugly stain. Behind her, Crow Feather holds up a pair of grinning, sightless heads that swing by the hair, spattering red droplets in the dust. White folks' heads: one a woman, the long, reddish hair stiff with blood. Justus eyes them steadily, licking lips that are suddenly parched and dry.

Close against him he hears Mary's shocked gasp, follows her staring gaze to where Red Wolf and 'Gator Head drag the prisoner forward, a thin, undersized white man who staggers in front of his captors, his hands bound. No shoes to his bloody feet, and the shirt and pants all but ripped from his body. The bare flesh over his ribs shows dark and bruised, and a long, slanting knifeslash mars the side of his face, the wound already crusting hard. Same moment, the man's head swings towards him. Justus meets the look, his face bare of expression, seeing thin, unshaven features a grey corpse colour; black eyes darting terror-stricken in the pallid face; the lips drawn back in a half-formed cry, showing stumps of darkly rotting teeth. Ain't much to look at, that fer sure.

Up against him, he senses rather than feels the sudden tremor that shakes Mary's body as that dark glance switches towards her in turn, a white woman in a crowd of hostile blacks and redskins. The faintest trace of hope showing in that pale, unshaven face as Mary meets his gaze. At sight of her the bound man throws himself clear of the Choctaws at his back, falling on his knees in front of her as his legs give way beneath him, rolling in the dust as he scrabbles vainly to clutch at her bare ankles. Fails. Drops back with the ropes sawing his bloody wrists.

'Lady,' his voice a sobbing whisper, muffled against the ground. 'Lady, you gotta help me . . . These niggers gonna kill me like they done the rest . . . Please, lady . . .'

Reaching again for her legs as he speaks, touching then falling back with a sharp grunt of pain as the Choctaws close in behind him.

At the brief contact Mary shivers, not moving, her own face flinching at the sound of his voice. Abruptly 'Gator Head moves in and a shod foot slams the white man in the ribs. He hunches over, yelping at the sudden pain.

'Git him up,' Shango says. 'He goin' see the god.'

Red Wolf grasps the man by his lank hair, drags him howling up on his feet. He and the older Indian haul their captive back into line, dragging him over the hard ground as he lashes frantically at thin air. Wild-eyed now in panic, he screams through the hard, brown hand that moves to cover his mouth.

'*Lady!*' A harsh, despairing cry, wavering as the redskins pull him away, lifting the thin body from the ground. '*Lady, help me.*'

Mary shaking visibly at the sound, lips trembling as her eyes fill with tears. At once Justus covers her hand with his own, feeling her shudder like a leaf at his touch. Aware too of his own breath heaving in his chest. This one, he knows, is marked for death.

'Yeah,' Soldier murmurs from the corner of his thin-lipped mouth. 'Look like he find out us nigras ain't all tame critters fer a whippin'.'

Justus doesn't answer. His eyes on Shango as he heads the line towards the long house, Mama Odu close at his back. The bunch of them by the stripped tree-pole, when Shango turns suddenly, the red cutlass lifting, the fouled point of the blade held level with the big man's breast.

'You, boy,' Shango says. Across the intervening space, his hard eyes bore like augers into Justus' own. 'The god in you. Best you come with us to the long house.'

He meets the fierce, bloodshot stare, unspeaking, feeling the blood chill sudden in his veins. Slowly he nods, stepping forward as the others move to let him by.

'Good 'nough, boy,' Shango grins. Turns his lean ebony back to stalk through the dust, making for the long house as the chant swells up again all around.

Justus stands in the open ground, thunder of blood in his head coming hard and fierce as the beat of the drums. His glance cuts back over his shoulder, to where Mary waits in silence with the bent figure of Soldier alongside. For a moment, his gaze rests there.

'Soldier,' his voice cutting harsh through the clamour of cries. 'She git touched *once*, I be back to eat yo' heart. You hear me good?'

At his words the veteran's broken face twists, cracking in a sudden grin.

'No call fer you to worry there, boy,' Soldier tells him, his green eye resting on the big man. 'Shango tole me to look after you good. She be here when you come back.'

Back of the stooped old man, other faces watching him, their eyes alert, questioning. Heron he sees, and Jewel, and Diamond; Cedar and Crow Feather. From them his look goes again to Mary. Struggling to still the hammering of his heart, Justus smiles.

'Stay put, honey,' he tells her. 'I be back soon 'nough.'

Mary nods in answer, forcing a shaky smile, and he turns, walking steady through the thick dust to where Shango stands waiting by the door of the long house, looking back towards him. Dust at his heels, puffing up at each tread of his feet, Justus keeps moving, slow and steady, his eyes level on the tall shape by the doors, the harsh sawing noise of his breath unusually loud to his ears. The drums seemingly drowned out by the sound of his heart thumping on his ribs.

The bow and arrows left behind him in the hut—the pistol, too, useless without its shells. But one weapon by him right now: the hoop-iron knife in his belt. His hand clenches on the thick twine haft as he walks, the feel of it solid and welcome against his palm.

Could be he'll use it if the chance come his way.

Up by the door, the Choctaws have turned the prisoner loose. He crouches, half-cowering against the log wall as Justus approaches, seeing in this huge, heavy-set black man a captor almost as fearsome as Shango himself. Beyond the wretched man, Justus hears the thick-throated laugh of Mama Odu, her squat, massive body planted like a boulder close to the doorway, the light catching her skin with a polished gleam. Justus takes in the rolls of bulging fat with a look of distaste. Over on the far side the Indians fall back as Shango towers to his full height, heaving back the great door.

'We go see the god, now,' the tall man says.

His harsh eyes on Justus, he turns, easing in by the open door, the dark of the long house swallowing him from sight.

Over by the wall the white man starts to whimpering. 'Oh, my god . . . *no* . . . what are you gonna do to me . . .?'

Mama Odu laughs again, fat flesh of her face wrinkling as she smiles. Her broad black hand grips the captive by the scruff of his neck. With the other she digs her knife hard at his back. The white man hollers out like a dog. Watching, Justus sees blood ooze out thick through the cloth of the shirt.

'Git on inside,' Mama Odu tells him.

She glances sideways, smiling to Justus as the two of them pass, going on for the darkened doorway. Meeting her look, he reads malice there. Something else, too, in the sharp glint of those eyes. cain't say what, but he hope it ain't what he thinks. He stands back in silence, as they too vanish into the gloom beyond.

For a moment he holds where he is, gripping hard to the knife-haft. He scans the stretch of black emptiness that waits for him. Shango in there now someplace, an' Mama Odu with him. The bound white man, too.

Yeah an' maybe the thing with the teeth. The thing that ate up Claw, and left only pieces. Sweat, thick and sudden at his brow, itching in the armpits, gliding slow and easy down the middle of his back. At once the chanting and the drums gone far away, his breathing the one noise in the new-fallen quiet.

You aimed to git inside here, one time. Looks like it happen sooner'n you thought.

At the thought his face clenches, hardening. Justus

101

breathes once, his lips tight together. Steps towards the looming arch of the door.

Goes in. To darkness.

'Shut the door, boy,' Shango says.

The voice comes to him out of the gloom. Smothering dark all around him, pressing in on him as he turns blindly for the door, reaching out. Wood meets his open hands, rough-hewn and splintery against the touch of his fingers. Gives back with a creaking groan as the weight of his body thrusts behind it. Slowly the door thuds shut. Justus stands back, breathing harshly in the stillness.

Dark lying on him thicker'n a cloak. Dry, stale stink of the place in his nostrils every way he turns. Thick, mingled scent of punk and rotted wood. Earth and dung, too, and the sickly smell of dried blood, like to an open graveyard. Justus swallows at the thought, trembling. He don't care to be in this place with the dark pushed up so close and the dead stink all about him. Got to be spirits here, that for sure.

Back of him comes a shifting movement and a sudden splutter of flame. Light flares from the heart of darkness, the shadows retreating but threatening still, thick and heavy, in the corners of the huge building. Beyond him, Shango takes the flaring pine torch, setting light to other knots of wood fixed in brackets slantwise from the wall. Closer in, the bound white man slumps groaning on hands and knees. Mama Odu standing over him, the dark-bladed knife held ready in her hand.

Eyes take in the room in the shaking light: carved beams overhead, hewn faces of wood that blend again to darkness where the flare of torches cannot reach. Twining snakes and thunderbolts patterned along the walls. Over against where Shango stood, a forked tree limb stands high as a man, set into the ground, a hollow log thrust into the fork of it, inset with polished hunks of stone. Some kind of altar, maybe. Back of it three carved stools are set, unoccupied; away to the side, a heavy dark shape. Tree stump, growin' right here underfoot, sawed down where it stood, the surface long since levelled off. As the torchlight shivers over

102

it, he sees the stump gleam, thick and smooth with a multitude of ugly dark stains. Back of his nostrils the smell of old blood threatens stronger than before.

Somewhere beyond Mama Odu and the white man, a huge circle of darkness. Seems to him, standin' here, that the darkness *moves* with a faintly lapping sound. Far side of the wall a fresh torch splutters, and he sees the glimmer of water, the light shimmering out across its surface. A pool, set deep into the ground in the centre of the long house. From it, a cut channel goes underground, disappearing from sight.

Must go all the way out under the compound, he reckons. What in hell *that* for?

'Good 'nough, I reckon,' Shango says. He turns, setting the last torch into the bracket on the wall, flamelight washing his body a tawny red as he starts back to Mama Odu and the prisoner. He still holds to the cutlass, its blade gleaming black in the glare of the torches all around. Abruptly his long head swings, looking to Justus by the door.

'Over here, boy,' the tall man says, the carved marks on his cheeks puckering as he grins, lips drawn back from his filed teeth. 'Don't want you should miss nothin' . . .'

Meeting that bloodshot stare, Justus feels his teeth clench, thud of his heart uneven against the wall of ribs. Shut in close, he senses the fearful power of the man across from him, drawing strength beyond his sinewy body from the dark and the stench of blood and rottenness all around. Taking power from the spirits in the carved beams, the stump, the forked tree limb. Dry-lipped, fists bunching by his sides, he takes a step forward.

From close by his foot, someplace in the darkness, comes a hissing sound.

Justus freezes. For a minute, feels like his heart stop altogether. Along his spine and the nape of his neck the hair stands, prickling, fear hitting him like a blow from a giant fist. For an instant he has to clench to hold his water. Across from him, rimmed in torchlight, the tall man smiles.

'Don' look too good, boy,' Shango says, his own voice low

103

and charged with malice, the dark stony eyes glinting. 'Somethin' wrong, huh?'

He doesn't answer, teeth clenched as he hears a rustle of movement on the ground. The hissing noise again. Abruptly the sound dies. Something cool and smooth slides over the side of his foot and away over the floor. Justus bears the touch for what seems an age, holding his breath. For a while, feels like his body is gone cold as stone. Then the slithering shape is by him, only the itch of contact left to set his flesh quivering. He breathes again, hearing Shango chuckle softly beyond him.

'Seems like he took to you, boy,' the tall man grins. He leans forward, stretching his long arms with their puckered fang-marks towards the coiling shape on the ground. Justus sees light strike on the markings of a cottonmouth and swallows hard, licking at his lips. In front of him Shango reaches down for the snake, heedless of the threatening hiss and the upraised head.

'Come here to me, spirit,' Shango murmurs. Picks up the swaying shape, the cottonmouth twining about his arms. Moves to where a wicker basket is set in the shadow of the forked altar, halfway hidden from sight. There, other shapes lie coiled together, the light quivering on their smoothly polished skins. From the midst, heads rear in darkness, hissing faintly. Shango chuckles, bends to let the snake slide from his arms and into the basket. Slowly the threatening heads sink back from sight. The tall man grinning keener as he turns, his hard eyes seeking out Justus across the darkened room.

'Spirits of the god-house,' Shango tells him, glancing once to his own scarred, snake-bitten arms before looking up again. Dark of those eyes bites into Justus like an auger-blade. 'Where Shango live, there plenty power.' Standing now, his broad chest heaving as his long hand gestures to the shapes around. 'Medicine in them stools yonder, an' here in the thunder-tree.' He points to the forked limb with its hollow log. 'Lightnin' spirit there, an' thunder-stones the god call down come the storm-time . . . That where we sacrifice . . .' Glancing to the blood-crusted stump and the pool beyond it. Pausing, he looks the big man in the eye for a long moment. Seems like there a sharp edge to that smile this time. 'Still,' Shango says. 'You'd know 'bout that, boy, wouldn't you? Bein' part of the god an' all?'

Justus meets the questing stare, keeping silent. Here in the dark house of the god, there no help for him. It between him an' Shango an' Mama Odu now, and the prisoner sobbing on his knees in the shadow ain't gonna be no use a–tall. Frowning, he stands where he is, willing his hand away from the twine haft of his knife, wary of showing any sign of weakness . . .

After a while Shango shrugs, the thin smile twisting. He moves back to the spot where Mama Odu stands ready above the bound man on the floor. Grasps the lank hair with one hand to pull the man's head back against the light. At the clutch of those fingers, the captive whimpers in sudden pain and terror. Straddle-legged above him, Shango grins.

'Lookit him good,' the tall man tells the watching Justus. 'This the overseer they have at Willow Bend. Shoulda seen him lay the hide on them black bucks in the canefield, 'fore we hit that place . . . Sure was one tough white sonofabitch!' Chuckling, he bares his teeth, giving a wrench to the hank of hair that he holds. 'Reckon he don't look so tough as he did, huh boy?'

Justus looks into the fear-stricken face, pasty and sweating in the livid torchlight, the mouth with its rotted teeth askew and ugly, still making its sick, whimpering sounds. Feels his own features flinch in distaste, his gut fluttering. He a long way from Sweet River, now, he figures. One time, he'd have hated this one hard as any. Right now, sight of the overseer grovelling in the dirt and begging for mercy is enough to turn his stomach.

Back of the tall man, Mama Odu laughs thickly, weighing the knife in her palm. Looking helpless into the face of Justus across from him, the white captive reads no hint of pity there. He begins to weep, his head sinking forward to the ground. His thin shoulders shaking horribly through the frayed cloth of his shirt. Shango snorts in contempt. Tightens his hold, dragging the man squealing back to his feet. Towering over his prisoner, Shango turns his glance to Justus again.

'Look like it time to go see the god,' Shango says, turning towards the pool as he speaks and dragging the choking white man after him by the hair. The prisoner howling, stumbling to stay on his feet as that fierce grip hauls him along. As he moves, the tall man signs to Mama Odu, and the fat goddess bends with a grunt of effort to a darkened space on the ground beyond the altar. Justus sees her come up grinning wide with something heavy in her hand. From here it look like a rotting haunch of meat. After a while it gits to smell like it, too.

He stands, his gaze following them to the stretch of flamelit water. Shango no longer pays him any mind. His back turned, he leans close to the overseer, whispering to him, pulling hard on the hair as he does so, until it seems he must tear it out by the roots.

'You wanta see the god, huh, big man?' Shango's voice falls hoarse, eager in the stillness of the room. Seems like they a world off from the drumming and chanting outside. He pushes his face close against that of the other man, laughs without mirth as the overseer recoils in terror. 'Yeah, you git to see him, sure 'nough . . . Call him, goddess!'

The massive black shape alongside him takes a waddling step forward, grinning deep in the creased thickness of her face. Pitches the stinking chunk of meat into the water. Justus hears the heavy splash as it hits the middle of the pool, already sinking.

'Oh, my God!' the overseer squeals like a stuck hog.

Abruptly, the water churns from below as a huge, gliding shape strikes upwards towards the light, surface ripples breaking back as a hooked fin cuts above the water, sleek outline of the body following after. Moment's touch of tawny flame on a smooth, monstrous flank, a round, massive bullet head, jaws gaping as it rolls sidelong to show teeth like row upon row of jagged knives. In the same moment, the haunch vanishes, the monster diving as its jaws clamp shut. Justus watches, shivering. Across from him he can hear their harsh, excited breathing.

'Yeah,' Shango's voice croons, thick with malice. 'Now you seen him, white trash. What you gonna tell me now, you sonofabitch?'

Held fast, the white man shudders in a frantic spasm, blubbering incoherently, his face awash with tears and sweat. At the crotch of his breeches a dark stain spreads, soaking the cloth. Justus puckers his lips at the stench, feeling the threatening lurch of bile in his throat. He figure he gonna be sick, pretty soon.

'Whitey done filled his breeches, I reckon,' Mama Odu chuck-

106

les behind them, shaking her bloated head, eyes glinting like live coals in the reflected light.

'Uhuh.' Shango's smile gives way to a snarl of impatient anger. Still gripping the lank hair of his victim, he tugs forward. Drags the screaming captive over the ground towards the rim of the pool, teeth gritted as he glares into the stricken face.

'Let's us go meet the god, big man!'

Justus looking on, helpless, frozen, the unbearable bellowing cries of the white man slicing knife-sharp through his every nerve, the stink of death and fear grown thick in his nostrils. In the flamelit water of the pool the long killer-shape breaks surface again, swimming back lazily the way it came, gliding swift and smooth, cutting the ripples with a flick of its powerful tail. The blunt bull head with its slit of mouth turned towards them as it comes. Like it waitin' for what about to happen.

Up by the pool's edge, the white man thrashes, shrieking high and loud, legs lashing out vainly to strike empty air. Bound hands scrabbling in the dirt, frantically searching for a hold. Shango snarls. Dumps the tied man hard down on the earth. Grabs him by hair and scruff to heave him on his feet again. For an instant he looses his hold.

Teetering on the lip of the pool, the white man fights and yells, struggling to hit out with his clubbed hands, bound fast with the ropes. Shango gives back, grinning. Braces one lifted foot against the doomed man's belly. Pushes almost carelessly, without force, knowing that one touch is enough.

Last wavering shriek as the white man falls, leaning out backward to hit the water. Same instant the whole surface of the pool churns over as the big fish strikes in quicker'n a whiplash, rolling to show its sleek, smooth belly, the mouth gashing open. Fleeting glimpse of those razor teeth, bared and gleaming, caught for an instant in the light of flames. No time for the luckless overseer to call out—he barely has time to fall before that huge mouth hits, slamming shut across him, teeth like a row of blades crushing and slicing the body apart at the waist. Justus sees the white man vanish in a spray of blood, a torso flung in the air as the great shape rolls to strike again. fragments of flesh, coiling ropes of gut, thick splotches of blood—all thrown out in a spattering curtain that fouls the dirt at the pool's edge. Justus fights back the heave in his throat, digs nails in his wet palms, sweating, shaking, wondering how in hell he keeps from throwing up.

In the pool the great beast turns, the huge head lifted to catch a mauled remnant of flesh as it falls. Swings over to plunge underwater. Behind it the surface boils, reddening. After a while there's nothing to be seen, only fragments and bloody foam left behind. Somewhere in the midst a stiff-fingered hand floats, palm upward, sawn off clean at the wrist, stretched out like it reachin' towards them. Justus shakes his head, swallows on the foul taste of vomit.

'Yeah.' Shango breathes the word, lips parted, the look of his eyes distant and glazed like to a sated beast after a killing. Abruptly he moves back to a wooden lever by the wall, leans hard against it. Somewhere out of sight Justus hears the screech as thick metal shifts, opening—must be that iron grille he seen a while back, when they come in with Soldier, he reckons. With the sound the surface of the water is disturbed once again, the offal fragments washing down along the cut channel and out of sight. Across the room the tall man eases away from the wooden lever. Steps to meet Mama Odu by the altar, smiling.

Outside he hears the throbbing of the drums, coming as from a vast distance, muffled by the long house walls, and with it the chanting: rhythmic, insistent, endlessly repeated. Justus clenches his slippery hands, the sickness ebbing to a drained, hollow feeling, like he's somehow empty of everything. No more in him than a block of hewed wood or stone.

Over by the forked thunder-tree, Shango glances back, still smiling.

'You look like you sick, boy,' the tall man tells him. The glazed expression has left his eyes now, their stare alert and probing as they touch on the heavier man opposite him. 'Ain't in nature for a god like you to lose power that way . . . Could be you better rest a while.'

Crosses to Mama Odu in the same moment, reaching to touch her heavy, pendulous breasts, stroking them softly upward from beneath. Cat-like, the obese black woman murmurs, eyes slitting as she arches herself to meet his hands.

108

'You an' me, we got us somethin' else to do . . . ain't that right, goddess?'

Blink of the metal moon-disc, caught in the light of the torches, as the fat woman moves, locking a thick, black arm round Shango's neck, drawing his face and its pointed teeth to her neck, her shoulders, her hanging breasts. Her belly and Shango's drawing together, fat and lean pressed close. Watching them, the echoes of that thrashing death in the pool still sounding in his ears, Justus checks on a fresh upsurge of vomit in his throat. Blind in the half-dark, breathing hard, he turns for the door.

Her half-shut eyes turn his way, catching the sudden move. Over the bent head of Shango, Mama Odu looks towards him.

'You goin' someplace, boy?' the fat woman asks. Soft as the voice falls, he hears it clearly enough.

Justus halts, his glance going back across the torchlit space to where they lean one against the other, aware as he turns that those half-lidded dark eyes are upon him.

'No call fer you to go yet,' Mama Odu is saying, her hands groping eagerly for Shango's loins, moving under the belt of skins to grasp what lies beneath. All the while her glinting gaze lies on him, measuring him from head to foot, like he's some kind of animal. 'Kin always stay to watch. Ain't that so, Shango?'

The tall man makes no answer, moving urgently to part her heavy thighs. Mama Odu lies back on the stained tree stump, Shango standing upright between her spread legs. Her hands on him, guiding the jutting staff of flesh into her open body. From where she lies, the fat woman turns her head sidelong, looking to Justus, smiling.

'You a well set-up young buck, I reckon,' the goddess says, her narrow stare on him, studying. 'When Shango through here, Mama Odu give you a try-out, huh?'

He forces himself to look back into that loathsome face as it creases into oily rolls of flesh, smiling, while Shango grunts in impatience, thrusting into her. Her eyes still on Justus as she begins to moan and writhe. Somehow her invitation comes as the most sickening shock of all—worse even than the last moments of the white prisoner as the fish chewed him apart in the water. He stay here any longer, he gonna puke for sure . . .

'Spirit in me tire out,' Justus says, the words coming from him dull and heavy as lead on the tongue.. 'Reckon I be goin' from here.'

Starting forward as he speaks, making for the dark slab of door where the shadow lies thickest. Conscious as he moves of his hurrying breath, the frantic thudding of the heart at his ribs like he been runnin' for miles an' just quit.

Over by the stump, the two locked shapes freeze to stillness.

Justus catches the change from the corner of his eye. Halts at the door, his hands laid flat to the wood, waiting. After an age of silence comes Shango's chilling voice.

'You in the god-house now, boy.' The sound prickles his flesh like the hiss of the snake by his foot in the darkness. 'Ain't no-one goes from here less the god tell him, you hear?'

Braced at the rough-hewn door, he feels a long breath heave in his chest, shaking him. Shuddering, anger rising in him now equal to the sickness and the fear, Justus grips hard on the splintered wood, grinding his teeth.

'God in me too, Shango,' the big man says at last, grinding the words out through his clenched teeth, not troubling to look around as he speaks. 'You tole me to go rest. I'm tellin' you I goin' from here.'

He waits a while after that, forcing himself to stand motionless by the door, his back to them in the fresh-fallen quiet. Daring them, waiting for the sudden move. The threat, the unexpected blow from behind. None comes. His words are followed by a long silence.

All the same, he feels it: knows their hatred sure as the trickle of sweat along his spine. Aware even as he speaks of Shango's harsh, unforgiving stare levelled on him. Of Mama Odu's slitted appraising glance. At once his belly knows the chill of terror.

Here in the god-house, the word is said. From now on there can be no going back.

He pushes fiercely , the door groaning back to let in the light and noise outside. Like a man stunned, he steps out into the glare of day to meet the throbbing clamour of the drums. His hands clenched to fists. Scowling, his mind in another place. He knows the way it has to be.

Sooner or later he gonna have to kill Shango, or die.

'You seen him, huh? That thing they got in there?' Soldier asks.

He nods in answer, silently. For the moment he doesn't trouble to speak. All day he's been restive, uneasy, standing apart in frowning quiet amid the shouted praises in the compound and the blood-beating pulse of the drums. Now, crouched up at the far wall of the hut, his look shows no sign of changing, the face still etched in hard, bitter lines.

Soldier meets the fierce stare of his eyes for a moment only. Look aside, his own leathery features puckered in thought.

'Yeah.' The word leaves Soldier's lips in a heavy sigh. He too sags back against the wall, his one eye closing, one hand resting on the grounded gun. Now he looks up to the roof overhead. 'Reckon you lucky enough as it is, boy. Ain't nobody come outen there alive, 'cept Shango an' the goddess . . .'

Over in the shadow of the far wall, Justus glances up towards him. Throbbing glare of the sunset reflected in the gleam of his narrowed eyes.

'I figure you seen him too, Soldier,' the young man says at last. 'Ain't that right?'

To the left of him he catches a sudden shift of movement as he speaks. Mary halting where she squats on her heels in the flattened dirt, doling out the corn mush on wooden platters. White of her freckled face, as she turns to look his way, her blue eyes questioning. Justus sees the look as it comes, ignores it. His own gaze fixed on the figure by the doorway, until the single green eye flickers open.

'Yeah, I seen him.' Soldier's mouth loses its crooked smile. Now he mutters uncertainly, glancing sidelong over his shoulder to where the dying sun floods the compound in a wash of blood-red light, like he ain't sure whether somethin' out there listenin' on him. 'Ask me don't do no good to talk 'bout that one . . . man says too much, sooner or later he gonna end up in the long house hisself . . .'

He pauses, scanning with his lone eye the husky, wide-shouldered man by the wall. Meeting that solitary stare, Justus reads fear in the veteran's dark face.

'Guess you ain't gonna say nothin', boy?' Soldier offers at last.

'You kin trust me,' Justus tells him.

For a while Soldier says nothing. Across the hut, Justus can see the old man's broad chest rise and fall. It's so quiet now he can almost hear the other's breathing. After a long age of silence, the veteran nods his grey head.

'Right enough, I reckon,' Soldier says. He breaks off at that, falling quiet again. His one eye resting on Justus, as if uncertain how best to begin. Across the room from them both, Mary turns her back as silence returns. Moves again to spoon out the mush.

'How long it been here?' Justus asks.

At his question the old man frowns once more. 'Year after we come to this place,' Soldier tells him, gaunt face wrinkling as his mind recalls that time. 'Early spring, I reckon. Cain't be sure . . . Anyhow, was one night an' he come callin' us from bed. Tole us he seen somethin' in the water yonder—some kind of spirit . . .'

'Shango—he saw it first, huh?' The young man's stare still harsh and cold.

At the mention of that name Soldier's humped shoulders quiver like a cold wind just passed over him.

'Don' sing out that name too loud, boy.' The veteran's face uneasy in the lowering sunlight. 'He got ears everyplace . . . Yeah, was Shango seen it first. Swimmin' out by the middle of the lagoon. We all of us seen that fin cuttin' through the water like to a knife in syrup, know what I mean? So Shango, he tell me an' some the others to bring nets an' bait an' git in our pirogues. That we goin' to fetch home the god . . .'

Justus nodding across from him, silent, his eyes fixed on the old man's face.

'As I recall, light was pretty fair,' Soldier says. 'Moon, stars an' all, you know? So we rowed outen the middle like he said an' put down the bait . . . an' that thing took it!' Draws in his breath with a shuddering sigh, grimacing at the memory. 'Ain't seen nothin' like that critter, boy, an' I ain't fixin' to see no more. Like to a devil he was; drug in one man to the water, took his arm off clean. Jes' the way a knife cuts, then one of his legs . . . Last off, took his haid 'fore we got the nets around him.' He shakes his grizzled head at the thought, lean mouth pursing close, feeling a momentary revulsion. 'Sure was glad when that boy died . . . He was hollerin' fit to bust for a while . . .'

Away to the side, he glimpses the faint tremor that moves through Mary's crouched frame. Senses his own unease like a crawling on the skin. Calling to mind those floating limbs, the sawed-off edges left by those fearsome jaws, Justus forces his lips to a grim, unsmiling line. Fixes his gaze on Soldier until the old man speaks again.

'Took us nigh on an hour to git them nets around him,' the veteran says, sweat slick on his forehead as he glances again over his shoulder towards the gathering dark. 'Once we had him tied, Shango made us drag him back 'cross the water an' uphill to the ditch yonder. Then we turned him loose into the water outside the stockade . . .' Grins, his lips moving shaky in the blood-rimmed doorway. 'Me, I couldn't loose hold from that thing fast enough, an' that the truth!' He draws breath again, a harsh, heaving sound. Looks to Justus questioningly.

'Guess it'd be after that he had the long house built, huh?' the young man asks.

'Yeah. An' the ditch dug under it to outside.' Soldier almost laughs, the noise a mirthless snort as his features clench, distorted still in fear. Now he's started, seems like he cain't go too fast, the words spilling out of him like a thunder-shower. 'Was but a few of us did the diggin' fer that, an' at nightfall. Shango didn't aim to have no other folks see it. Tole us if we talked, we was for the god, come the time . . . Way he got it fixed, the critter stays up in the pool by the long house mostly—kin swim out only when he lets it loose. That's the way it was done . . .'

He sags against the wall, gasping, his one eye sober and hard now, his face paled to an ugly grey colour.

'Eight of us brung him in,' Soldier says, his voice dull, measuring the words in his mind. 'Same eight dug the channel. Two of those fellers were killed in plantation raids. Other five went to the god. Claw was last, I reckon. He take me, ain't no-one gonna be left to tell it. You hear me, boy?'

Quaver of fear in his voice as he speaks. Justus facing him, grows thoughtful. Now he sees why Soldier is so afraid.

'You already done tole it, I reckon,' Justus says.

'Guess so,' a mumbled whisper, passing almost unheard. Soldier's hand wavers over his sweating face, drops listless to his side. When he glances to Justus again, though, the look in his lone eye is of warning.

'Hear me good, boy,' Soldier mutters, swallowing as he speaks, his body hunched as if fearing a blow. 'You got sense, you git outen here first chance that comes. Shango aim to kill you, sure. You a good enough young feller, I reckon. Wouldn't care to see you comin' out in pieces from that channel yonder, know what I mean.'

'I hear you,' Justus says.

In his mind other visions, their power stronger than the dark itself: Shango's shape, looming like a young tree in his path, charged and murderous in its strength; Mama Odu's obscene, gleaming bulk. And back of them, the knife-jawed monster in the pool.

His gaze comes back at last to the figure of the old man squatting by the door, his head and shoulders outlined in black against the setting sun. Reading from those careworn features the effort it has cost him to speak the last words aloud.

'Thanks for the warning, Soldier,' Justus tells him. For an instant the grim mask eases, showing the faintest trace of a smile. 'Come the time, I'll remember.'

Uneasy behind the humour as he speaks, knowing that for all Soldier has told him, it makes no difference. Ain't just himself— he got Mary to think of, too. And the pair of them are hedged in by this stockade, imprisoned surer than back on Sweet River. One word from Shango, and there are close on a hundred folks out there, ready to tear them to pieces. Soldier might help, or Jewel—and then, maybe not. Shango is a hard man to go up against. He himself knows it. Somehow, he cain't see Jewel or the old man trying that.

An' if he gits out from here, where in hell he gonna go?.

He shakes his head at the thought, crushes a snarling sound that threatens low in his throat. Across from him, Soldier has sunk

114

back on the wall, the gun laid by as Mary hands the platter to him. The old man eats in silence, his grey head bowed. Avoids looking at Justus. Watching, the big man shrugs resignedly. Could be Soldier figures he said too much, as it is. Justus leans at the wall almost wearily, hands down flat to his thighs. His look is thoughtful still as he takes the offered platter from Mary's hand.

'Thanks, honey,' the big man says.

Spooning the corn mush, he eyes her as she eats, marking the white-blonde hair in its horsetail at her neck, glinting as it catches the last fires of the sun. Sees the smooth, supple curving of back and haunch, gleam of her bared legs with their faint, pale covering of downy hairs. Going back once more to the face that watches him, expectant, questioning. Justus lets his own glance rest, saying nothing. Feeling the slow fierce lapping of bloodflame through his limbs.

He been a long time without her.

Taste of the corn mush coarse and gritty against his teeth. Barely warm now, it been left so long. All the same he eats, hardly noticing the food as it passes down his gullet. His eyes on her still, waiting for the night.

'Sounds like a bull shark, from what you say,' Mary says.

Sun gone down behind the row of huts, beyond the stockade. Outside, the compound lies quiet in starless dark, no wind stirring. They too lying still on the rush mat by the wall, their bodies close, facing. As yet they do not touch.

Bull shark . . . His mind takes the words in, not fully accepting them. Justus nods, eyes on her face. Still he does not speak.

'Never seen one myself,' Mary admits, her pale features grown thoughtful as she remembers. 'Was Caleb told me of it, back at Butler's Fork. Said they come upriver from the ocean sometimes. Only shark he know of that swim in freshwater that way. Grow to ten foot or so, was what he said. Told me I wasn't like to meet one, but if I ever did to look out, on account of they were worse than any gators . . .' Looking to him, uncertain now, trying to read the harsh mask of his face close to hers. 'Never did think of it till now.'

'Uhuh.' His own look doesn't alter. As well as the horror of the

long house, of the shape with its gleaming jaws, he feelin'
somethin' else now: anger—at himself, mostly; once she git to
talkin' of Caleb, he cain't help feelin' how dumb he is. Seems like
he don't know nothin' a–tall. An somethin' of that feeling showing
in his eyes. Seeing it, Mary checks for a moment, then goes on.

'That business with the snakes, too,' the white woman says.
'Don't know exactly how it's done, but Caleb used to say he'd
known it in Galveston once. Seems you can be bit and still live, if
you do it right. Somethin' about how so much poison in the blood
protects you, kind of fights any more poison you take in . . . Never
did understand that rightly, but that's what he said . . .'

'Use to know quite a bit, huh? That Caleb?' Justus says.

For an instant Mary frowns, a brief glint of anger in the blue of
her eyes. 'He taught school,' she says. 'He knew more than most, I
guess.'

At his sullen glance, her own look softens, her hand moving to
cover his.

'Don't be sore, Justus,' the white girl tells him, her voice soft
now, gentle as her touch on the back of his fisted hand. 'It don't
signify so much. Besides, that's long over now.'

Under her hold the bunched black hand opens, the scowl
disappearing as he nods his bushy head. Justus looks down to her
hand resting on him. Up again into her face.

'We got to git from here somehow, girl,' Justus says.

'I know it.' A shadow clouds her face as she replies. Unsought
remembrance of the sacked plantation at Blackwater, the butchered family, and the girl with her empty, staring eyes; and after
them, the wretched overseer, grovelling in the compound dirt
before they dragged him away . . . abruptly her lip trembles,
Mary shaking her head as her eyes fill up with tears.

'How we goin' to do that, Justus?'

Right now that's somethin' he ain't figured either. Still, he
forces himself to smile. Under her open hand, his own turns palm
upward, closing its long fingers to clasp her woman's hand.

'We think of somethin',' Justus tells her. 'Jes' trust me, girl, is
all.'

Soldier turned on his side away from them, one shoulder humped, twitching a little as he sleeps. The two of them lie still for a

116

moment, hands clasped, faces so close that their breath warms each other's flesh. Watching. Silent. About them the darkness grows deeper than before.

Pulsing heat of the blood-rhythm in his veins as he lies, feeling the torment, the ache of unsated flesh. His need drawn to a white-hot core at his groin, where the manhood throbs and swells tight against the cloth of his breeches. Her own warmth inches from him, motionless. Seems like an age before she moves at last, her free hand coming up to touch lightly on the side of his face . . .

At that first touch, Justus freezes where he lies, his eyes meeting hers. For a while, neither of them speaks.

'You want to, Justus?' she says at last.

Justus makes no answer. Reaches instead to touch her hand to his lips.

Mary smiles. 'Me too,' she says.

She leans back from him slowly, arching to pull the torn dress over her head. He reaches upward to clasp the white globes of her breasts in his hands, palms stroking the smooth, pale flesh, fingers moving light over the soft-textured skin to where her nipples thrust out in budding points against him. At his touch Mary smiles afresh, easing out of her drawers, taking his hand to guide it gently between her thighs, her touch gliding swift along the muscles of his flanks and belly, down to the point where his jutting maleness strains beneath the buckled belt of his pants. Movement of her hands rapid and assured, unbelting him, laying him bare.

Her eyes on him as he lies, breath coming hard, fingers finding her wet and trembling, ready for him. Mary gasps, shivers against his hand, her eyes half-closed. For her, too, it has been a long time.

Her hand closing on him as her own need quickens. Mary kneels above him, leans to kiss the column of his manhood as it rises, her mouth taking the tip of the hot, pulsing staff, warmth of its soft inner surfaces closing on the throbbing flesh. Mary swings her body, moving out across him. Thighs spread to lower the wet heat of her loins to his face.

Scent of her woman's body strong in his nostrils as her thighs enfold him, Justus kisses, enters the moist heat of her flesh, gasping. Dark and pale of their joined bodies twined fiercely

117

together now, limbs locked as they shudder and groan. Comes the long-awaited moment of release. With the last light flutter of her tongue he crows and shoots, rearing helpless in the clutch of the orgasm, her mouth taking the hot rush of his seed. A moment more and she comes like a ripe fruit bursting across his mouth, taste of her warm juices sweeter than syrup to his tongue.

Later she slides down and takes him into her body. Straddling him to ride his fresh-risen maleness until the two of them come again. Sinking to cover him at last, her body gleaming white, she lies over his darkness, the two of them sweating, smiling, sated. His black arm about her. She with one white hand in his bush of hair as they drift towards sleep at last.

White and black alike imprisoned. In danger of their lives. But no longer alone.

Together now.

Reason enough to smile as they lie close, joined by the warmth of their loving.

'LAFAYETTE HERALD', SEPTEMBER 25th, 1865.
Punitive expedition formed.

FOLLOWING THE DASTARDLY ATTACK AND MASSACRE BY
RENEGADE BLACKS AT THE LACOURBE PLANTATION AT WILLOW
BEND, THE MILITARY AUTHORITIES HAVE AT LAST RESOLVED
UPON ACTION. THIS LATEST IN A SERIES OF MURDEROUS ATTACKS
BY RENEGADES OF THE SAME BAND ON FOUR PLANTATIONS IN THE
REGION BRINGS THE TOTAL OF WHITES KILLED TO THIRTEEN,
WITH OTHERS YET TO BE ACCOUNTED FOR. IN EVERY CASE
SURVIVORS HAVE TESTIFIED TO THE APPALLING CRUELTIES
INFLICTED BY THESE SAVAGES ON THOSE UNFORTUNATE ENOUGH
TO FALL INTO THEIR HANDS.

IN THE OPINION OF THIS PAPER, ACTION HAS LONG BEEN
OVERDUE. THE EARLIER EFFORTS OF SHERIFF WHITESIDE AND
MR JOHN LAWRENCE OF SWEET RIVER TO RAISE AN ARMED
FORCE, THOUGH ONLY PARTIALLY SUCCESSFUL, HAVE RECEIVED
OUR STRONG SUPPORT. NOW IT SEEMS THAT THE MILITARY HAVE
AT LAST SEEN SENSE. AT ANY RATE, A FORCE OF MORE THAN A
HUNDRED AND FIFTY MEN IS TO TAKE THE FIELD AGAINST THE
RAIDERS, UNDER THE LEADERSHIP OF CAPTAIN JAMES A.
MAITLAND. AN ARMED VIGILANTE FORCE SWORN IN BY SHERIFF
WHITESIDE AND CO–LED BY HIMSELF AND MR LAWRENCE, HAS
ASSURED THE MILITARY OF THEIR FULL CO-OPERATION. THE
JOINT PUNITIVE EXPEDITION PLANS TO MOVE IMMEDIATELY
AGAINST THE MURDERERS, WHO ARE BELIEVED TO HAVE THEIR
BASE IN THE MARSHLANDS FURTHER SOUTH.

WE AND OUR NORTHERN KINSMEN HAVE HAD OUR
DIFFERENCES IN THE PAST, AND MUCH BITTERNESS REMAINS
FROM THE RECENT CONFLICT BETWEEN THE STATES. NEVERTHE-
LESS, THIS PAPER WELCOMES THE LATEST MOVE BY THE
MILITARY, AND WISHES THEM EVERY SUCCESS IN THE FIELD.
NORTH OR SOUTH, WE ARE ALL OF US AMERICANS, AND THE
TRAGEDY OF WILLOW BEND BRINGS HOME OUR NEED TO JOIN
TOGETHER AND PUNISH THESE SAVAGES FOR THEIR ATROCIOUS
CRIMES.

In the grey time before morning he rouses, woken by some half-heard sound.

Shadows hold to the corners of the hut as he turns his head. Light in the doorway sunless, greyer than iron. Away from the threshold, Soldier sleeps on, his body humped close to the wall, his face turned from them, halflight touching ghostly on the knitted scars of his back as the darkness thins all around. Apart from the shifting shadow, nothing moves.

Mary lying against him, heavy and slack-limbed in sleep, her head resting on his chest. Here and there their bodies cling, the warm flesh joined by sweat and the moisture of their lovemaking. Justus grins softly at the memory. Lifts one dark hand, fingers spread, to stroke the hair that fans silver-white on the black of his chest, feeling her breath touch him as he moves. All the time listening for the sound.

Nothing answers. Only silence, and the eerie halflight spreading from the open door.

Justus grunts, unsatisfied, feeling the pull of weariness begin to claim him, dragging at the lids of his eyes, sapping the strength from his limbs. Slowly he settles over on one shoulder, his eyes starting to close.

One faint slither of sound warns him, rasping along the fibres of his nerves. His eyes open in a moment, seeing it plain: the dark, coiled shape like a length of rope in the dirt, inches from his face. The shape he didn't see before, when it went on its belly, lost in the shadow. The shape that now lifts up slowly, hissing, as the flat-fanged head poises in readiness to strike for his unprotected eyes and mouth.

Freezing like stone at the sight of it, unable to move, he stares in terror. Fear paralysing him as he gazes mesmerised at the smoothly gleaming skin, the bared fangs and black, unwavering eyes. Not a hope for him, he knows. Cottonmouth kin hit faster 'n lightnin'. Inwardly, somewhere in the midst of his terror, he finds time to hope it strikes him first. Maybe then Mary at least will have a chance.

Wills himself to be still as fresh sweat beads out on his skin, stinging him as it runs into his eyes. The smooth, poised head

120

of the snake dips backward. Justus clenches on the urge to scream aloud.

Beyond them, a sudden blur of movement: long shadow coming swift across the grey light in the doorway. From where he lies rooted, he catches a glimpse of a lithe, moving shape and the bright gleam of a blade. Whistle of a broad cane knife drowns out the snake's hiss, cutting through air and on beyond, its honed blade shearing through bone and flesh. Watching, he sees the cottonmouth's severed head fly from its body with a splutter of blood, eyes and fanged mouth glaring in the moment of death, the knife itself thudding into the far wall as the lashing headless shape splays out, its tail brushing lightly on the flesh of his arm. Justus bears the touch, his dark face flinching in distaste. Unable as yet to take in the fact he's still alive.

He lies, making no move, as the lithe figure steps by him, tugging the knife from the wall. Turning, grey light playing down the sleek, bronzed outline of her body. Jewel bends close above him, smiling, her bared teeth gleaming white in the darkness of her face. Justus meets the Indian woman's predatory look, holding still to the sleeping Mary. Jewel grins tighter, leans in to wipe her darkened blade on the leg of her breeches. Her hand touches the hard-muscled flesh of his belly in passing.

'Come the time, you for me,' Jewel says.

She rises swiftly, without a sound, darting quiet as a shadow towards the doorway.

Against him Mary stirs, murmuring as she turns sidelong in her sleep. Justus holds her to him, his hand stroking the white-blonde cloud of her hair, eyes still wary as the bronzed, black-haired figure vanishes out by the open door. Stunned as he is, his mind takes in all that it needs for the present.

Shango wants him dead. And from the look of it he ain't in a mind to wait overlong.

Jewel wants him alive for herself, and now it looks like he owes her somethin'.

The big man frowns, the hand on the white woman's hair bunching to a fist. Slowly he eases Mary away from him, laying her back as he gets to his feet. Picking up the hacked fragments of the snake, he crosses to the doorway. Hurls head and body out into the compound.

Best that Shango should know the way it went, he thinks.

Justus forces his lips to a dry, tired smile. Sure has been one hell of a night.

He leans on the low sill of the door, waiting for morning.

Beneath him the horse ploughs leg-deep into water, floundering. Maitland goes with it, muttering under his breath as the wash hits the animal's belly, features twisted into a grimace as a spray of green muck spatters his boots. In front, and around him, his vision blurs under the thrashing downpour of rain, grey solid sheets of it slamming down, whipping up the surface of the marsh, drawing a veil across the flat stretches of water and the tall banks of reeds, the marooned islands with their thickets and stunted trees. He scowls, touches heels to the creature's flanks. The big horse fights on, splashing through the shallows and up the far bank, hooves slithering in the mud and reeds. There on the rim he draws rein, hunching as the downpour hammers back off his head and shoulders, warm heavy droplets spatting on his face and sluicing down inside the neck of his cavalry blouse to soak him through his breeches. Maitland shakes a blond head, his brows weeping into his eyes. Glances back to where the other horsemen follow, plunging their mounts into the water.

Maitland watches as his troop swim the stretch of marsh, their horses disappearing almost up to their saddle-cinches in the water and the thick scum that coats its surface. Frowning stoop-shouldered figures, their head bent in weariness, the rain turning the blue of their uniforms to a sodden black and spreading a wet sheen over saddle leathers and the gleaming flanks of their beasts. The Captain's eye marking them, one by one: Sergeant Elliott, Corporal Rose, Troopers Taggart, Moody, Johnson, Craig . . .

Back of his own detail, another bunch of horsemen without uniforms: men in denims and cords, their faces hidden under broad-brimmed hats, all of them with knives and hand-guns belted down. Maitland eyes them as they approach the far edge

122

of the marsh, his frown deepening. These fellers he could do without, and that's for sure.

Beyond the horsemen, already blurred by the sheets of rain, a long, straggling column of men on foot. Somewhere behind them, at a point no longer visible to him, two gun teams are at work, struggling to drag their wheeled weapons forward through the mud.

Maitland shakes his head, sighing, forgetting for an instant the drenching fall of the rain. What in hell's name is he doing out here? he wonders. Thirty-strong cavalry detail, full company of infantry and two light field pieces—plus these damned Louisiana riders. And all of it for the sake of a handful of ignorant blacks.

He draws the dipping slicker about him, feeling the force of the rain that sprays at the back of his neck. Even now, in the middle of the downpour, he finds he's sweating hard, warmth and damp combining to clamp the sodden clothes to his flesh like a second skin. Maitland endures the sticky discomfort, scowling. No doubt of it, he'll be glad to get out from this godforsaken territory and back to Indiana.

Down below him, Elliott and his mount break from the shallow water, man and horse alike streaming wet as they gain the bank, forcing a way up through the clinging mud. The half-breed Cherokee tracker close behind the sergeant as he climbs, digging heels to the flanks of his thin pony. A spatter of wet muck flies back from Elliott's horse, drenching the rider below. Maitland looks on sourly in silence as the two of them join him on the crest, Rose and the other men of the detail hammering through the shallows in a cloud of brownish-green spray.

'Have the troop halt, Sergeant,' the officer says.

His glance travels on as he speaks, beyond Elliott to where the Indian sits astride his narrow-hipped pinto, turning the animal slowly in circling movements along the crest, scanning the drenched earth for sign. Maitland studies the hunched shape coldly, unsmiling. The tracker lean and shapeless under a frayed old Union reatcoat that hides him to the knees, stained leggings and moccasins hanging loose beneath the pony's belly, the battered black hat leaking water in a freshet to the ground, its brown eagle feather bedraggled under the rain. Beneath the spouting brim, the

123

features are harsh and dark, the eyes glinting from hooded slits in the flesh, the greased black hair tied in a thick knot at the shoulder. Maitland breathes out, turning abruptly from the unkempt horseman, feeling his annoyance grow keener. He knows as well as the Indian that whatever sign there was will have been washed out of this ground long ago.

'What do you think?' Maitland asks the sergeant, who has pulled in alongside and now sits with his head bent to the rain, looking out through his horse's ears to the half-hidden land ahead. At the sound of his voice, Elliott glances up, eyeing the officer narrowly from under the peak of his dripping forage cap.

'Ain't showed themselves yet, sir.' A wry smile puckering as he speaks, droplets of water gleaming in the grey-wired stubble of his beard, Elliott shifts upright in the stirrups, easing his breeches from the clinging wet of his saddle. 'Could be we ain't about to see these folks at all . . . Can't say as I seen too many black heroes in these parts, you take my meaning?'

Maitland frowns, nodding back without a word. Truth to tell, he's pretty much of Elliott's mind himself. No way he can see a rabble of black runaways and a few badly-armed redskins standing to fight against the kind of strength he's brought along. With the weather taking a turn for the worse, the chances are that the whole exercise will prove a wild goose chase, like most other missions he's had down here since the war ended.

Then again, he can't discount the evidence of these massacres. From all accounts, the renegades did a thorough job of slaughtering there. And since his column entered the marshes, there have been other, disquieting signs. Those mangled fragments they found in the water a few days back were enough to turn anyone sick. Rotted and flyblown as they were, there was no mistaking what they had once been. And a man's bound to ask himself how that kind of thing must have come about . . . Just what kind of people are they? he wonders. Somehow, he can't relate this style of butchery with the blacks he has seen, so servile, grovelling almost—scarcely like men at all. Must be some difference between them and these others. Has to be, if what they say is true . . .

'They're already murderers, Sergeant,' the captain says.

124

'Heroes or not, their crimes must be accounted for.' Turning aside, he shakes off a trickle of water from the end of his nose. 'It may be they'll fight to stay free, after all.'

Elliott scowls, pouting his lips in thought. Rakes one hand through his glittering stubble to wipe it clean of sweat and rain.

'It ain't the same, Captain,' the sergeant tells him. 'Way I see it, they ain't had nothing to fight this far. No more than three or four white men at a time, most of 'em with old guns . . . No sir, farmers is one thing; regulars, that's a whole peck of difference. They see us, they're like to run far and fast sooner than fight. That's my opinion, sir.'

Maitland nods, but doesn't answer. The continual hiss of rain sounding on as he looks over the waiting horsemen in their soaked uniforms, reining in along the crest. His gaze moves on to the Cherokee tracker, who now nudges his gaunt pony to a walk, moving in towards the captain with shoulders slumped, the black-hatted head sunk forward almost on his chest.

'You find sign, Owl Man?' The captain's voice curt, impatient, knowing already that his words are wasted.

As he speaks, the Indian lifts his head slowly, measuring the officer with his dark, hooded eyes.

'No sign,' Owl Man answers. He stretches, shaking himself like a dog in the wet, dark, deep-set stare of the eyes holding to the captain as he moves. 'Best we try further south. Pick up trail there, maybe . . .'

He falls silent, sitting there hunched, with both hands laid flat to the pony's mane, the frayed cuffs dribbling water from the sleeves, his glance on the captain. Waiting . . .

'Thank you, scout.' Maitland's face shows his weariness. He edges the horse around, looking away through the grey, drumming curtain of rain to where hummocks of land rear in the distance, blurred and indistinct. Alongside him, Elliott squints uncertainly into the downpour, his harsh features grown sober in reflection.

'Looks like the ground firms up yonder,' the sergeant offers at last, his voice vying with the rain as it strikes and rebounds from their slickered shoulders. 'Give us more of a foothold, maybe . . .'

125

'Won't be much help to Riordan's guns,' Maitland says. 'Or the ammunition waggon.' He swings round abruptly, swatting water from the rim of his cap, glancing towards the clustered horsemen of the detail, further along the crest. 'Corporal! Over here!'

Rose comes riding over, stiffening upright in his stirrups beneath the rain, his arm snapping up in a keen salute that flings droplets on his horse's neck.

'*Sir!*'

Not much more than a boy, even now. Barely twenty, the captain judges. Still, he's been through these past years of fighting with the rest.

Met by that youthful earnest face, Maitland almost smiles.

'My compliments to Lieutenant Pfister, Corporal. Have him detail parties for tree-felling at the double. We're going to need rafts for the guns and the waggon.'

'*Yessir!*'

Swinging his mount away, he salutes once more, then forcing the animal downslope at the gallop, spray washing high along the horse's flanks, he takes to the water. Maitland looks to the vanishing horseman, slim and erect in his saddle under the thrash of rain. A faint smile begins to inch its way over the officer's smooth-slicked face.. They don't come any keener than Rose, he guesses.

At once he is back in the present, aware of their searching eyes upon him. Owl Man and the grim-faced sergeant, and back of them the troopers of his detail. Moody, stocky and wide in the shoulder, leans forward on his animal's neck, his blue-jowled features twisting in the wryest of grins. Behind him, the taller, sour-looking Taggart, and Craig with his red hair plastered down into his eyes. All of them watching the captain as he smiles, waiting.

Maitland lets out his breath in a sigh, feeling the clammy trickle of the water down his spine. The smile fading as he turns from them, glancing back the way Rose has gone, across the wallow of green, stagnant water.

Lawrence's bunch are halfway to meet him by now, their mounts swimming at the deepest point. Maitland watches them come, strung out wide in a ragged line, riding six or seven abreast, their long-skirted dusters dark and sodden from the rain that hits

126

across them now in brief, squalling gusts, drenching men and beasts alike. Lawrence himself up at the head, the long whip coiled on his saddlehorn, his hand-gun belted out of sight under the wet coat. Alongside of him, the big-bellied, grizzled figure of Whiteside, gripping a sawed-down shotgun whose shape is outlined under the duster's dripping folds. About and behind them the rest of the party in their coats and slickers, their denims and cords. One man on Lawrence's far side reins in his mount, waist-deep in water, tilting his head to a whisky-jug he holds at the shoulder, rain hammering down on his upturned eyes and mouth as he drinks; already swaying in the saddle.

Up beside him on the crest Elliott watches, saying nothing. But Maitland reads the contempt in the sergeant's narrowed eyes.

The group of riders make way as Rose thrusts his mount past them at a lurching run, not looking to left or right as he heads through the shallows for the distant column of infantry. Lawrence's lean hatchet-face tautens briefly as the youngster throws up a wake of scummy water in passing, the anger giving way to a vicious, mocking grin that spreads over those narrow, hard features. An eddy of laughter fans out along the line of horsemen as Rose spatters ashore on the far bank.

'Sure in one hell of a hurry, that Yankee boy!' Munson calls out.

He sways again, the horse moving forward beneath him, all but pitching him from the saddle. Munson cackles, clinging to the jug as he hits against the mane, Lawrence reaching sidelong to haul him up in the stirrups. He and another of the riders steady their drunken friend as the bunch of horsemen gains the bank, still laughing among themselves as they push their horses uphill through the mud.

'Y'all see that kid, Jared?' Munson still singing out with the full force of his lungs as he reels, fighting to keep his saddle. 'Ain't seen a Yankee run that way since we come up agin them yellow-britches over by Shiloh . . . Sure run from us, that time . . .'

Maitland has done smiling. Away to the side of him, Elliott's whiskered features are as hard and pitiless as hewn stone. Further off, Owl Man sits with shoulders humped, his dark head drooping on his chest as the rain streams from the brim of his hat. The Cherokee is already tired: of the soldiers, the posse, the rain, the lack of sign. Gonna be glad once this jumped-up bluecoat captain gives the word to turn back, he figures.

'Mister Lawrence!' Maitland's voice cutting sharp against the fall of rain. The captain's eyes fix pale and cold on the foremost of the riders. At the sound of his words they haul rein below him, looking upward.

'Mister Lawrence, you would be well advised to send that man home under guard. As I see it, he is in no fit state for further travelling!'

The downpour slackening as he speaks, splashing over Lawrence as the plantation owner turns his head sidelong to the uniformed officer above him. Maitland sees one hand clench a moment on the coiled blacksnake whip in front of him, but it's for a moment only. After a time the dark man's mouth resumes its mocking smile.

'Don't trouble none about him, captain,' Lawrence says, his grin touching on the men about him now as he looks from one to the other. 'Ole Munson craves his liquor a mite fierce, I'll allow, but comes a chance of a fight, you kin depend on him. Ain't that so, boys?'

A murmur of agreement from the horsemen around. Sight of their grinning faces under the rain is beginning to saw on the captain's nerves. Munson laughs harshly, gives out with a raucous Rebel yell. One of the other riders grabs him as he once more threatens to pitch over the animal's neck to the ground.

'He's right, sure enough,' Whiteside tells the soldier. 'Never yet seen a nigra could look old Munson in the eye, an' live on after.'

Maitland appraises the sheriff with the briefest glance. The body with its big shoulders and heavy gut swelling over the clasped leather belt that holds up his breeches; the massive head with its grey, cropped hair and thick moustaches; the eyes like cold, pale stones in the dark, seamed leather of the face. Whiteside chews on a frayed wood toothpick, meeting the officer's look with a chill stare of his own. Sight of his dark, discoloured teeth at work on the wood stub is enough to turn the captain's stomach.

'That's as may be.' Maitland's voice stays cold, his glance

128

leaving Whiteside again for Lawrence. 'This man is your charge, Mr Lawrence. Should any harm come to him, the responsibility will also be yours.'

'Ain't gonna be no trouble, captain,' Lawrence grins in answer, fondling the smooth coils of the whip. In the dull light his eyes glint black and keen as shards of rock. 'Nigras is dumb anytime. We run 'em down, they give us no more hardship than a turkey-shoot, I reckon.' Turning halfway to the rider on his far side, his thin-lipped smile broadens. 'Jared here was thinkin' to bring his hounds along, first off, only we took pity after a while. Thought we'd give the dumb sons a chance, ain't that so, Jared?'

'Sure is, Mr Lawrence,' Jared chuckles in answer. His eyes, too, have a vicious, hungry look.

'That's the way of it, captain.' Lawrence grins on beneath the spattering rain, his hand laid to the whipstock. 'Once we catch up with 'em, you jes' stand away an' give us the room to shoot. We'll clean them nigras out for you, sure enough . . .'

Maitland hears out their laughter, his smooth features suddenly turned hard and cold.

'Command of this punitive expedition rests with me, Mr Lawrence,' the captain says at last, looking the Southerner level in the eye. 'Should you and these other . . . *gentlemen* . . . choose to accompany us, you will do so under my orders. Furthermore,' the hand in its soaked white gauntlet clenches on the saddle-horn, tight almost as the sound of his voice, 'should the renegades we are in pursuit of show themselves willing to surrender, they will be given every opportunity to lay down their arms. This is a military force, sir, and not a vigilante patrol.'

In front of him the laughter stills. Only the steady slackening fall of rain to be heard now; that, and the snorting of the horses. Abruptly Lawrence's smile vanishes, his thin lips clamping themselves into a hard, bitter line. Maitland endures the harsh stare of his eyes, unflinching.

'I trust that I am fully understood,' the captain says.

For a moment the plantation owner doesn't reply, struggling with his anger. Then Lawrence lets out a hissing breath. Grips on the whipstock with whitened finger-ends.

'Reckon I catch your drift, captain.' His voice comes low and calm, belying the hatred that flares in his eyes and the taut-clenched muscles of his jaw. All the same there is venom in his speech, and Maitland feels the sting of it along his nerves.

'Have it your way, mister,' Lawrence says, then turns, glancing to the silent riders all about him, unsmiling now. 'Let's git from this wallow, you boys.'

He jabs his heels to the sides of his horse and the big stallion heaves from the water, surges up the bank in a spray of mud, other horsemen following him, one by one. Whiteside, the gun pressed close against his chest; the reeling figure of Munson, the one they call Jared still holding to his arm. Then the rest: Clayt and Sims, and a man named Hooker. All keeping one arm free as they ride, in close reach of the belted hand-guns and knives.

The group of riders gather again, further along the crest, holding to a distance from the cavalry detail on the same stretch of mud. Maitland eyes their retreating backs, silently.

'Don't do to pay them no mind, sir.' Elliott's voice coming suddenly from alongside, barely heard in the fall of rain. 'Bunch of no-account hellions, is how I got them figured.' Digs down under the slicker as he speaks, going for the bulge in his pocket. 'captain's permission?'

'Carry on, Sergeant.' Maitland forces his lips to a smile.

'Sir.' Elliott unships the corncob pipe from its hiding-place, tamps tobacco into the bowl, fingers working deftly to shield it from the rain. Maitland looks on as the veteran strikes a match on his thumbnail, touches the glowing flame to the fuel in the bowl. He smokes on for a while in quiet, neither one of them speaking.

'There are times,' Maitland says at last, 'when I wonder just what it is we're doing here.' He scans the dark, marshy spread of land, the far islands blurred still under the dull curtain of rain. His boyish features frown, the look of his blue, youthful eyes suddenly unsure. 'Before, the other battles we were in, the business was straightforward. We had a job to do, to preserve the Union, bring the Rebels into line . . . Nowadays,' he shakes his head, still frowning, 'I'm less certain. There's something about this kind of venture that doesn't appeal to me at all . . .'

He breaks off, falling silent all at once. Across from him,

130

Elliott nods, eyeing the officer over the glowing bowl of his pipe. The sergeant gives a wintry smile.

'Guess headquarters know what they're about, sir,' Elliott says.

Faced by that level stare, Maitland's own look sobers. The young officer shrugs, as if shaking off the mood, draws himself up in his stirrups, straight-backed under the rain.

'You're right,' Maitland says. 'We have a job to do here, like we did before. And it will be done.'

Looks away from Elliott as he speaks, his glance cutting back towards the infantry, the way Rose went. Seeing how the distant column slows to a halt, details of men peeling off towards the islands with their sparse covering of brush and trees.

'All the same,' Maitland says. 'I wish it wasn't us.'

Beside him the whiskered sergeant breathes pipesmoke into the dull air. He doesn't answer.

'Come on down, you sonofabitch,' Voorhees says.

He swings, the tree bole ringing as the axe bites into it, stunted timber shuddering under his blows. Up on the far side, Benton grunts, his own axeblade slamming deep into the wood. The tree keels sideways in the slant of rain. Goes down slow with a dry, creaking groan. The pair of them stand back from it, breathing hard, resting on their long-handled axes as the heavy drops of water fall warm on their sweating shoulders.

'Looks like the worst of it's over, now,' Benton says, glancing up and drawing a wet sleeve over his face. Out of breath for the moment, Voorhees nods, not speaking.

On the island slope around them, the other men of the wood-felling detail work on, hewing down the trees and brush, lopping boughs and limbs, stacking the finished lengths together in heaps. Schwab is the nearest, laying into the trunk of a stunted fir. From where they stand, Voorhees can see the wide spread of his shoulders and his thick corn-coloured mop of hair. The crossed white galluses strain as he leans into the blow, the army blouse clinging tight across his powerful back. Good enough man, Schwab, even if he ain't too bright. Voorhees looks on that

131

huge figure for a while, then his glance returns to Benton and the tree they have felled.

'Good thing the lieutenant had us bring the axes along,' he says, and the dark man across from him grins slyly, his head set to one side.

'Army thinks of everything, soldier,' Benton tells him. 'Ain't you learned that yet?'

Voorhees grunts sourly, not answering. Picks up the axe again to start on one of the thicker boughs, treading the upper clusters of thorns underfoot as the wood shakes to his blows. Benton shrugs, moving to join him.

'Wish they'd tell us what in hell we're doing out here,' Voorhees says.

At the sound of his voice, big Schwab leaves off, turning with the axe laid back to his shoulder. From deep in the whiskered ploughboy face, his blue eyes fix on Voorhees, frowning reproachfully towards him.

'Reckon your folks wouldn't care to hear you talk that way, son,' Schwab tells him.

'Ah, to hell . . .' Voorhees' voice runs out, exasperated. He slams the axe hard into the wood by his feet, letting go the helve as it sticks fast. That same moment feeling a twinge of shame that this dumb farmhand should be telling him how to behave. The worst of it is, that Schwab is right. Voorhees' people are Philadelphia Quakers who wouldn't take kindly to hearing curses from the lips of their only son. Come to think, he never used to swear overmuch himself before he joined up.

The young man falls silent, leaning again on his axe to draw breath, watching the big heavy-shouldered man across from him as Schwab talks on.

'Way I see it, it's simple,' Schwab is saying, brushing at his wet face with the back of his hand. 'These blacks have murdered innocent folk, and we got to put an end to it. Nothin' out the way about that . . .'

'Guess not,' Benton agrees, smiling still, half-amused at the annoyance of his friend. Voorhees is a mite touchy at times, he figures; comes with being a Quaker, or something like that. 'All the same, ain't like to a regular soldierin' job, I'd say . . .'

132

'Had us somethin' like it, back in Iowa.' Schwab's face creases, remembering. 'War-party run off our hogs, killed 'em some for the meat . . . I was no more'n a kid then, but I went along. They was a bunch of us—my old man, uncle and so on. We took out for the woods an' run 'em down. Killed us a few before they run . . .' Frowning yet, as he scans the faces of the other two men. 'Don't see as this is no different.'

'Blacks ain't the same as Injuns,' Voorhees says, but he knows as he speaks that what he says has nothing to do with it.

'No, that ain't it,' Benton puts in. 'They got Injuns in with 'em anyhow, from what I heard. Fact is, Schwab, you got to consider how these blacks been treated 'fore we come down here. From what I seen, your hogs get better back in Iowa. Ain't that right?'

'That's right!' Voorhees' young face glows, eager and excited, glad, too, of the chance to get back at Schwab for once. 'We all of us come down here to put slavery down—leastways, that's the way I heard it. Far as I'm concerned, the blacks are men, same as us . . .'

Once more his words tail off as Schwab looks him in the eye, the big Iowa farmer seeing through him so clear, it's almost painful to meet that stare of his without flinching.

'Maybe they're men,' Schwab says. 'But they ain't like us, an' that's for sure. Me, I don't know nothin' about slavery, and I ain't any too interested. All I know is what they done to them farms back yonder . . .'

'Plantations, they called,' Benton says, but the big man ignores him, his pale hard eyes still on the slim, fresh-faced figure of Voorhees across from him.

'Was they to come at a farm back home, I know how I'd feel about that,' Schwab says. By now there's an edge to his voice, and his grip tightens on the handle of the axe. 'Maybe you fellows come south to finish slavery. Not me. I fought to preserve the Union, an' hold this country in one piece 'fore the Rebs tore it apart. Now we won that fight, an' if a bunch of niggers think they about to take us on, we got the same answer for them. That's the way I see it!'

He turns from them, setting his great shoulders wide, and swings viciously into the trunk of a fir tree, the sound of his axe ringing back to them as he strikes again. Thwarted by the sight of that massive frame, Voorhees scowls, hot and sweating in the last skittering drops of rain. Across from him, Benton looks to his grounded axe, still smiling.

'Don't take it to heart, boy,' the dark man says. 'It don't signify nothing.'

Voorhees is about to reply in anger, when thorn brush crunches at his back, abd he looks round to find the lieutenant behind him, his hand on the hilt of his belted sword, Sergeant Gifford coming up to join him as Voorhees turns.

'We're working to a schedule here, soldier,' Pfister says. He's of a build with Voorhees, slim and medium tall, his uniform tightly belted at the waist. Hearing the calm tone of his voice, the two men come swiftly to attention.

'Next time wait till you hear the word before you ground axes,' Pfister tells them, his gaze level and cold on each man in turn. 'Now get to it, on the double!'

Pfister watches as they take up the long-handled axes once more, striking at the half-hewn tree limb on the ground. He smiles wearily, his thin face streaked with rain and sweat, then signs to Gifford to take over, and turns, his high boots creaking as he steps back through the trodden brush and the mud that clings thick to halfway up the calf. Gifford's bellow sounds after him as he moves.

'C'mon, you dumb sonsabitches! Swing to it! We ain't got all day!'

Pfister steps on, looking out for thorny lopped boughs in the mud, reaching to tug the peak of his blue forage cap lower on his brow. Set tight in this weather, it starts to itching him after a while.

Lieutenant Julius Pfister. Thought of that name sets him smiling despite the clammy grip of shirt and breeches, the stray droplets that strike on his face. Barely four years ago he was still teaching school back in Massachusetts, wondering if he'd ever make it to college lecturer. Seems like an age ago, nowadays. After the first bloody reverses of the Union armies, finding it harder to keep his peacetime job with a quiet mind, he enlisted in the State Volunteers and fought his way up to a couple of stripes. His commission came later, won in the carnage at Shiloh. After

134

that, a few skirmishes here and there. And now this punitive expedition against the renegades.

Shiloh. He stands a while, eyes half-closed in thought. Even now it comes as a surprise to him that he was able to look hard into the smoking Rebel volleys without coming apart. Better yet, when the regiment broke, he held a bunch of infantry together and counter-charged. Looking back, he figures they must all of them have been a little crazy, but it worked. Held the line, for a while.

Shakes his head, chuckling softly. Yes, Pfister, you were crazy at that—scared to hell even when you made them run. Could scarcely hold your water afterwards, just about made it behind that tree out of sight . . .

Still, it was good for a lieutenant's bars. And it won him the respect of his new command. More important, his own respect for himself.

Under the sodden blouse, the silver locket chafes on his sweating chest with its faint scattering of blond hair. He smiles softer, touching the place. He and Laurie haven't known each other for more than a couple of years, and most of that time he's been away fighting, but he isn't likely to forget her. From the time he saw her at that ball in Springfield, he knew she was the girl for him, and she seemed to feel the same. Last time he got back on furlough he bought her a ring. Soon as he gets home, they aim to be married.

Dear Laurie! Pfister's hand closes tight upon the locket on its chain. Calling her to mind, he knows a momentary anguish: that she should be so far from him, and the two of them unable to touch, to kiss. In the nights his body aches for her beside him, even now . . .

A heavy drop spangs from the peak of his cap, and his face sobers in a moment. Pfister grasps the hilt of his sword. Stalks on in silence through the brushwood and the thick mud of the island bank.

The sooner this business is over with, the better, he thinks to himself.

*

Further back along the line, Sergeant Riordan looks on as his second crew fight to haul the nine-pounder out of the mud.

By now the rain has stopped altogether, moisture and warmth hanging in the dull grey atmosphere that remains. The wet uniforms of the artillery troopers steam visibly as they bunch and heave, up to their waists in the scummy water. Under their weight the gun trembles, edges a short distance up the bank, before settling back on its bogged wheels to stick fast. Riordan swears under his breath.

'Not a chance,' Copeland says from beside him, the weather-beaten face of the corporal creasing like leather as he speaks. He scratches at his stubbled throat, frowning. 'Have to lay a rope on if we want to get her clear.'

'Then get to it, soldier,' Riordan tells him, swinging round abruptly, his hard-eyed glance cutting to where the rest of the detail wait in silence on a ridge of mud, topped by a thick bank of reeds and brush. The driver of the waggon slumps at his reins, the crew of the first nine-pounder leaning on the gun itself. At the sergeant's shout the group of them breaks suddenly to life.

'Lay out the ropes!' Riordan bellows.

Measured beside most of his men, he's on the small side, dark and thin, his hair black and shining as an Indian's under the tilted cap, his eyes a stony grey in the brown of his face. All the same, when he sings out, the detail jumps. They know better than to run foul of Irish Mike.

He moves at a run to join them, sliding on his heels towards the water, the others following on the double. Riordan hits the shallows, sucking in his breath as the slimy muck engulfs him to the waist. He grasps the rope that is flung to him, drags it over the barrel of the gun, hands of the second crew reaching to help him as he makes it fast. Riordan stands back, breathing hard, starting to sweat again under his arms.

'Copeland! Harris!' he barks to the men on the bank above him. 'Take the far end and give it a coupla turns around that tree yonder. Whan I call out, haul on that line!'

He watches for a moment as the corporal and four or five men take the rope twice around the bole of the tree before tying it securely. Riordan scans the stunted trunk thoughtfully, lips puckered. Nods at last, spitting into the water. It's low to the ground, deep-rooted. Chances are it'll hold.

'Get ready to heave like hell,' he shouts to the troopers in the water.

Wading out around the bulk of the wedged gun, he joins the bunch of sodden, sweating troopers beyond and puts his shoulders to the bogged-down wheel, testing the stubborn resistance that meets the thrust of his body. Hunched back of the gun, he nods.

'Haul away!'

The mass of blue uniforms heaves forward, pushing and lifting as the rope sings taut overhead. Greenish water swills at the sergeant's waist, thick mud gripping his boots out of sight lower down. Riordan sets his wiry strength at the wheel, fighting as with a living enemy, cursing through his teeth as the metal bites into his shoulder. Above and around him, the grunts of the gun team mingle with his own.

Lift, you bitch! the sergeant urges in his mind.

Abruptly the heavy gun shudders, lurching, rumbling forward. The wheels clear out of the mud with a loud sucking noise, rolling towards the bank, while the troopers pack in and heave to the limit of their strength. Riordan grunts, recoiling as the gun hits the base of the slope and shudders back, the rope taking the strain for an instant as the gunners struggle to get in beneath it and thrust upward.

'Get to it!' the sergeant yells, diving chest-deep in the foul water to bunch his slight body back of the gun. Above him, he can see the rope fraying, and for a moment it looks like it might slip the hitch altogether. Riordan catches a glimpse of Copeland's scared, sweating face close overhead, and tries not to think too hard of the gun coming down on them in the water.

The rope holds, though for what seems like an age he can still feel its vibration throbbing back through the metal against his hands. Slowly the wheels pull out from the shallows, and the rest of the first gun team dives in to haul it up the bank, tugging and heaving as the second crew flounder soaking from the shallows to lend a hand. Riordan himself clambers out after them, hands in the mud, his filled boots leaking water at every step. By now his uniform is spattered with green and he smells as high as any of the gunners. All the same he grins, topping the rim of the bank to lean a moment on the barrel of the rescued gun.

'You bitch,' Riordan says, but this time there is no rancour in his tone. He smiles as he speaks the words, stroking the metal with a grimy, affectionate hand.

'Looks like we made it, anyhow,' Copeland says, and the Sergeant nods, his grin fading.

'Loose off the rope,' Riordan tells him. 'An' get some of the filth cleaned off this here weapon. Gun ain't no use once it rusts over!'

He leaves the nine-pounder where it stands, walking away slowly along the crest, while the gun teams move in to clean off the worst of the mud. Riordan halts by the twisted tree, loosed now from its rope. He leans a moment by the gnarled trunk, his shoulder aching a little where the bark digs into the flesh, looking out across the reedbeds and the thicketed shapes of islands in the water. The land beginning to emerge afresh out of the rain-mist. Faint shafts of sunlight filtering through the clouds, striking fire from the droplets that hang in the branches overhead, touching reeds and water with a smooth, white sheen. Riordan takes in the sight, his dark features closed and sombre in thought.

Praise be the rain's left off, anyhow, the sergeant thinks. Lord, what a country! Thought he'd seen the last of rain like this when he left Ireland nearly twenty years ago. Back there in Kerry they used to have rain, all right. Times, it seemed like it would never end. The whole world sodden with it: fields bogged and hills awash, the thatch of every roof wet and stinking with mould. Warm rain, too, like here. That's where the likeness ended, though. In Kerry he saw famine, starvation, murder. Leaving Ireland was the best thing he ever did. Reaching for the tobacco pouch on its thong inside his shirt, Riordan smiles gently. He hasn't ever regretted changing Kerry for New York. Sooner he gets back to Albany, and Kathleen and the kids, the happier he'll be.

Over on the islands, the infantry are moving now. Using their woodmen's axes to fell the thorny bush. Rafts, huh? Riordan sighs, getting a hunk of tobacco loose. About time, too. His guns are going to need them pretty soon, and the waggon. Must be the

captain's idea, he figures. Doubts if the lieutenant had anything to do with it. Pfister's all right, he supposes, but not
what you'd call a regular soldier. Brave enough, sure, but not
cut out for this kind of life. Schoolmaster, that's more his
line. Can't beat a good noncom, he reckons: man like Gifford, or Master Sergeant Hale in the infantry company yonder. That Elliott, too, the cavalry sergeant with Maitland.
Good man, Elliott. He'll keep the captain in order, no
trouble there . . .

He grins now, reaching for his knife and springing the clasp
to bring the blade free. Backbone of this man's army, good
sergeants. He's one himself. He ought to know.

From the thickest part of the reeds below, a covey of wild
geese take flight, spurting up suddenly towards the dark reaches of the clouds. At the sound of their flurried wing-beats
the sergeant turns, his glance following the arrowed shapes as
they pass overhead into the distance. After a while they too
are lost, swallowed by that sun-drizzled haze where the
islands loom above the level of the reeds.

Riordan frowns, his knife cutting through the tobacco plug.
Inwardly he hopes they get this renegade business settled
before long. Tracking them down should be the hardest part
of it, he reckons. Never did have too much time for niggers
as fighting men. Towards the end of the war he heard tell of a
few, here and there, but never did see one. Only blacks he's
met have been sutlers, teamsters or servants, like these folk
in the South. Cutting down a few plantation owners is one
thing, but he doubts they'll stand up to a regular charge. And
with his pair of nine-pounders along, they got no chance at
all. Once those guns start to firing, it'll be the finish.

And once it's over, he'll be headed straight back for
Albany.

His wet clothes are beginning to steam in sunlight. Riordan
scratches the itch of slow-drying flesh. Swallows a chew of
tobacco, pocketing the knife, savouring the taste as he crushes it to juice against his tongue. Chaw of tobacco cures
most things, he finds. And for what's coming, the guns will be
answer enough.

139

He leans, feeling the bark of the tree rasp him through his sodden shirt and breeches, his eyes lidding as the warmth of the sun fans on him through the stunted boughs overhead.

Gator slithers from the reeds, plunging into the green, foul-smelling water as the column starts up again. Cavalry ploughing their horses fetlock-deep; infantry wading nearly to the waist in places, holding their long rifles above their heads; further back, the guns and the waggon, lashed to makeshift rafts and hauled along by rope teams using the banks that rise up on either side. All around, the ground firming, rising from the water now. Bedded in muddy shallows, the gator watches them go, his cold eyes slitting. The scummed water splashes back. Westering sun glinting bright on weapons and harness, stirrups, barrels of the guns. Gator lets them out of sight before settling at last, sinking in mud, his great jaws levering open, grey-black of his scaled body all but hidden among the reeds. The black, unblinking stare of his eyes takes in the desolation left behind.

This his country, not theirs. And he be here when they long gone.

Here in the compound, the heat presses on him, moist and stifling. Blasts of blinding sunlight slanting through a red pall of dust that fills the open ground. Inside the stockade, the air rings with chants and the thunder of drums, the ground shaken by the tread of many feet. And in the midst of that smothering cloud, outlines of dancing figures. Shapes that stamp and sway, hidden in the murk, loose-limbed, circling the trunk of that massive, unbranched tree, white with its burden of skulls. Somewhere at the heart of the dust-cloud, Shango is standing, himself tall and treelike in the shadow of that stripped tree. The medicine stools from the long house set out around him as symbols of his power, and beside him, Mama Odu: the god and the goddess together, core of that throbbing life that wheels and shifts about them to the pulsing beat of the drums.

This is the time. The festival of the god.

Justus sits, his back to the sun-warmed wall, eyes squinting against the glare and the swirl of dust beyond. Sweat gleams on the black spread of his chest and shoulders, pearling his face and brow at every pore. Justus tastes its saltness at his lips, grimaces as it stings in his eyes. On the thighs of his worn breeches, his palms lie flat, soaking through the cloth to the flesh beneath. And not from the heat alone: unease in him now, and that disturbance of the blood that comes with drums and dancing, the thoughts in his mind driven out by the blast of bone whistles and the clamour of beaten gongs, low whirring drone of swung bull-roarers, and the endless, hammering tide-race of the talking drums. The dancers and their high, shrill-voiced chanting:

'SHAN–GO! O–DU! SHAN–GO! O–DU!'

But for Shango, no men dance in that smother of dust. All are women. From where he sits, Justus watches their weaving, sinuous bodies as they glide by him, moving with a proud, floating grace, their narrow feet turned in. Sees the tautness of firm breasts lifted, slender arms outspread, heads held high on the columns of their necks. Calling on the god as they clap and whirl in that spinning circle. Smooth, sweating texture of their flesh shining black or red through its coating of dust. Tremor of that flesh carries to him, throbbing in the haze of heat. Justus sweating harder as his own blood turns to flame.

This the time when god and goddess come together, and each woman seeks out the man of her choosing.

Mary crouched by him at the wall of the hut, sun catching harsh on the tanned white of her skin, freckling the bared shoulders, tinting the ash-blonde hair with tawny reddish lights. Her pale eyes look resolutely ahead into the dust-pall, showing no sign of the fear she feels. All the same she stays close alongside him, squatting, arms hugging her knees, warmth of her crouched body no more than a breath away from his own.

Mary the one woman seated. On the far side of him, Soldier hunches, his upthrust back ridging the sunlit wall. Face frozen to a dark, mahogany mask, the one green eye glaring at the circle of dancers. Over beyond him, the thin-limbed Heron, the long spear sloped back against his shoulder, his dark, lean face hard and intent on the swaying shapes in front. All around the outer rim of

141

that circle, the figures of squatting men: the Choctaws together with the blacks. Crow Feather, he sees there, and grey-maned 'Gator Head. Red Wolf, with his fierce, hawkish face turned towards the women in the dust. Each of them silent. Watching. Waiting.

At the edge of the circling dancers, two lithe figures take his eye: Jewel, and her sister Diamond—smooth, slender outlines that twist and twine to the blood-throb of the chant. Raven-black hair flying wild to hide their faces, bronze of their bodies gleaming through the smoking swirl of dust. So like, even now, he has trouble telling them apart . . .

Sight of Jewel brings back that other time: the shadow-shape in the doorway before daylight, the hewn sacred snake he flung out in the compound afterwards. Wet blood from the cane knife's blade, wiped clean on his breeches as he lay there, feeling the force of her eyes upon him, sensing the power of the bond between them.

Since that time, Shango has said nothing, keeping his distance from the man he took into the long house: the man who walked out from it, daring the power of the god. Only by a chance look of those stony eyes, of a fanged smile, has the tall man given any hint of what might have been. All the same, Justus knows it, feels it surely as the pulse in his veins: the snake came from Shango as a parting gift. He is not meant to be living right now. Soon, the tall one will think of another way.

Thus far, only Jewel has held off the god from his prey.

Her head lifting towards him as the thought crosses his mind. Warm dark of her probing eyes full upon him, as her body shivers in the rhythm of the dance. Jewel smiles, her full lips parted, breathing hard. Justus sees the sweat that bathes her features, the shimmer of moisture that gathers at her naked breasts. Clenches hands on the damp breeches as his own senses send a jolt of recognition along the nerves, his breath coming shorter as he feels the answering fire in the blood.

'Lookit that,' Soldier murmurs from alongside, the thin mouth twisting into a mocking grin. 'That one fer you sure 'nough . . .'

Justus frowns, not answering. From his feeling of inner hunger, and from Mary's hard-eyed glance towards him, he knows well enough that Soldier is right. Knows too well than Jewel's lithe body has its own magic, no less powerful than that of Shango. At his far side, Soldier grins wider, shrugging his dusty shoulders against the wall.

'Have it your way, boy. But she be comin' over 'fore long . . .'

Heron darting a rapid glance as the words are spoken. Justus bears with the grim stare, recalling the old man's words: how Heron don't like for any man to tell his sister no. The big man's face holds to harshness, his gaze and Heron's locking together. That the way it goin' have to be. Pretty soon the slim man scowls, looking away. Justus breathes again, fighting to disregard the tremor in his limbs.

Beyond them, the chanting dies suddenly, the drums stilled now to a low, muttering sound. From the heart of the wafting dust-cloud, Shango rears, his tall, black body limned in the glare of the sun, light glinting on the snakeskins hanging at his waist, striking grains of fire from the sweat-beads on his ebony skin. The tall man holds a gourd, cupping it in both hands. About him the circle of swaying women slows, their faces turned to him as he brings the gourd to his mouth . . .

'This the time.' Soldier grins. 'God water the women with his seed—get their sap to runnin' high. Make fer good breedin', boy . . .'

Justus stays silent, watching as Shango drinks from the hollow gourd. Spins to spray the liquid from his mouth, jets of it hitting the bodies of the dancers. He drinks and spits again. At once a shrilling call goes up from the women. They whirl and leap in a frenzy, shuddering in paroxysms as the power of the god enters them. From their midst he sees Jewel as she swings towards him, stepping high to stamp in the dust. Between her raised breasts, the water flows in a runnel, trickling down over the mound of her belly. Seeing her closed eyes, her rapt ecstatic face, he's suddenly afraid.

'The god give strength!' Shango yells out from the swirling dust, and from all around the answering shout rings back to him:

'SHAN–GO! SHAN–GO! TO THE GOD!'

The chant setting up afresh, drums stuttering to life again as Shango turns, pouring out the remnant on the ground before the stools. The liquid spatters, puddling the dry earth as the stamping dancers raise dust all around. From the far side of the circle Mama Odu steps, pacing along the ranks of waiting men. She too holding up a filled gourd, from which she drinks, spraying each of them in turn.

'Sap from the goddess.' Soldier's voice coming hoarser now, stare of his one green eye fixed on one of the whirling figures about the skull-strewn tree. The veteran licks his parched lips, starting to smile again. ''Fore we git that, ain't none of 'em gonna come after us . . .'

Justus saying nothing, waiting in silence as the fat, waddling shape of the goddess crosses ahead. Bulk of Mama Odu's body blocks out the light of the sun, shading him as the negress puckers and spits. He draws in his breath, hearing Mary's cry as the liquid sprays over him, spilling warm and wet on his face and chest. The big man glares back into that gross, smiling face, his teeth setting hard together. Above him Mama Odu chuckles thickly in the throat, looks on him once, appraisingly, then moves on.

Sits where he is, hearing Soldier grunt as his face is sprayed in turn, feeling the sticky warmth trickle down over his cheek and chin, a harsh rasp of breath coming from deep in his chest like he just felt a noose come tight at his neck, choking him: a reminder that he's a prisoner in this place, him and Mary both. And no way out of it.

Worse yet, he senses surely that this time they gonna push him harder up agin the wall. And he still ain't figured out what he gonna do about it.

In the centre of the compound, Shango whirls, flings the empty gourd hard at the bole of the tree. It hits a nailed skull, breaking to shards. The dancers shriek together and abruptly the circle opens, scattering, thick dust flying upward as the women spread out in search of the seated men. The latter come swiftly to their feet as soon as they are approached. At once the compound fills afresh, packed with couples who cling together, swaying, their feet shuffling in dust, their harsh, gasping breath fighting the frenzied clamour of the drums.

Jewel standing in front of him, bronzed gleam of her body dripping with sweat, shaking with the shuddering force of her breathing. All the same she smiles, her open hands reaching out towards him, black-sloed glint of her narrowed eyes upon him, holding him fast. Faced with the probing stare, Justus swallows uneasily, watching the last of the sprayed water as it trickles from her belly, downward out of sight where the breech-clout hides the darkening fleece of hair, stray drops shining on her thighs.

'You for me, Justus,' the woman says, her voice low, husky in her throat, the eyes half-closed as she reaches to him, teeth glinting behind the parted lips. 'You come with me, now, big man . . . We got us things to do . . .'

Beside him he hears Mary's indrawn breath, glimpses the tremor that goes through the white girl's body as she tenses, leaning out from the wall, ready to spring for the dark woman's throat. Justus' own breath heaves, his teeth grinding together a moment. Meeting Jewel's eye, he shakes his bushy head.

'No, Jewel,' the big man tells her, his words low-voiced but firm. 'I got me a woman here. Ain't no call fer you to take me, I reckon.'

Across from him he catches Heron's look of anger and gathers his legs in hard under him in readiness. Heron, though, doesn't stay to look. A slim young negress in a yellow headtie grasps him by the arm, dragging him into the mill of dancers. Soldier, chosen by a hard-limbed, stocky Choctaw woman, has already joined them. Even as he watches, several of the twined couples sink to the ground, locked together, dust covering them as their naked bodies join, rising and falling fiercely against the ground.

In front of him, Jewel still stands, her eyes narrowed cat-like, lips drawn back from the teeth. Justus reads the coiled tension in her body, its lithe, balanced strength. The sound of her breath hissing now as she faces him, her hands clenching into fists.

'You owe me, remember?' Jewel says, her voice biting into him the way the flung knife speared through the snake. 'Now, you come with me, you hear?'

Heat of the woman-smell close to him, rank in his nostrils. Justus fights down the urging of his blood, glancing sidelong towards Mary as he speaks.

'*No!*' His voice grating, the teeth clenched tight. 'Mary my woman, Jewel! Best you go find somebody else . . .'

145

At his words she sinks back in a crouch, teeth bared, her dark eyes opening wide. She's about to answer when a shout goes up beyond them and Shango comes darting through the dancers at a run, looking ghost-tall above men and women alike, his black body gleaming through the coating of red dust. Justus takes in a fleeting glimpse of the gaunt, sunken-cheeked face, the carved tattoos puckering as Shango draws back his lips from the filed teeth, the staring bloodshot eyes. Next moment, the tall man shoulders past him, his long arm stretching for Mary where she cowers away from him against the wall.

'This time the god choose!' Shango yells, his grip fastening on her as the words come from him, hauling her bodily upright from the wall. Dragging her to him with a bruising hold on her wrists as she cries out in fear and pain, helpless in his hands.

'Justus!' Her voice ringing shrilly above the noise of drums and dancers. *'Help me, Justus!'*

At her first cry he's up from the ground, lunging forward, Jewel, the festival, the hungering of his own blood all forgotten. The sharp-edged note of fear in her voice cutting through him to the core. Justus feels the swift onrush of hate and anger flower up within him as he springs, beating in blood at the back of his eye, thundering in his veins. Knowing as he moves that this is the time. It him and Shango now, and no way he kin go back.

He goes into Shango hard, his head and the wide wedge of his shoulder smashing the god across the middle and driving the breath from him as his greater weight slams him backward. Justus grabs for those thin haunches, feeling the bunched muscles fight him as his fingers dig for a hold. His rush takes Shango out and down, the tall man letting go his grip on Mary as he claws for Justus' face. Justus grunts, weaving his head away from the blow as the two of them thud against the ground. The wave of onlookers retreats as he and Shango roll thrashing in the dust. From somewhere above him he hears Mary's scream.

Beneath him, Shango's breath comes harsh and rasping, the stink of it rank against his face. He slams his head hard in the other's chest, feeling the thin body give as Shango twists from under. Teeth scrape, stinging the scars on his back, and he hacks with one elbow to where the face was a moment ago. Same instant

146

a knee jolts up into his groin, and Justus sets teeth on a yelp of agony. He pitches off the tall man to the ground, bunching his body as both hands clutch to the place, face twisting as he fights the sickening pain.

Shango on him in a flash, gripping with one strong hand in his bushy hair to drag him over on his back, his gaunt face thrusting closer, the filed teeth baring for a bite at the throat. Struggling against the pain, Justus takes the chance: batters his head viciously into that face as the teeth come glinting towards him, feeling a crunch of impact as his skull hits the other man across the bridge of the nose. Shango howls, recoiling, his nose splayed and pumping blood, his lips torn raw by splinters from his busted teeth. Justus pulls clear, coming to his knees, swings his bunched fist in a looping blow from the shoulder. All his body's force back of it as it strikes Shango full in the throat. The sound of the fist on flesh thudding back to the ears of the onlookers all around. Shango croaks, eyes bulging as he fights for breath. A second clubbing blow slams against the side of his head. Shango sighs hoarsely, thuds to earth like a loose sack, hands to his throat as the thin body heaves, gulping for air.

Pain still howling through him, clutching his groin with fiery fingers as his gut lurches. Foulness of blood and bile in his ripped mouth as he spits and shakes his bushy head. Justus snarls, seeing Shango sprawled helpless in the dirt. Black of his body coated with the dust, whose red mingles with the throbbing red haze in front of his eyes. Still on his knees he starts in again, heedless of pain as he throws himself forward.

Gonna fix you good this time, you sonofabitch!

Sudden weight hits him from behind, flattens him with his face against the ground. Justus growls like a mad dog, biting dirt as he struggles to get loose. Fails. His arms pinned, twisted behind him, a knee digging hard into his back. Somebody gets a grip on his hair, yanking his head back, making his eyes water. Men grunting in effort, holding him fast, hauling him up on his feet, pinioning him by his arms and hair. In front of him, Shango lifts with a painful slowness from hands and knees, standing at last.

Silence in his ears like to a thundering tide. The drumsong and chanting stilled. Uneasy quiet fallen over the compound where the coupled dancers stare in horror. The one sound in the stillness the harsh, laboured breathing of the god before him. Shango's thin face convulsed as he sucks in welcome air, massaging his throat, shaking his head and spattering blood in the trodden dirt. Meeting the black glare of those eyes, Justus feels the hate in him give way to a paralysing terror.

'You raise yo' hand 'gainst the god, boy,' Shango says. The sound of his voice comes hoarse and ragged through the torn lips, the words themselves distorted as the splayed nose swells bloody and bruised against the carved patterns of the face. All the same the eyes hold level on him, harsh and merciless.

'But one answer fer what you done,' the tall man tells him. 'It mean death!'

He stays quiet, holding the stare of the eyes, the breath rasping harsh in his throat, his mouth stinging raw. Pain still stabs at his hammered crotch, and a bruise is forming at the right side of his face where the head went in. Justus clenches his fists, the nails biting into his palms. From the corner of his eye he catches sight of Mary's pale, stricken face, hears her faint moan of shock. Soldier grasping her by the arm, back against the wall of the hut. Red Wolf and Heron still gripping his own imprisoned arms. As yet, he can't see Jewel or her sister. Not that any of it matters no more. He made his bid, and lost.

Now it the finish, for sure.

From some empty place back of his mind, he watches as Shango takes a heavy cutlass from the hand of Mama Odu. Fighting to hold his gaze level, he watches as the tall man straightens and swings back, the blade whistling up in an arc of edged white light. Justus sucks in his breath sharply, teeth clenching.

Halfway down the blow halts, suddenly. Shango lets the cutlass fall. Thin lips drawn from bloody, sharpened teeth as he smiles for the first time.

'That way too easy, boy,' Shango says, his dark eyes glinting with malice. 'Reckon I got somethin' better in mind for you, right now . . . Jewel! Diamond! Over here!!'

Sound of his voice brings them over at a run. The two women stand as the crowd ebbs back around them, looking to the god, their dark eyes wary and unsure.

148

Reading those faces, the tall man grins crueller than before.

'You choose this man, huh, Jewel?' Shango asks.

Eyes on him, the woman nods. 'Yeah.' The word breathed slow, a lizard hiss of sound.

Shango turns to where the big man still struggles in the grip of Red Wolf and Heron, grinning evil through the ruin of his busted mouth.

'You gonna git him, sister,' Shango tells her. 'You an' yo' sister both. You have him, an' we gonna see it. After you done, we take him to the long house. You hear me good?'

Wordless, the tawny-skinned woman bows her head. Her eyes got a hot, glazed look.

Held tight in their grip, Justus feels the chill of those knifing words go through him. Thought of the long house. That fin-backed shape with its slanting, razor jaws. That, and what they aim to do to him before he goes . . .

Makes to speak, but don't no sound come. Instead he snarls, wild-eyed, fighting in vain to haul free of the men who hold him. Up ahead, looming tree-tall over him, the god smiles again.

'Don't trouble over your woman, boy,' Shango says. 'Once I see how they make out with you, be my turn. She take seed from the god . . .'

Justus yells out in anguished rage, dragging his captors as he heaves forward again. Fresh hands slam down on him from all sides, hauling him back. Weight of bodies pressing on him, forcing him to the ground. Above him he hears Mary's whimpered cries, and the low, thickening chuckle of the god.

'Hold him down good,' the tall man says. Then in a hoarse, eager voice: 'Go git him!'

Justus snarls again, wrestling with the hands that hold him pinned to the ground by arms and legs, spreadeagled, helpless. Justus hears the grate of his own teeth as they grind together. Light cut off sudden as two lithe, slim shapes break through and fling themselves upon him.

'This time you for me,' Jewel says,

Feels the swift movement of her hands as they reach downward, unbelting him, drawing back the sweaty breeches from his loins. Justus rages, bristling up like a hound as he tries to move aside

149

from those hands. Failing as he is held to earth. Touch of her hands finds him, strokes at the heated column of his flesh. Spite of his hate and anger, spite of the gnawing ache from Shango's blow, he feels that urgent flesh respond. Back of his mind, the first flickering tongue of animal need uncurls itself . . .

'God damn you, leave him be!' That Mary calling out. Her voice, though, a world away. Nothing she kin do, no more'n him. Not now.

Feels the cool stroke of Jewel's hand withdrawn, catches sight of her raven-black hair over his belly as she bends over him. At once the soft, moist warmth of her mouth engulfs him, teasing at his manhood with lips and tongue until he throbs up huge and stiff. Unable any longer to rule the hunger at his flesh, he groans out as she flicks him with her tongue, his head falling back.

Above his face, Diamond crouches, sliding soft palms over her sister's sweat-slicked breasts.

Jewel rears up, her mouth leaving him. Now she lifts up, crouching over him where his maleness heaves, pulsing up towards her. Slides on to him, straddling him, her hand guiding him in as she eases down. He fights the slow, slithery uprush of pleasure, shaking his head against the ground, grinding his teeth hard, biting on his lip. No use: that pleasure starts to pulse up through his body, slow, steady, unalterable. Poised above him, Jewel smiles, cat-like, her dark eyes lidded. Starts to move herself on him, her smooth thighs gripping at his flanks.

Gasps now, the effort of holding out too much for him to bear. Justus breathes harshly, arching up to the sweetness that engulfs him, driving deeper into her as she thrusts and cries above him. Dark covers him sudden as Diamond kneels over his face, reaching to touch her sister as she lowers herself down on him. Musky woman-scent drowns his senses as her loins cover him.

Wet, open heat of her sex forces his mouth open, rank taste of her inner flesh firing him, driving out all other thoughts. Probes for that opening with his tongue, tasting the sweet honey of her as she shivers and cries, already near to her coming. Justus mouths at her, frantic, slavering at her lips, at the hardening bud of flesh. Already, lower down, feels the surge of his own pleasure lift up and race like a curling wave. Above him, Diamond shrills out, keen as a blade. Slumps, jerking at him as she rolls clear, her juices sticky down the side of his face. Now he sees Jewel straddling over him, hands gripping the bush of his hair as she arches and drives, sweat falling from her in a fine spray as she too hollers and yells, her hot, sweet muscle tightening on him, drawing the hot jissom up along the straining column of his flesh, hidden deep inside her. Justus draws a sharp, unsteady breath, howls as the moment takes him, bucking to meet her as he heaves and shoots off, filling her in spasm after draining spasm. She screeching out in the moment before she gasps and sinks down upon him . . .

Black-red circles ebbing from front of his eyes. He lies spent, gasping, hearing from some immense distance the chanted shouts of those who look on, and above them all, Mary's stricken cries. Sound of that voice rouses his anger afresh, reminding him of that other time, when they brought him to the wenches at Sweet River. Then, it was white men who looked on and laughed. Now they black, but what they doin' is sure as hell the same . . .

Goes limp, the last rage ebbing. No use. They gonna have their way with him, jes' like they aimed to do.

An', like an animal, he got to take his pleasure along with them. Before he dies.

Jewel's lithe weight lifts from him and she moves aside as Diamond slides tawny and smooth down over his body, aiming for the place where his shrunken maleness lies, slack now, against his thigh. Jewel shifts over him. He feels the smooth touch of her sister as she clasps his manhood between her breasts, moving herself against him until the aching pleasure starts to rise once more. Jewel reaches backward, sliding long fingers into the wet, open flesh of her sister's loins where she lies. With her free hand she grasps him by his mane of hair and moves over him in turn, bringing that heated warmth to his face.

Down below, his root swells afresh, arching upward as Diamond murmurs and slides against him. Another musk of woman covering him as Jewel sinks upon him, opening hot over his searching mouth. Not woman only he tastes, this time: probing, lapping, he tastes *himself* with her, rank mind-busting scent and taste of lust, of his animal need. Clamour of voices about him, but he no longer heeds them, his mouth attacking her as Diamond hefts his uprisen rod, squats on him, his manhood entering her in her turn.

Above him, Jewel bucks and plunges, sawing sound of her breath one with his as they labour together. Opens for his mouth to drive deep inside her as she hollers and comes, christening his face a second time. Justus groans as she rolls aside from him, his huge body arching upward now to meet Diamond as she thrusts in a frenzy on his upright maleness, hurrying to her time. Roar of their other voices the echo of the pleasure as it looms and rushes once again. Drives, yelling out through his clenched teeth as the moment takes him soaring, flying high above the world, his thick seed spurting in her as she too cries and comes . . .

Lies drained, feeling the last pangs of pleasure ebb from him. Feels only the emptiness and pain now, aware for the second time of Mary's sobs, the cries of onlookers, their leering laughter. Groans again, but not from pleasure.

They done it to him, sure enough. And now he gonna die . . .

Far above them all, the deep, lowing sound of the bull-horn on the rampart. He lies, gasping, flung on his side. Darkness rolling back from him as they loose their hold, his body sheathed thick with sweat that pours in his eyes, blinding him for the moment. As the crowd wavers back, he sees they are all looking up to the rampart. Even Shango's lean head turned from him as he follows the sound of the horn.

Overhead, the giant figure of Cedar looms against the skull-decked wall of the stockade, his hawkish, Indian features meeting Shango's gaze, at once eager and troubled.

'Soljers!' Cedar's voice hoarse, excited. 'Plenty blue soljers comin', out past the water! Look like they got 'em some big guns along!'

At the sound of his words, Shango's lean face clenches, hardening, the dark eyes slitted. The tall man springs for the ladder, mounting the rungs swiftly to join Cedar on the rampart, the rest of them keeping silent as he looks out over the lagoon.

When he turns from the wall at last, the look on his face is enough.

'Load up them slingshots!' the tall man bellows at the nearest of the men below. 'Rest of you, go get yo' guns! We got us a fight on here!'

Justus staggers to his feet as the group scatters for the huts. Within seconds the compound is deserted, the drummers and the dancers gone. The big man heaves a shuddering breath, wincing as a fresh stab of pain goes forking through him at the groin. Aware that same moment of Shango's fierce eyes upon him.

'Soldier!' Shango's harsh voice stays the veteran in the doorway of the hut. The hump-backed figure turns, his one-eyed glance shifting again for the rampart. 'Count off fifty-some of the folk here, an' take 'em cross the water. I want them soljers hit 'fore they git as far's the lagoon, you hear me?'

Soldier nods wordlessly, his leathern features bare of expression. Ducks again inside the darkness of the hut. Shango smiles, one hand on the rampart with its crop of skulls.

'Cedar!' His glance shifting from Justus to the white-faced figure of Mary, pressed still at the hut wall. 'Go take a hold of that woman yonder. She for me—later.'

Justus watches the face with its thin-lipped smile, feeling the rage build again in him, warring with the sickness and the pain. Not a hope, he knows. Already men and women pour out from the huts on every side, gripping their guns and bows. Ain't no way he gonna fight 'em all . . .

Still, when Cedar lays hold on Mary and the white girl flinches from him with a whimper of pain, the big man starts forward. Finds Soldier's shotgun blocking his path. The black twin barrels huge as judgment, levelled on his gut. Overhead on the rampart, Shango chuckles softly.

'Ain't forgot you, boy,' the god says, grinning now despite his swelled nose and busted mouth, his dark eyes narrowed and shrewd, empty of mercy. 'You claim you got a strong spirit, huh? You kin go with Soldier in the ambush, I reckon. Kill you some whites. If you git to come back,' the thin smile grows keener than a blade, 'you gonna feed the god fer sure. *Soldier!*' The tall man's voice harshens again, barking. 'You stay close by him. He try anythin', don't miss!'

'I hear you, lord,' the veteran says, his green eye holding steady on the man in front of his gun.

Looking back at him, Justus reads no hint of friendship there. Soldier got his own skin to save, he reckons. He stands, keeping silent as Soldier tells off the remaining men and women for the attack, feeling his mauled hands clench to fists down by his sides, helpless in the heat of his rage.

They backed him to the wall, an' now there no way out. He marked for death.

Soldier looking to him, handing him the bow and the sheaf of palmetto arrows, the hoop-iron knife. Not the empty gun, that no use anyhow. Justus takes the weapons from the veteran's hand, his rage ebbing, leaving a sick feeling of emptiness at the pit of his stomach. Marking the sombre doomed look on his face, the old man nods.

'Let's be goin',' Soldier tells him, then turns away.

Justus stands a moment, unsure even now, his trapped glance going to where Mary huddles in the giant Cedar's grasp. Her wide-eyed, frightened stare is answer enough for him.

He goes forward, head down as the gate swings open, following the humped back of Soldier towards the daylight beyond.

On his back the sun strikes harder, piercing the network of thorns. Justus lies motionless, though the sweat slicks his body and the heat sets his scars itching afresh. The thorn bush branches over him with its thin scatter of shade. His arms are stretched out in front, the hickory bow laid flat, with the first of his arrows already fitted to the string. The palmetto sheaf hung at his neck, the iron knife stuck into his belt. Soldier crouched in cover ahead and to the left, sunlight glinting on his grey, salty hair, picking out the livid scars on his malformed shoulder-blade. Out beyond, the oncoming noise of hooves in the soft ground grows closer.

Shango knowed his job, Justus reckons, plantin' that stockade where he did. That way, he seen the soljers comin' when they was miles off. Give the ambush party time to cross the lagoon an' git settled. No trouble a–tall. Now the pirogues grounded in the reeds back of these thickets, and the bunch of them ready for whatever comin' in.

Jewel and Diamond to one side of him where he lies, Heron on the other, his long spear hefted in readiness. Any other time the sisters with their smooth, strong limbs laid so close would be disturbing; now they ignore him, and he them. Their dark faces turned from him, the black eyes fixed on the approaching horsemen out in front.

The first of the riders are already into sight, topping the low rise in the ground some forty paces off from where the ambushers lie hidden, moving at a steady walk through the thickets that line the slope. From where he lies, his glance picks out some figures ahead of the rest: the slim officer in his peaked cap and campaign blouse, mopping his brow with the back of his hand; the scarecrow shape of the Indian tracker, hunched in his saddle, the black hat all but hiding his face; after them the lean, hard-looking sergeant and the corporal with his boyish face. Further back, beyond the column of mounted troopers, other horsemen follow: men in cord jackets, hunting shirts, denims, faces shaded by wide-brimmed hats. As yet, he can't be sure who they are, but he has a fair suspicion. The thought of it enough to clench his teeth, biting back the snarl that threatens from low in his throat.

'Plenty of 'em, sure enough,' Heron mutters from alongside him. His dark features are sober, thoughtful. 'Must be close to a hundred back of these riders. An' they got guns, too . . .'

Yeah, guns. Justus remembers Sweet River—the grey-clad column on the road, the noise like thunder he heard when he set his snares, back in the wilderness. Inwardly he wonders what chance they got agin that kind of stuff. All right for Nestor to tell him 'bout that Toussaint feller, but soljers is somethin' else. With or without the guns, it goin' to be hard, he figures.

Remembering then in the midst of his thoughts how he fixed, thinking back to Mary at the stockade, an' what Shango got in mind for her. Him, too. Chill of the thought striking him suddenly. Whichever way this goes, he be lucky to come out alive. An' without Mary, he ain't goin' nowhere.

At that he snarls, his teeth grating together. Anger at the trapped feeling inside him building fit to bust him apart, wanting to hit out, to kill and smash what in his way. Right now don't matter if it Shango or the whites: they *both* out to kill him. He git in there first, he gonna make it count—that fer sure.

Back of him he hears the breathing of Crow Feather, the stocky Choctaw crouched in a thicket a few paces behind and to his right. Beyond him the line of ambush spreads in a wide-spaced arc, curving to take in the oncoming horsemen from front and flank. Red Wolf and 'Gator Head lie way out to the side, almost on the far side of the slope. Most of the men with them are armed with bows. The guns are with Soldier's party, here in the thickets.

Fresh itching above his eyes as a fly settles, floundering in the thick sweat that trickles from the roots of his hair. Justus grimaces, eyes narrowed to the torment, not daring to risk everything by a move. His gaze still on the bunched group of horsemen as they start down towards him from the crest. By now they're close enough for their voices to carry, and he can hear the clink and jingle of the harnesses.

'Here they come.' Heron's voice low almost as a whisper, staring ahead of him as he speaks, his hard eyes still with the riders in front.

Justus says nothing, lash of the sun shifting over the scarred back as he lies, watching them come, waiting. Hands out ahead of him, gripping to the strung bow and the arrow-flight. Gaze of his eyes harsh and bitter as the thorns, hating them all.

White trash sonsabitches, all of 'em. They had him where they wanted, one time. Now it his turn—an' they gonna pay.

He edges forward on to hands and knees, bringing up the bow as the hooves beat in closer, hidden in the sparse shade of the thorns.

'The place is well sited,' Maitland says, half-turning in the saddle; looking out over the wide span of the lagoon, where light makes a fierce haze on the water, to where the stockade stands outlined against the wooded green slopes beyond.

'A natural strongpoint, and no way of coming at it without exposing our men to fire.'

He frowns, turning again to glance between the ears of his horse as the animal picks his way down the thicketed slope. Elliott close to him on the left, sitting easily astride his sway-backed mount, his teeth gripping the stem of his pipe, one hand resting on the butt of his holstered sidearm. On the far side comes Owl Man, leaning hunch-shouldered on the saddle-horn to let his pony find its own way down. Then Rose near in at his back, and the other riders of the detail strung out behind. By now he guesses, they too must have some idea of the task in front of them.

'Looks like we'll need the guns brought up,' Elliott says at last, glancing ahead towards the far stockade, his grim, stubbled features betraying nothing of his thoughts.

'I guess so, Sergeant.' Maitland sucks his teeth in exasperation, wincing a little as thorns claw the leather of his boot in passing. 'But right now that's only a part of the problem. If we're to cross that stretch of water, the infantry are going to have to fell more timber—a good deal more timber, Sergeant.'

Falls silent as the words end, his irritation burning out. Pointless, this giving way to annoyance in front of the man; they feel it as much as he does himself, he knows. Only solution is to get on with what has to be done, and keep complaints to a minimum.

Sound of hooves thudding in the soft ground along the crest brings him twisting around in the saddle. Maitland watches, unsmiling, as Lawrence and his horsemen top the rise, coming downhill at a canter to join the column of soldiers. Remembering his resolution of a moment past, the captain holds on to the rags of his temper. But confronted by the hard, lean-lipped smile from the dark man in the planter's rig, he finds it isn't any easier than before.

'Well now, Captain,' Lawrence grins, a faint sneer on his lips and glittering from the hard depths of his eyes. He leans back as he speaks, pushing the skirt of his long coat away from the holstered butt of his weapon. 'Looks like we run 'em down at last, sir. When you suppose we gonna git to grips with them savages, Mr Maitland?'

In spite of his resolve, the captain feels his face grow hot, aware all at once of the stiff set of his body in the saddle. Something about this man never fails to have this effect on him. Like a brush rubbing up against the fur of an angry dog. Meeting the stupid,

157

grinning faces of the Southerners grouped around him, Maitland draws a careful breath, holding back on his anger as it rises afresh to the bait.

'First of all, we shall need to cross the lagoon,' the officer says in as calm a voice as he can manage, aware as he speaks of his clenched hands on the rein. 'That means more brushwood to be felled for rafts for ourselves and the infantry. That, Mr Lawrence, means time—in my opinion, another hour at best.' His lips tighten, as his voice slips its bonds, now cutting coldly at the lean-faced planter. 'It would appear that you and your friends will have to wait a little longer for their ... turkey-shoot.'

Watching the grins wiped from their faces, he's almost pleased for a time. The bunch of armed riders lower their heads at his words, muttering. Big-gutted Whiteside turns to spit in the mud, rubbing the shotgun barrel on his sleeve. Lawrence, as ever, shields his rage to better effect than the rest. For an instant Maitland sees the dark features tense at the barbed answer he has given, but just as swiftly the thin-lipped smile returns, dark eyes gleaming keen and hard as slivers of rock.

'We kin wait, I reckon,' the plantation boss says. And the quiet tone and level look he gives to Maitland are insult enough in themselves.

The captain frowns, conscious once more of his face and its blushing heat, betraying him. Turns about to present his back to the Southerner, the breath hissing viciously through his clenched teeth.

'Rose!' At his shout the young corporal salutes, riding over. 'Compliments to Lieutenant Pfister! Have him set the company to felling more timber immediately. His men are going to need all the rafts they can put together ...'

Out beyond them, Owl Man's harsh features crease into a frown, some inner feeling flickering danger along his nerves. Next moment the pony pricks its ears at something lying low in the thickets and rears at its halter-rope, snorting.

'Captain!' The voice of the Cherokee tracker brings all their heads round towards him. Their arguments forgotten at sight of his taut-strung figure in the saddle. 'Captain, we got trouble ...'

Turning at the sound. Hands dipping swift for holstered guns. And the same instant, the ambush breaks in on them from every side.

Watching, Justus follows the second group of horsemen as they ride easily down the near slope to join the waiting soldiers. His eyes on them, narrowing to merciless slits as he marks each hated face: Jared he sees, who held the dogs, and Hooker. Clayt and Sims, and the cackling Munson, swaying to keep his mount and with the corn-jug at his shoulder—the men who ran him into the bayou at Sweet River. Up beyond them comes the bulky figure of Whiteside, but Justus' glance passes him over, fixing instead on that thin dark-faced man in the long-skirted coat and broad-rimmed planter's hat. The man who smiles now, hand to his gun-butt, as he talks to the soldier captain, the free hand resting on that thick, blacksnake whip.

Lawrence!

Justus snarls like a vicious dog, the back hairs stiffening along his neck, the hand that grasps the bow lifting a fraction as instinct answers. Heron turning his head sidelong at the low-throated sound, his look startled and uncertain at the sudden ferocity that meets his gaze. Jewel too reads the look, half-smiling. Justus himself seeing neither one; his savage stare for Lawrence alone as that bow starts to lift . . .

Same instant, the tracker's pony pricks its ears, snorting in unease and terror, and at once the Cherokee rider yells out to the rest. And Justus knows that it is time . . .

'Kill fer the god!' Soldier calls.

The long-barrelled gun blasts, the sound deafening as it shatters the stillness. Rose, swinging in towards the captain as Soldier fires, reels as the slugs smash into his body. Before he can cry out, the blast hurls him sideways and down from his plunging horse, hitting the ground heavy and loose as a sack.

Roar of other guns about him as Justus takes aim and lets fly, and from further out the low, whistling whip of arrows in flight. His own shot is hurried, the palmetto shaft loosed before he's on his feet. He snarls wolflike as he sees it hit the peak of Lawrence's saddle, glancing to strike with the flat stem at his shoulder before flipping away to the ground. He's reaching another as Lawrence curses, dragging his tall mount back upslope, pulling the holstered gun. Back of him Crow Feather's ancient muzzle-loader crashes, and the stricken horse of Whiteside squeals like a woman, collapsing on its knees. The sheriff throwing his bulky body clear as the beast goes over, his shotgun blasting wildly over their heads as he falls.

Up in front of him the riders mill together, confused, uncertain. Their horses bunching close as men haul their guns and turn, desperately seeking a way out, while shots and a sleet of arrows clatter in on them from front and flank. Justus sees the rearmost horsemen waver to a volley from the Choctaw bows. A struck horse crashes on its neck, pitching its army rider headlong to the dirt. Further out, one of Lawrence's denimed vigilantes flings his arms wide as an arrow hits him square between the shoulders, the bloody snout jutting from his chest as he clutches and falls. Justus hears the shrill yelling of the attackers, the hoarse oaths of the startled troopers. He lines on Munson as the horseman grips for his holstered gun, his free hand still holding to the whisky-jug as he turns. With the whip of the loosed string he feels the bow vibrate, stinging his palm. Munson croaks, folding, the feathered palmetto wand standing out from him, low beneath the armpit. The pistol explodes in his holster in the moment he is hit, the slug ripping the toe from his boot. The white man sags, leaning sideways across his mount as the animal swings away, still trying to get the gun from leather, seemingly unable to fall. Justus grits his teeth, reaches in haste to string another arrow. From the far side he glimpses the cavalry officer turning towards him. Hears the crack and whine of the shot as it burns the air close above his head. Justus lines the bow, shooting agáin. The shaft takes Munson low through the ribs as he wheels, and he slithers to the ground, dropping the corn-jug which shatters somewhere under the hooves of his mount.

Heron goes by him at a run, the long spear hefted, stabbing viciously at a trooper whose horse stumbles, all but foundering, with an arrow sunk into its flank. The soldier yelps as the iron blade strikes in, fighting against the pain to bring up his gun.

Heron grabs at him, hauling him down, Jewel and Diamond springing out to join him as the trooper falls, hacking at him with their heavy-bladed cane knives. Their shouts drown the trooper's yells as the body rolls loose, ribboned with blood and dirt. Other mounted soldiers up beyond, blazing back into the volleys from Red Wolf and 'Gator Head: Craig and the lanky Taggart, guns in their hands. A shot from the taller man hits a Choctaw bowman who stands in the open, smashing him over backwards to the ground. Craig, his red hair flying about his face, has his own weapon lifted, when two feathered arrows bristle suddenly from his chest. The trooper sags, gasping, firing uselessly into the ground as a third arrow thuds into his back. The panicked horse carries him five or six paces further on before he slides off, hitting the dirt.

Up ahead, Soldier's gun booms again, and a trooper scrambling up from his felled horse, sabre drawn, is flung to the ground, the charge tearing him apart. Justus catches a glimpse of Whiteside, his broad face paler now from dust and terror, running awkwardly through the litter of men and animals. He still clutches the useless shotgun. Lawrence has turned back, coming in for the Sheriff at a gallop, his levelled gun throwing flame. Dirt pocks up in front of his feet, and Justus clenches his teeth. He dives for where Munson's fallen gun lies unattended, flung out from the prone figure of its owner. Letting go his grip of the bow, he hurls himself forward.

His hand closes swiftly on the grip of the gun, recognizing the feel of the weapon: a long-barrelled pistol, not unlike the one he took from Burns in the wilderness. He comes up with it from the ground, rolling aside as Lawrence thunders past him, his second shot buzzing wild over the tops of the bushes. Whiteside leaping for the offered stirrup, his bulky shape hanging halfway across the horse as Lawrence drags back on the rein. Crouched in cover of the thorns, Justus moves fast, cocking the hammer afresh for a shot at the planter just as Lawrence brings the horse around. Same instant another hand-gun blasts from further out, the shot crashing through the thorns. Justus pivots on his heels, raising the pistol in both hands as a second horseman ploughs in towards him, firing over his horse's neck as he comes. Another of Lawrence's riders, the patroller they call Sims.

Thunder of the horseman's gun all but blinds him with its

smoke, cordite reeking in his nostrils. A slug whistles past him and into the thicket, the impact slapping at his face. Justus lines on the oncoming rider and pulls the trigger, wincing as the gun blasts, thudding back against his palms. Sims jerk-reins his mount to a halt, leans forward with a choking sound, dropping his gun. Sweating hard, Justus cocks and fires afresh, the shot slamming the hit man back over the crupper to earth. Caught by one foot in the stirrup, he's dragged away through the dirt.

Lawrence is clear when he looks around, lunging away over the crest with Whiteside hung like a sack of flour over the saddle. Justus shudders, lowering the pistol, aware all at once of his harsh breathing, the cooling moisture of sweat against his skin. In front of him the maul of riders has begun to clear, most of the horsemen already heading back upslope at the gallop, not halting to fire back. Justus sees another soldier go down where the Choctaws ply their bows in the thickets. A riderless horse plunging by him, maddened. Foaming at the mouth and flinging up its head, a smear of blood along its flank where the rider clung before falling at last. Squinting into the dust, he makes out the hunched figure of Owl Man, fighting his way clear. A tall black dives in, grabbing for the halter-rope, aiming to strike with the clubbed butt of his gun. The Cherokee twists in the saddle, a long-bladed knife in his hand. He slashes the attacker with a back-handed blow that lays the flesh open near the shoulder. The man howls and retreats, gripping the wounded arm, blood spilling bright through his fingers. Owl Man swinging away uphill, holding the knife.

Back of him Crow Feather grunts, ramming home a second charge to the barrel of his gun. By now the horsemen are nearly all gone, strung out in a ragged line as they gallop for the crest. The grim, whiskered sergeant is last. Half-blinded by dust, Justus sees the lean face harden as the horseman turns halfway in the saddle. Elliott raises the pistol in his hand, taking aim over his forearm and firing. The blast is so close as to be deafening. From the corner of his eye, Justus sees the stump-legged Indian spun round by the force of the shot, the long muzzle-loader sagging in his grip. Crow Feather ploughs over to the ground, the gun falling away beyond him. Justus fires blind into the shrouding smoke, but some instinct tells him the shot was wasted.

When he looks again Elliott is gone after the rest, and the ambushers are left with only dead men and horses.

'That's it!' Soldier's shout rings huge in the new-fallen stillness. The twisted figure turns, ducking back through the thorns, shucking fresh loads to his gun as he moves. Close to, the splayed features tauten in a fierce grin. His breathing harsh, excited, the one eye glittering as it narrows against the light.

'We hit 'em good, sure 'nough! Now git on back to them pirogues, you hear me?'

On his knees by the fallen Munson, wrestling off the gunbelt and its shells, Justus senses a grey-black flicker of movement as Soldier goes on by him. Others already turning to follow him, Heron and his sisters among them, loping downhill through the thickets towards the water's edge. Further out, the Choctaws are starting back down the slope, slinging their bows, more than one carrying plunder stripped from the dead horsemen: a broad-brimmed hat or hunting shirt, maybe, or a peaked cavalry cap. Like Justus himself, several brandish looted pistols and shell belts, or the short carbines the soldiers carried. Fitting the heavy belt around his hips, the big man slides his gun to leather and scans the litter of dead horses and men in the open space beyond. The baby-faced corporal sprawls where the shotgun blast flung him, his body crooked over at an awkward angle to the ground. Flesh and uniform alike dissolved to a mess of blood at the waist. A red-headed trooper lying face-down, stuck with Choctaw arrows . . . Justus spares them hardly a look, his glance cutting back to the fallen Louisiana riders. Munson down to him now, and Sims. Right now, the worst of the hate gone from him. He doesn't feel too much about it. They would just as soon have killed him. He got in first, and they're dead.

But Lawrence isn't. He got clear, and chances are he'll be back.

At that he pauses a while, glowering over towards the thickets by the crest, the way Lawrence took. His mind recalling the image of the horse galloping past him, Whiteside slung over the saddle-horn. The lean, harsh face turned towards him as the shot ripped through the brush overhead. Eyeing the empty skyline, the big man frowns, willing Lawrence back again within reach of the bow or the looted gun.

'You comin', boy?' Soldier yells.

Justus shakes his bushy head as if to rid his mind of the thought. Gets to his feet, picking up the bow from the ground. By now the bunch of them are at the waterline, wading out to get the pirogues launched. Heron and his sisters up to their waists in the green, scummed water, pushing, while others climb aboard with their stolen weapons. Justus breathes out once, slowly. Sets back downhill to join them at a loping run, glancing back one time in passing as he takes in the crumpled body of Crow Feather from the corner of his eye. Soldier's hard stare upon him as he ploughs through the shallows and into the bed of the canoe. The prow of the pirogue cleaving water as it skims out over the lagoon. Headed back for the stockade.

Up on the thorn-bushed slope the spilled bodies lie quiet. One with the stillness and the throbbing heat. The land beyond them shimmering in a haze before being lost from sight.

When the horsemen come over the ridge for a second time, the pirogues are already afloat. Sitting astride his horse above the thickets, Maitland watches the narrow, sleek shapes in the water, the upright figures in the stern of each craft sinking their long poles. Black, sweating bodies agleam in harsh sunlight as they pull out across the lagoon. Moving, it seems to him, with a studied slowness, already out of range. Maitland grips on the rein, his teeth setting hard together. Feeling the change in his face as it blanches whiter than a bone.

'Well, they're clear.' Elliott says.

He turns aside, his whiskered features bare of expression, refilling his spilled pipe from the tobacco sack in his blouse. Maitland sits silently, still pale as he sweats in the heat. His eyes are for the sprawl of bodies and downed horses that strew the earth down below. The flies have already begun to settle, clustering dark at eyes and open mouths, setting down amid the spreading stains of blood. Their low, hovering drone the one sound in the newly fallen stillness.

Nine men down to the ambush: five of his own troopers, four of Lawrence's riders. And three horses killed. The attackers have

164

left only three bodies behind: the Indians shot by Elliott and Taggart, and the black Moody killed. Owl Man looked to have wounded another with his knife. So far, that's the limit of their success. Maitland breathes hard, his eyes welling suddenly, his face growing hot. Good men lost, and himself to blame. Walking into a trap with his eyes wide open. He glances once to the mauled corpse of Rose, where the flies gather thickest, and chokes down on a surge of bile in his throat.

God damn them to hell, he thinks, the black, murdering bastards.

'Looks like we found us some niggers who can fight, after all,' the sergeant says, his stare flinty-hard as he lights up his pipe afresh and looks out over the water.

From the other side, Lawrence crowds in close, dark eyes narrow-slitted as he seeks out the captain's attention. His first shock of fear passed, the planter's face shows hard and motionless, vindictive, eager for the chance to hit back more viciously than before.

'One of them I seen before, sir.' His voice grates in the ear of the captain as Maitland looks out ahead of him to the litter of bodies. 'Big bush-headed buck, he took down Munson an' Sims. Name of Justus. He run off my plantation a while back . . .' Pausing as his glance rakes again at the silent soldier. 'Give me a peck of pleasure to see that desperado hang, Mr Maitland.'

Seems to him that Maitland's breath comes shorter for a time. The captain, though, makes him no answer. Turns instead to the grim-faced sergeant on his other side.

'Sergeant.' Maitland's blue eyes have the chill of ice. 'Have Pfister step up the timber-felling. And get Sergeant Riordan to bring up his guns to the ridge. I want that place under fire within the hour, you hear?'

For a moment Elliott meets the level stare of his commander, his leathery face unchanged. Then the whiskered noncom takes the pipe from his mouth, tamps it out and slips it into his pocket.

'Sir!' He salutes, his arm holding there for an instant as he endures that chill blue gaze. Then Elliott swings his mount, moves at a canter back over the crest and out of sight, the sound of hooves dying in the muddy, sun-scorched earth.

Maitland watches until he's gone, then turns to face the open water and the stockade. The boats are almost home by now, dipping in beneath the overhanging greenery at the rim of the island. Light comes blinding off the flat lagoon, white sunbursts glinting from the rifles brandished overhead. The captain breathes out slowly, his grip tightening on the rein.

'They've had their chance,' Maitland says. He speaks to no-one in particular, but he's heard by them all as they sit their horses around him. At the look on his face, even Lawrence draws back. The young officer ignores him as he ignores them all, glaring out across the water, his bloodless lips set hard together.

'Before I'm through here, they'll be sorry,' the captain says.

He sits, his white face beaded with sweat as his mount twitches and flicks its ears at the gathering flies. Looking hard-eyed into the glare of the sun on the yellow-green surface of the lagoon.

'So you got back, huh?' Shango says.

Inside the walled stockade, hearing the gate slam shut behind him, Justus feels his mouth go suddenly dry, like he come back all at once from sunlight into the dark. Sight of those black, stony eyes looking him over don't make him no happier.

'Spirit brung me through, I guess,' the big man answers, wondering as he says it where he finds strength for the words. At that Shango nods, grinning, his keen-eyed stare hooding over. His carved face is still flecked with blood from his splayed nose, and the gashes in his lips show raw as the features move. Some teeth busted jagged too, but those long filed fangs are still there, points glinting where they catch the light.

'Yeah. Guess it did, at that.' The gaunt man breathes the words, his voice hoarse, thick with malice. The narrowed eyes glint like to crumbs of black glass. 'This time, though, you for the god. You hear me?'

'I hear you,' he says.

Swallowing almost as he speaks, feeling his throat knot hard as a tree growth, shutting off his breath for the moment. Scans the faces round him in one fleeting blur of sight: Mary pale and wide-eyed across from him at the hut wall; Cedar standing back of her, his great hands on her shoulders; the smooth, sweat-slicked features of Mama Odu, grinning back towards him. And behind him the others, closing in. One-eyed Soldier is nearest, his shotgun only halfway lowered—the gun that killed two soldiers of another kind, not too long since. Then Heron and his sisters, holding to their blood-stained knives. And Red Wolf's Choctaws.

Like before. Not a hope for him.

Justus thinks back to the moving shape whose fin sliced the waters of the pool. The bull head. The lipless mouth gaping to show the rows of knife-edged teeth. Spite of the sun's heat, the sick fear-feeling chills his gut.

'Whipped them soljers good!' Heron crows out from behind him. 'Ain't gonna be back fo' a while . . .'

His words tail off in a moment, giving way to a silence that presses unbearably on them all as Shango turns his bloodshot stare on the young spearman. Heron swallows, looking down.

'God talk, you stay quiet.' Shango speaks low, but the venom in his voice has lost none of its sting. The gaunt man's lips curl back from his jutting teeth in the most vicious of smiles. 'Less'n you fixin' to go where this one already haided . . .'

His glance cuts away from the figure of Heron and settles afresh on Justus, who stands with one hand clenched on the gun at his belt, glaring back into the eyes of the god.

'Yeah,' Shango says, and his pitiless stare rakes the big man through to his backbone. 'Reckon we waited long enough . . .'

Tensed at the words, Justus spans the distance between Mary and himself. But even as he looks, he knows it's hopeless. Sensing their movements about him, crowding in at the sudden move, he barely has a chance to reach the pistol half from leather before both his arms are pinned from behind. The muzzle of Soldier's long-barrelled gun touches him cold along the spine. The big man stiffens, motionless.

Up in front of him, Shango smiles again, comes in with the cutlass hefted, reaching for him with a long-fingered hand. Justus feels a sudden searing pain as those fingers grasp his hair, jerking his head back. The fierce eyes glaring inches from his own. Held fast, the big man grits his teeth, willing the water back from his eyes. Inwardly, he wonders how long they'll take to drag him to that pool . . .

'Shango!'

The shout breaks the stillness, ringing like blasphemy through the compound as all heads turn in answer. On the rampart overhead the lookout swallows, paling grey before Shango's hard-eyed stare, knowing too late that he has spoken the name of the god. At sight of his fear, the gaunt man almost grins.

'Tell it,' Shango says.

'Lord, them soljers comin' back!' The man dares one glance backward over his shoulder, then licks at his lips, terrified. 'Lord . . . it look like they bringin' up the guns!'

In the moment of quiet that follows, Justus feels the bunched group of bodies withdraw from him, and with it the touch of the gun. Shango leaves hold on his hair, and the big man shakes his head, his eyes still blurred from the pain. Around him the blacks and the Indians murmur, uncertain, looking from one to the other. For a while the harsh face of the god himself shows surprise. Then the eyes hood over, and Shango bares his teeth.

'Let me up there, an' fast!' the tall man yells.

He swings away, his long shadow crossing Justus as he moves. Dives into the crowd ahead. Flung back as the others part to let the god through, Justus finds himself breathing a shade freer than before, aware all at once of the sweat running into his eyes and mouth. Shakes his head, half-turning as the grip on his arms relaxes. No place he kin run, anyhow. From the corner of his eye he sees a black spectral flicker of movement as Shango climbs hand over hand up the rampart ladder. The big man sighs, letting the vision pass, watching the faces turn towards him, the glances questioning. Jewel, her eyes touching on him slyly from a distance; Diamond like a mirror-image at her shoulder, only to be told apart from her sister by her sullen look. After them, Red Wolf and the scowling Heron. At his back, the low voice of Soldier.

'Look like you bought yo'self another minute,' the veteran mutters.

Justus ignores him. Right now he kin do without Soldier's grudging friendship. That ain't gonna be no use to him, come the

168

time. His look is for Mary, pinned still by Cedar's hands. Her mute, stricken stare is answer enough. Justus grimaces, looking down.

Above his head, he hears the voice of the god.

'Yeah, they linin' up, right enough,' Shango says, a sneer in his voice, like he don't reckon too much to what he seen. 'They got but two guns, is all. Cain't see how they gonna reach all the way 'cross the water . . .'

Almost as the words leave his lips comes a thunderous explosion. The lookout howls, going flat on the rampart walk with his hands over his ears. The air torn open as the shell whistles towards them. Down below, in the compound, all of them duck to the sound. Shango alone stands upright, staring out over the parapet of skulls. The shell falls short, blasting into woodland halfway down the hillside. At the shattering noise, the earth shakes a moment underfoot, Shango looking on as splintered trees fly upward, pattering fragments on the wall of the stockade.

'Tole you,' the tall man crows into the blast, his feathered head flung back. 'I tole you! They cain't hit us from where they stood! Ain't a thing they kin do . . .'

A second explosion follows hard on the echoes of the first. This time the noise keeps right on coming, rising to a shriek as the shell hurtles in over the stockade. The grip on Justus' arm is loosened and all around him men and women run scattering, screaming against the deafening noise of the shell. Halfway across the compound, a row of huts erupts in a sheet of flame. For an instant the world vanishes under a rain of flung spars and splinters, blazing thatch and showers of stony earth.

In a moment he's down, flat to the dirt, earth in his mouth, spitting and cursing, eyes shut against the glare of flame. Underneath him the ground shudders like it run wild, bucks to throw him sideways across the compound. Blast of the explosion goes on forever, seems like, numbing his ears, echoes racketing back and forth over the lagoon. Then, as it passes, he kin hear the screamin' from all around.

'Oh, ma Lawd! Ma Lawd!'

'Sweet Jesus, lookit that!'

'Done kill us all with them guns!'

'Somebody help me—ma laig! Ma laig!'

Other wordless howlings—crazed sounds that go on and on, as he scrambles on hands and knees, looking about him. Where the huts once stood, there is now a huge, smoking crater in the ground, its outer edges scattered with flung debris of every kind. In among the charred splinters and rubble he sees other shapes that do not move: torn fragments, blackened and splotched with blood. From the scorched, shrivelled remnants he cain't tell them for men or women, or even children. Enough to know they once were people. Justus shakes his head, gags on the taste of bile.

Over beyond him, the rest are getting to their feet. One woman stands howling like a maddened beast in the open ground, arms crossed on her breasts. Somewhere through the smoke a man crawls feebly, dragging a shattered leg. Most of those who crowded him a moment before are still living. Now they stand dumb-struck, gazing at the terrible hole in the ground. Justus sees Mary upright and unharmed with Cedar holding to her, and breathes a sigh of relief. Pushes to his feet, licking away the sweat from his lips.

'Git on over here!' Shango's voice comes shrill above the howling of the woman. The tall figure turning, bloodshot eyes staring wide as he grips at the stakes, flecks of foam already at the corners of his mouth. 'Git to them catapults, less'n you aim to go for the god! You hear me?'

The shocked mass below have scarcely begun to move when the guns open fire again, two thudding explosions coming close together. The group scatters afresh, the lone woman still yelling as the shells come over. Justus is stumbling in towards Mary and her captor, when the first one hits, ploughing to earth outside the stockade. With the blinding flash of flame he is thrown down for a second time, the skull-hung rampart disappearing from sight, the reek of smoke clearing to show daylight through a gap in the stockade. Stakes blown out and smashed to matchwood. The busted gate hanging sideways on its pins. Beyond the crater of the shell is a hole wide enough to drive a four-hoss waggon through. Same instant he looks, a fresh eruption rocks the ground under him, a deafening blast drowning out the other cries. Dark falls on him suddenly, a heavy, smothering weight that pins him to the ground. Justus snarls, fighting to get his face up from the dirt, hitting out in panic at the thing above him, aware of the sound of falling debris, pattering down on them like soft rain. The stink of the weight above him becomes a harsh man-reek of sweat and flesh, and with it the more acrid, charred smell of something burned.

Justus heaves and the weight slides from him, thudding to the ground. Getting to his knees, the big man finds his own body foul and sticky with blood. The hook-nosed face of Red Wolf glares up at him from the dirt, eyes wide, teeth bared in a snarl of rage. His blackened body ends at the waist, the near arm blown ragged from its socket. Lower down, his ribs show palely through a bloody gash in the flesh. A jagged wound in the throat twists the head askew, all but severed from the stump of the neck. Justus looks once and turns away, his mouth gone dry.

Stink of blood clings to him as he rises, giddy from the din of bursting shells and the sight and smell of death. In front of him bodies litter the compound, scorched and smoking where the blast took them down. He catches sight of Mary, cowering on her haunches, her face hidden. Back of her, the next row of huts are blazing now, fire leaping along the dry thatch as it takes a hold. Further off, Soldier and 'Gator Head are leading a bunch of armed men towards the gap in the stockade. Right now he cain't see Heron nor his sisters. Justus breathes out, the sound harsh and tearing in his own ears. Starts for where his woman crouches in the shadow of the flame.

Cedar raises up from the ground as he nears her, lifting upright to bar his path, both hands outstretched. The giant's body is coated with dust and filth, his eyes glaring wild as a dog's. In the moment his looming figure blocks off the light, Justus sees a fearful splinter-wound that lays his gut open, the frayed edges of flesh peeled back to show the blue-white gleam of intestines beneath. Cedar makes as if to speak, chokes, his mouth filling with blood. Bright droplets spatter the dirt as he reels, lurching forward. Justus weaves aside, letting the big man fall. Cedar goes down hard, shuddering against the ground before he lies still.

Over by the burning huts, Mary sobs, hiding her face with her hands. Even as he reaches out for her the guns boom afresh. Up above him he glimpses the skeletal outline of Shango himself, poised on the lip of the quaking rampart as the shells scream in. The lookout clings to him, wide-eyed in a frenzy of terror. As he looks on, the tall man pulls away, hacking his cutlass into the wretch's neck. The lookout shrieks, pitches from sight over the line of stakes, Shango springing down like a cat in the instant before the shells strike the compound.

The first explosion hits over by the far wall, stakes flung in the air like busted twigs, showering down on the huts beyond. Justus sees the thatched roofs cave in, the walls sagging under the sudden weight. Splinters whine and hiss across the open ground, scything into those wretches too slow to outrun them. Watching, he sees them struck by the murderous fragments: a hobbling, grey-haired negress hit from behind, throwing her arms wide to fall without a sound; brown-skin kid who leaps in the air, screaming out as the razor-sharp blades of wood rip through his spine. In his mouth the vile taste grows hard to bear . . .

He stands, earth shaking underfoot with the volley of blasts. Through a drifting skein of smoke Jewel and Diamond run together, bronze of their bared limbs gleaming in the murk. Next shell drops close in back of them, the blast throwing up a fountain of dirt and stones. With the gush of flame both running figures go down. Jewel rolls, gasping, hair in her eyes as she claws herself up on all fours. Diamond stays down, her arms flung out stiff to either side.

'*Diamond!*'

The word comes from Jewel as a harsh animal cry, sawing at the nerves. She leans, cradling the slack-limbed figure in her arms, blood puddling in her lap as she crouches there, rocking back and forth over the shape that does not move. For the first time Justus sees the hideous splinter-wound that must have struck the girl from behind, lifting off the top of her skull, killing her instantly. Hunched over the body of her sister, Jewel looks up sudden, her black stare locking with his own.

'The god fail!' Jewel screams, like one demented, her face twisted ugly in rage and fear. 'Hear me? *The god fail!*'

Sound of her voice cuts through the shrieks of torment and loss, heard above the echoes of the bursting shells, the howls of the hit and dying. For an instant the shock of it roots him to the spot, held by her terrible eyes.

That same instant, Shango seizes his chance.

He glimpses the gaunt, upright figure, lunging for him out of the smoke, a split-second before the blow falls. Swinging half around, Justus ducks his head, the blade of the cutlass slashing air inches from him, the haft and Shango's clenched fist thudding hard on the bone of his skull. The big man grunts, one shoulder slamming to earth as he goes down, rolling. Pain inside his head threatening to bust the skull wide open. As if from a world off, he senses the rush of that tall shape overleaping him, making for Mary, who shrinks back from him with a cry of terror. Justus snarls. Struggles to his knees, fighting the pain. He's a way too late. Already Shango grasps the white girl roughly by the arm, his fearful strength all but lifting her from the ground. Drags her back over the hard, rutted earth, headed already towards the long house.

'This white bitch to blame!' Shango screams over the clamour of sounds, his lean face twisted so the carved patterns writhe like snakes in the flesh. His blood-veined eyes stare crazily as the gaunt head swings to left and right. He lifts the blood-spattered cutlass above his head, foam flecking thick at the corners of his mouth. 'Hear me? She for the god!'

'No!' Justus yells the word back into the din of shells and stricken cries, pain stabbing white-hot through his head as he calls out. He gathers himself, lurching up again to his feet as Shango hauls Mary away across the littered compound, reaching for his holstered pistol in the same moment. Too late, now, for a shot. Screaming shapes flitting back and forth through the smoke keep coming across his line of fire, and all the time Shango drags Mary closer to that carved wooden door. For the briefest of seconds he catches a glimpse of the two struggling figures: Mary off-balance, kicking out helplessly, before she's dragged off her feet again, her strength useless against the gaunt man gripping her arm. Then smoke fans across, drifting back again to hide them. Justus clenches his teeth with a harsh, grinding sound, momentarily heedless of pain.

God damn you, Shango. This time the finish, sure enough.

He pulls the gun and moves, plunging forward into the smoke, the way Shango and Mary gone. Back of him, amid the echoing rumble of explosions, he hears Soldier's raised voice.

'Lord help us, they comin'!' the veteran yells out. 'Looks like hundreds of 'em! They comin' out on rafts, 'crost the water!'

Any other time the words would have sent a chill through to the pit of his belly. But not now. Justus turns from the sound, growling savagely as a rabid dog, pushing on at a run into the smoke as Shango gains the door of the long house and levers it open, pulling Mary inside.

Across the far side of the lagoon, the guns open fire again.

Voorhees shoves back hard, the water sucking at his pole as it works free of the mud. Thrust on by Schwab and himself, the clumsy raft lurches closer in towards the land. Up in front he sees the grinning figure of Benton, crouched over his rifle with the rest, and beyond him, the thin, upright shape of Lieutenant Pfister, gazing out to where the first green branches of the island hang down into the water. The lagoon around is thick with makeshift craft, felled trees lashed together into platforms to accommodate fifteen or twenty men at a time, crowded together with their rifles lifted, water seeping through the cracks to well over their feet in places. Across from them it's Master-Sergeant Hale who leads, and on the far side Sergeant Gifford. Apart from the artillery crews, every man fit to stand is on the crossing. Maitland himself is following Pfister's raft, and back of him the Southern posse under Lawrence and Whiteside. From away behind them all the guns thunder out again, shells crashing into the far stockade as the echoes shiver out across the water.

Ain't gonna be too much work for us, once we get over, Voorhees thinks to himself.

He moves, steadying the long pole, grimacing as water and slime stream from it back into the lagoon. Voorhees spits, sinks the pole again, sweating in the harsh warmth, his uniform sticking to him like a second skin. Across from him, the heavy-set ploughboy catches his eye a moment. Schwab winks an eye, grinning. Voorhees nods back, smiling uncertainly. Guess the

174

sodbuster ain't so bad, at that—even if he would sooner be up there with Benton in the middle of the raft.

He doesn't turn to look over his shoulder towards the stockade. First thing is to get this goddamned raft to land. What trouble is left up there can keep for a moment.

But right now he don't figure it will amount to much.

Under his booted feet a tide of water glides backward against the thrust of the raft, a thin, greenish scum slopping over the toes of his boots. Pfister ignores it, looking out ahead. On the island itself shells burst in geysers of flame, smoke rolling sullenly upward from the stockade and the shrubbery lower down. A wonder the place hasn't been blown apart, Pfister thinks. For a moment the look that crosses his thin face is almost disapproving. Inwardly he finds time to question the need for so many shells to be fired. As yet, the infantry on their rafts have drawn no answering fire from the island. With only small arms to rely upon, the renegades must surely realise the senselessness of it all. Enough blood has been spilt already, he feels. Besides, sight of the burning stockade raises uneasy thoughts of women or children up there, cowering under the shells.

Soldiering was bad enough, but this is worse than war. The sooner it's all over, the better.

Ah Laurie, what wouldn't I give to be back home with you right now?

They're close in, almost within reach of the foliage at the water's edge, when he hears Gifford sing out from the raft on their right.

'Look out overhead!' the sergeant yells.

At the shout Pfister stiffens, clutching his sheathed sword, feeling a jolt as the two infantrymen at the back ship their long poles, the raft lifting to the swell beneath. Same instant comes a heavy hissing noise, and a huge rock ploughs by them and into the water. Between his raft and Hale's, a pillar of green scum towers up, curling over to drench them with the wet, stinking spray. Pfister grimaces in distaste as a fleck of it spatters on his face.

'Push in to land!' the officer calls out to Voorhees and Schwab behind him. 'We're under fire!'

Even now he feels no sense of excitement, still less fear. The whole thing is too far away somehow, seen and felt from a distance. He finds himself wondering what kind of machine could have hurled the projectile down on them. Some primitive type of catapult, he supposes. Pfister shakes his head, the raft sliding in beneath the green overhang of the boughs. Poor savages, he thinks. What chance do they stand?

Above them, the same hissing plunge, the fleeting glimpse of a boulder that crashes by them from overhead, faces fanned by the wind as it sails past. Further back comes a harsh splintering and the sound of frantic screams. Turning, Pfister sees a raft hit and sinking, men yelling as they plunge into the water. Glimpses others who make no move, smashed to a wet ugly pulp on the stoved-in platform. Force of the rock takes it down, the wood shelving up for an instant before it goes under, men floundering and calling out as they struggle for land, some of them, caught by the vortex and their own weighty clothing, dragged under with the raft.

Looking on, Pfister feels his gut clench the way it did back at Shiloh, before the charge. Knows in that moment that he is at war again.

'Follow me!' the lieutenant calls. Leans under the probing branches to drag out his sword, grasping with his free hand at a thick-leafed bough to pull himself ashore. He lands in ankle-deep mud, crouched under the trees, the others springing to firm ground after him with their rifles lifted and ready. Voorhees and Schwab are last, grabbing their weapons and scrambling off the raft as another boulder strikes the lagoon and showers them afresh with liquid filth from the surface. Out beyond them, Gifford leads his men ashore.

The sound of the bursting shells comes louder in their ears now, screaming down to explode inside the stockade. Pfister struggles up the slope, grabbing hold of what brush offers itself. Wedging himself in between clefts in the rock, he comes in sight of the trees near to the summit, hearing harsh breathing and a clatter of booted feet behind him that tells him they're following. From where he is, it sounds as though the catapults have ceased firing. Pfister smiles tightly, edging out from cover. Once it's begun, he never feels quite so bad. The waiting is over; now he's free to act.

They're three parts of the way uphill, when the flat crack of a rifle blasts out from overhead: sharp, snapping sound, unlike the old guns they had. More like a cavalry carbine, Pfister thinks, as the bullet sizzles past his face. Behind him, a climbing soldier topples without a sound, his rifle clattering loose as the body slithers down the slope. At the sight of the stricken man the rest of the troopers freeze a moment, standing.

'Come on! Get moving!' Pfister yells, leaping from cover as he calls out and starting uphill at a run, his upheld sword catching the light as he moves.

The black marksman is set in a tree fork to the right of the stockade, maybe twenty feet above the soldiers as they climb the slope, his back pressed firm against the bole, the Springfield carbine he snatched from a fallen cavalry trooper resting over a stout limb. When the officer breaks cover, running uphill, he takes careful aim. Squeezes the trigger.

Scrambling through the last of the undergrowth, Pfister sees the blazing stockade loom up ahead, glimpses the outline of its shattered walls for an instant through the murk. He's started forward again when something lashes him hard in the breast, the force of the impact knocking his feet from under him. When the answering crack of the shot sounds, he's already down, sprawled over the rocks, the sword slipping from his hand.

Over his head the tree crowns form a branching net through which the sun pours down in a drizzle of flame. Pfister closes his eyes to the glare. Somehow he can't seem to move his limbs. No pain as yet, but when he reaches towards his chest, the hand meets a thick, spreading stain. Somewhere, miles away, comes Gifford's voice, yelling out to shoot the bastard down. With the rattle of the volley, he catches sight of a blurred shape toppling out of a tree fork on the crest, hitting the ground away from sight. Pfister grunts, struggles to raise himself on his elbows. Sinks back, the treetops wheeling madly above his head.

Faces shut out the dazzle of light, crowding to peer down at him. Gifford he sees, and the dark-faced Benton. And the young Dutch boy from Philadelphia. What's he called? Pfister struggles for the name, can't find it somehow. And when he tries to speak, his lips refuse to move. Above him the fair-haired kid watches his efforts, the boy's face pale and scared. For a moment Pfister wonders what's the matter with him.

'You all right, sir?' Voorhees falters, his blue eyes welling with tears as he speaks.

All at once weariness overcomes him. The strength draining from his limbs with the slow seep of blood from the hole in his chest. Why can't they go away, and let him sleep? he thinks. Somewhere in that last, dragging tide comes memory of Laurie, and how it was. Pfister fights to rise again, eyes opening, lips trembling, about to form a word . . .

'He's dead,' Benton says, reaching to close the staring eyes as the officer's head rolls sidelong against his shoulder. He and Voorhees get to their feet, the younger man brushing awkwardly at his face with the back of his hand.

'What do you reckon he was trying to say?' the Dutchman asks, his own voice muffled as he turns his head away. Benton frowns, uncertain. Shrugs as he picks up his rifle.

'Some girl's name, I guess . . . Can't say as I heard him too good . . .'

'We ain't through yet!' Gifford's shout breaks in on them suddenly, jarring them to life. The face of the sergeant colours to a furious red, anger in his voice all but choking him. 'The lieutenant's dead! Now hang on to your rifles and git up that slope. We got unfinished business up there, remember?'

Stung by the harshness of his tone, Voorhees swings halfway round to meet him, hurt and anger struggling together in his look. But Gifford doesn't wait for him. Grabs his own rifle and heads leaping up the incline, loose rocks and dirt sliding out from his booted feet as he climbs. The rest of the infantry follow at a stumbling run, each man with his rifle held crosswise in front of his body. Voorhees glimpses the burly figure of Schwab among them, the Iowa farmer moving slow and heavy as a bear in the wake of his fellows. The young man frowns, shaking his head to clear the water from his eyes. Turns again as a hand falls lightly on his sleeve.

'Stick by me, Dutchy,' Benton tells him. 'I'll see you don't come to no harm.'

Voorhees lets out a breath in a shuddering sigh. Aware of the dark man's eyes upon him, he nods slowly, gathers up his rifle from the ground. His sight clearing now as he makes after the lithe figure of his friend, scrambling up through the screen of bushes overhead. He spares one look for the still corpse of the lieutenant, outlined against the foliage with the red blotch at his breast. Voorhees shivers, his back hairs prickling. Turns away to fling himself at the thicketed slope.

In front of them smoke from the burning stockade drifts out along the crest. Back across the water, the guns set up their relentless pounding once again.

The open door of the long house looms against him, leading into unlit darkness. Justus plunges headlong through the gap, drawing the pistol from its holster as he moves.

Sound batters from a bursting shell outside, drowning out all else and making his head ring. Justus stands, pressed to the shuddering wall, watching earth shower down from the roof as the explosion shakes the ground beneath, eyes straining to single out one set of shadows from the rest.

In the wake of the shell-burst comes Mary's high-pitched scream.

At the sound he whirls cat-like on his heels, guessing the distance. By now his eyes are used to the darkness and he sees them plain. Over by the forked altar, Shango rears upright, outlined tall against the shadows, grasping Mary by the thick, pale hair of her head, dragging her backwards on the ground so as to shield him from the gun. A short distance from them, the light at his back reflects the gleam of water, and a moving fin cuts the surface like a blade.

'Hold on, Mary!' Justus yells.

Dives forward as he calls, raising the long gun. Same inst-ant, a dark whiplash shape curves in for him from somewhere to the side. Whirling about, he fires, the roar of the pistol racketing in the enclosed space, hearing her scream out again. The snake strikes, falling short to hit the ground back of him, head and body splattered by the force of the close-ranged slugs. Justus gasps, ploughs on over the rutted earth, looking in vain for the chance of a shot as Shango drags the white girl to the water.

They're at the lip of the pool now, Mary yelling, twisting her head against the brutal grip that holds her fast, arms flailing; Justus standing helpless, the gun wavering in his hand, unable to see past her to Shango who struggles to swing her bodily in over the rim of earth. The big man brings up the gun, sweating, feeling the thunder of his heart hammering against his ribs.

'Git loose from him, gal!' Justus shouts. Thumbs hammer again to aim at the thing in the water. The boom of the shot swings Shango halfway round, echoes cracking across the pool. He sees it fetch up a whitish fan of spray, but the grey, half-glimpsed shape turns to swim around once more, and he knows he's missed.

Mary fights loose from the tall man as he turns, twisting her head about, but his grip rips strands of hair loose and she howls with the pain. She sinks her teeth savagely into the flesh of his wrist, Shango yelling now as he fights to throw her off. A blow from his forearm sends her clear, sprawling to the ground, his free hand bringing up the cutlass as Justus comes plunging in, head down, throwing the smoking gun aside.

Goes in hard beneath the upswept arm, his head battering at the tall man's chest, dodging clear of the two spread fingers that come jabbing for his eyes. The blow misses, ripping the skin of his cheek, blood from the wounded flesh spattering salty in his mouth. He grabs with both hands at the arm that holds the cutlass, wrenches it down to beat hard on the point of his knee. Shango grunts, his fingers splaying open as the weapon goes skittering from him across the ground. Brings up his own knee into the bigger man's crotch. Justus turns sideways on, takes the blow and its numbing pain high on the hip. He grabs hurriedly for a hold on the thin man's neck, his hand slipping on sweat and grease to find empty air. Next minute Shango is up close, rank smell of him thick in his nostrils, vying with the stench of blood and rot all around. Justus catches a glimpse of those long, bared teeth as they lunge for his throat. Turns fast away from the bite, his right shoulder thrusting up to ward off the descending blow. Pain like to jagged knives slices into the flesh, Justus yelling out as Shango locks teeth and hangs on. Blood running warm and thick over his arm and breast, the big man gasps, grinds his teeth hard, fighting the pain. Head down, he gets a bruising grip about the lean waist of the god.

Hard strength meets him, muscles like steel resisting the force of his arms. The tall man rears to bite again, teeth sinking viciously into the old wound, the blood running freely now. His long hands clawing, beating at the back and neck of the man below him, Justus hangs on, choking for breath. Crooks a leg back of the gaunt man as he takes a hold, wrenching to lift Shango halfway from the ground. Grunts as the pair of them smash into the altar, the tree limb falling with a splintered crash, flints scattering. Justus treads on an edged stone, flinches, kicks it aside, feeling the momentum carry him forward as Shango's feet leave the floor. The big man mows ahead, drives for the hewn tree stump beyond. Shango's clawing hands loose hold, Justus swinging to batter him hard into the wood. He feels the sickening thump of impact come back through the palms of his hands, Shango going limp as the breath whooshes out of him. Justus snarls, hoisting him way off the ground, wheeling him around towards the rim of the pool.

Scream of a falling shell like a world ending overhead. Blast of the explosion has the long house rocking, a vivid glare lighting up the place as dust showers down in a cloud. For a jagged instant he sees the place alive: the coiling snakes and lightnings carved into the beams; the metal brackets on the walls. Back of him, Mary is on her feet, firing with the pistol at other moving shapes on the ground. And only feet away, that grey bull-snouted thing turns at the pool's edge, slicing the surface of the water. Abruptly the light shivers out, the room plunged again to darkness.

Above fists thud into his neck, fingers grasping to claw at his bush of hair. The big man breathes out, hanging on. He has Shango lifted now, too far for his teeth to reach again. Justus snarls like a dog, bunches the great muscles of shoulders and back to squeeze in with all his strength. Crack in his ears like to busting wood, Shango screaming out as his ribs give way, hands clutching and hammering at the man under him in the last of a despairing rage. Justus feels the blows as they hit and rebound from his flesh, blind alike to pain and pity, tears loose from the clinging hands that slip and slide in the sticky blood from his bitten shoulder, swings to heave outward with the last of his strength, then lets go . . .

Shango takes the fall headlong, yelling as he goes, long arms and legs splayed out as he hits the water. Rolling awkwardly to his hands and knees by the earthen lip, Justus sees the sleek, grey body of the shark drive in, the bull head slamming into the god at the level of the waist. Shango screams, high and harsh as a trapped critter, as the great jaws close on him, teeth shredding flesh to ribbons, slicing home through bone and tendon alike. For an instant he looks to Justus and the big man meets his look. Glare of white eyes rolled back in the head. Black, yelling hole of mouth, and upflung arms. The water churns, spattering, the shark diving to take him under, blood ribboning dark and thick to cloud the surface of the pool.

The god comes up one more time, calling out, his body torn away below the waist now. The bull shark swings, shows a glimpse of gleaming belly, then strikes in again, the heavy snout thudding into Shango between the shoulders, bladed teeth slashing through him. He goes down without a sound, the beast shaking him like a dog shaking a rat, the remnant of human being flying apart in spatters of bloody flesh. Blood and filth litter the pool and foul the earth at its edge as the shark turns, dives, stirring up a wave of dark foam, the hideous fragments scattered further as the water boils, then slowly settles.

Justus gains his feet, staggers across to throw the lever. The grille screeches up, a wash of bloody water following, then the sleek shape plunges, vanishing underground. After a while only the blood and the gobbets of flesh remain. Justus stands, breathing hard, feeling for the first time the dull, numbing pain in his shoulder and the ripped skin of his face.

With the fall of the god the place echoes, hollow, empty. The big tree down, leaving him in open space. Justus swallows, his gut trembling. Stumbles to where Mary stands waiting beyond the churned pool, her face a pale blur against the dark that presses in upon them, the pistol trailing smoke in her

182

hand. Before he gets halfway to her she is moving. Flings herself into his arms, holding to him as to life itself.

'Justus . . .' Sobbing openly on his sweat-slicked black chest, heedless of the congealing blood that clings to her hair. 'Oh God, Justus . . . I was so scared . . .'

He stands, holding her to him, shuddering with relief. Despite the pain and the trickling flow of blood, he forces himself to smile.

'Me too, honey,' Justus says. He reaches down to take the pistol from her hand. Works left-handed to shuck the dead shells and fit fresh loads from the belt at his waist. His glance goes on over her head to where the doorway shows grey against the blackness around. 'Right now, though, we best git on out of here . . .'

The flow of blood slows to a sullen trickle, some of it already drying to coat his upper body. High on the shoulder Shango's teeth have left raw, bloody gashes in the flesh. Justus ignores the knifing throb of pain. Reaches to clasp Mary's small hand in his own.

'Let's go!' the big man tells her.

Heads for the open door, breaking into a run, careless of the snakes that still move half-seen across the ground. Mary going with him, gasping to keep pace, their bare feet slapping on the earth and the strewn thunder-stones.

Outside, the compound still shudders as the shells burst. And in the wake of the explosions, another gathering roar: sound of white soldiers, charging over the crest.

'Cease fire!' Riordan calls.

He stands, the breath heaving in his thin chest, watching as the second nine-pounder rocks back and settles after the shot, smoke from its hot muzzle drifting out over the water. Beyond him the sweating crews pull back, blouses steaming in the heat. Riordan grins tightly, satisfied. Reaches to dash the sweat from his brow with a wet sleeve.

'Yeah,' Riordan says quietly to himself. 'Ought to be good enough, I reckon.'

Glances away from them as he speaks, his look raking out over the lagoon to the island beyond. There smoke from the shellbursts rolls black and thick, shrouding the wooded slopes, the wrecked stockade all but hidden in the murk as the last echoes quiver across the water. From somewhere in the heart of that smoke, Riordan glimpses the blue-clad figures as they climb, picking out the gleam of bayonets and swords and the barrels of rifles. The sound of shooting comes back faintly towards him, hanging a while in the still afternoon air.

Can't be much left of them now, Riordan guesses. Place is shot all to hell. Just a matter of time now before the boys get in there and finish the job. Either way, he's done what he was brought out here to do.

'You done your job,' he tells the men by the guns. For a moment the grey eyes hold a glint of humour. 'Near as good as I could wish. Have them stand down, Corporal. All we got to do now is wait, I guess.'

He turns, stalking away along the ridge, hearing Copeland's voice issue orders behind him. Riordan grins. Leans by the stunted tree to look out again over the flat green of the water, forgetting the reek of sweat and scum that clings to his body.

Pretty soon he'll be out of this godforsaken country. Back in Albany with Kathleen and the children.

He reaches to roll himself a cigarette. Squints into the drifting smoke yonder as he touches the match to flame.

Guns still racketing from inside the stockade as Maitland comes on at a run over the crest, air above his head thick with arrows, bullets, crude shotgun slugs. Noise like a nest of hornets about his ears. Maitland feels something tug his sleeve, hears a man yell as he stumbles and falls. Heads on towards the water of the ditch, the long pistol held out ahead of him, unfired as yet. So far, he's seen nothing to hit.

God damn them all, the captain thinks.

Elliott up alongside as he gains the edge of the ditch, his whiskered, unsmiling face harder than stone. Hunched figure of Owl Man, holding his long-bladed knife. And close in behind, the men of his dismounted troop: blue-jowled Moody, tall Taggart and the rest.

184

Ploughing in filthy water up to his knees, Maitland frowns. Shouldn't have brought Owl Man along, he guesses. Going to need a good scout to lead them out of this maze of a country once the job's done. He shakes away the thought, flinching as a stray arrow hits water only a foot or so from him. Too late to worry over it, now.

The infantry are already crossing, he sees, wading waist-deep, their rifles above their heads. Maitland catches a brief glimpse of Master-Sergeant Hale and Gifford at the front of the ragged line. Wonders uneasily what happened to Pfister. Over on the right comes a high-pitched yelling as Lawrence leads his armed posse splashing through the muddy shallows. Eager for his turkey-shoot, no doubt. Maitland scowls. Guns still blasting from the stockade. Midway across, an infantryman throws up his arms and sinks, floating half-submerged as the others wade on past him. Floundering almost to his waist in the greenish muck, the captain swallows hard. Even after so many years of war, thought of those hand-made slugs ripping into him is enough to turn his belly over.

'Keep it goin'!' Elliott yells from beside him, the pace quickening as the green tide laps at their chests, bullets and arrows spattering into the water all around. On the broken walls over-head the catapults stay silent, unmanned, already useless at this range. Maitland bites into his lip, feeling his anger rise as the blood runs to his chin. The savages are done for now, trapped in their own stockade. Once he gets inside to them, he doesn't feel like being any too merciful.

Smoke wafts thick in his nostrils from the burning walls, the acrid stink causing him to cough and shake his head to clear his streaming eyes. Through it the sound of gunfire slackens, the spouts from the stricken water thinning out. At a gap in the wall a dark, indistinct figure lurches into view lifting an old muzzle-load gun. Elliott's long-barrelled pistol booms and the shape flops over, sliding for the water.

'Our boys goin' in there!' Moody shouts.

Watching, Maitland sees the infantry pour out from the far side of the ditch, blue of their uniforms fouled and green with stinking weed. Rattle of rifle volleys as they gain the nearest gap in the defences. The line checks a moment, reeling halfway back as

185

though pushed bodily out by some unseen force. Then the blue wave rolls forward, men dropping here and there as the infantry thrust their way inside. Beyond the gap a yelling shout goes up, and with it the sudden clash of arms.

Turning as Moody calls out, Maitland finds himself staring open-mouthed. On the far side, the water of the ditch foams suddenly crimson with blood, an ugly tide washing towards them from below the stockade wall. The captain glimpses floating shards of flesh on the water's surface, and fights down a vile taste in his mouth. He barely has time to take in the first shocking vision, when Lawrence yells out, leading his men back in a rush from the reddening water. Same instant the surface boils and churns, and Maitland's eyes grow wide at sight of a sleek, fin-backed shape striking like an arrow straight towards him.

My God, am I going crazy? Maitland thinks.

'*Shark in the water!*' Elliott's voice hoarse at his back. But just as the words come from him, the beast rolls in and hits.

Moody half-turning, his mouth still open. In the split-second the shark cuts the water, Maitland sees the stare of the trooper's eyes: black and wet as sloes, they fill with raw terror and disbelief as the round bull head breaks surface, teeth gashing wide to reflect the glare of the sun. Moody howls, struck by a vicious hammer-blow that tears both legs out from under. Both arms jerk up under the impact as the shark ploughs on, dragging him down, his death-cry lost as he vanishes below the surface in a bloody cloud of spray. The long-backed beast dives, then breaks surface a second time, its jaws running red. Some distance beyond, Moody's upper body rolls in the waters of the ditch. Below the chest is a ragged strip of flesh, through which the bone gleams, white and splintered.

'Kill it! Kill the goddam thing!' Maitland's voice rises to a shriek. He takes aim, firing into the water as the head comes up again, triggering off all the loads in succession, frantic in haste and fear. Hit from above, the great creature shudders, blood flowering suddenly from the holes in its skull. The noise of gunfire is deafening now as Elliott and the rest of the troop pour their shots into it. The stricken fish thrashes, the water round it darkening by a shade. Desperate, maddened, the creature turns, biting at its own mangled flanks and tail.

'Kill it! Kill it!' Maitland still yelling above the gunshots, jamming fresh loads to his pistol as the body of the shark jerks and leaps under the hail of bullets. He has the hammer cocked again when at last he sees that it floats belly-up, jaws gaping to show the knife-like rows of teeth, hung still with shreds of flesh and bone. Maitland pauses, aware all at once of his shuddering breath, the sweat that drenches him from head to foot. The hand that holds the gun trembles like a leaf in the wind.

'Jesus God!' Taggart's horrified murmur chokes off suddenly as the tall man doubles up to puke in the water. Maitland shudders, grimacing, the taste of vomit washing at the back of his throat. Tries not to look at Moody's mangled corpse as it floats past them, the eyes in the dead face still staring upward. Over beyond him Owl Man hacks his knife into the flank of the lifeless shark, spilling the creatures's guts loose. A lone infantryman, stumbling by, jabs at the thing with his bayonet in passing. Maitland stands, frozen, his breath heaving at the wall of his chest.

'C'mon, move it!' Elliott's fierce shout penetrates the waking dream, jerking him abruptly back to life. 'Git on 'cross the goddam ditch, you hear? You want the infantry to have it all?'

The sergeant reloading as he speaks, his harsh face bare of expression, shoving at the men around him until they move at last, floundering on through the shallows and up towards the gaping shell-holes in the stockade. Elliott sets his hammer on a fresh-filled chamber. Looks to the captain, his keen stare questioning.

'I'm obliged to you, Sergeant.' Still gasping for breath, Maitland smiles and starts forward through the bloody wash, the level falling already to his knees. His hand is sweating still, but his grip is steadier than before on the newly-loaded pistol. 'Let's get in there before it's all over, shall we?'

'Sir!' Elliott nods, his problem solved; the captain shaken from his momentary daze. He and Owl Man fall in alongside Maitland as the young officer gains the bank of mud beyond. The din of shots and cries washing back and forth from within the stockade above them.

Climbing, slithering in the thick mud for a hold, Maitland

remembers young Rose. Craig, too, and Moody, floating in the red water beneath. His friends through years of war, now all of them dead. He grips the butt of the pistol, his youthful face hardening in its turn. Once inside, he'll make these renegades remember him.

He gains the top of the bank, the others close behind as he plunges into the shroud of smoke beyond.

Gifford is up with the first wave of infantry as it charges in through the gap. Only the burly figure of Master-Sergeant Hale is ahead of him, shouldering his rifle like the rest. Underfoot the ground is uncertain: ragged from smoking shell-holes, strewn with shards of wood, and the blood-spattered fragments of bodies. Gifford treads on something soft that gives under him, rolling to pitch him down. He's still struggling to get up as the opening ahead of them erupts into a wall of smoke and flame. Gifford stays put, hearing the whine and spat of the volley that lashes into the luckless infantry, slugs and arrows, thudding into unresisting flesh. From where he is, the gunflashes seem to be stabbing at his eyes, blinding him for the moment. Gifford scrambles up, gripping his unfired rifle as the noise of the volley comes racketing back again, seeing as he moves the huge shape of Hale flung sideways and down by the force of close-ranged shots, heavy slugs smashing through him, blasting the body to rags. Other men leaning and toppling down, blouses flowering to an ugly red as arrows and metal hunks strike home, some of them not falling at once, held upright by the weight of men behind them. For a fleeting instant he catches sight of the renegades, crouched back of a makeshift barricade inside the wall, hurrying to reload. In that brief space of time he senses the line of his own men wavering, uncertain under that first, withering fire, their officer and top noncom already downed.

I'm in command of this bunch, Gifford thinks. And with that thought, the hard, cold feeling overcomes him, the need to act conquering his fear.

'Charge!' Gifford yells. Leaps the last of the rubble and the spilled bodies, the rifle with its long bayonet up and poised for the

188

thrust, hearing a baying noise as the bunch of them come after him. Up ahead he can see them plain: a line of blacks and Indians, most of them naked to the waist, reloading ancient guns or setting fresh arrows to their bows. A few, sensing it's too late for a second volley, heft the guns like clubs, or turn aside to reach for axes and cane knives. A lone gun thuds from away to the side, and a private screams and lurches, clasping his shattered arm. Next minute the charge smashes into the flimsy barricade and the brushwood goes scattering down, soldiers leaping the boughs and shards and wielding bayonets and gun-butts at close range.

A thin shape swings up in front of him, a young black kid, his scrawny body half-grown, chopping at him with a curved sickle-blade. Can't be more'n fifteen, Gifford reckons. He goes in fast under the blow, lunging with the bayonet to take the boy high in the throat, all but ripping the head from his body as the kid gurgles and slumps away. Gifford kicks him off the bloodied blade, turns to sidestep the onrush of a second from the right, jarring the butt of his rifle hard into the newcomer's ribs. As the lithe shape folds, he sees the unusual slenderness of belly and flanks, the fullness of the naked breasts.

A woman, the sergeant thinks. Then: dear God!

His assailant turns, grunting, doubled up against the pain of busted ribs. Gifford sees the hate in her dark Indian face as she fights to bring up the long-bladed knife in her hand. Sets himself behind the bayonet as she comes in again. His thrust goes through her at chest height as she flings herself forward, and the body falls limp. Gifford takes a step back, shaking her off from the reeking steel. Turns to spit against the ground.

What in hell we here for? he asks himself in the back of his mind.

'C'mon, you men!' Yelling harder as he drives at the scattering group in front, as if to drown out the questions in his head. 'We got 'em! Give 'em the steel, you hear me?'

Ploughing on as the words leave his lips, striking out viciously at every shape that moves or calls out ahead.

Voorhees stumbles in as the echo of that first volley dies, already gasping for breath, the long-barrelled rifle weighing down his arms. Staggers on a blue-clad rolling body that howls and flinches under his feet. Voorhees retches, swaying to keep his balance. Benton reaching to steady him in the same instant, his dark face half-amused.

'Stay close, Dutchy,' Benton says.

They're into the smoke-hung compound now, mowing into the barricade. It gives way, falling with a smash of brushwood as they trample it underfoot. From the corner of his eye, Voorhees glimpses a white-faced soldier who sags by the wall, blood pumping from an arm blown almost to splinters. Clenches teeth against the lurch of his stomach. Up ahead, two men are fighting to regroup the savages as they fall back, reloading. One, a grizzle-headed black with a strangely twisted shoulder, rams fresh slugs into his shotgun. The other, an old Indian in buckskins, hair flying white about his face, has a fresh arrow laid to his string. Voorhees is on one knee, levelling to shoot, when the shaft whips loose.

'Look out!' Benton calls.

Chokes the same moment, the arrow taking him low in the side. Benton keels over, spitting blood, snapping the shaft with a convulsive movement as he falls. Voorhees half-turns at the sight of his friend, his own shot falling wide, ploughing up the compound dust. In a moment the two old renegades are lost from sight.

'Goddammit! I missed!' A scream of anguish. Voorhees turning, hands gripped white-knuckled on the barrel of the rifle, his pale eyes awash with tears of pain and rage. Schwab is down, kneeling by the dark man, lifting the fallen head, blood running from the corners of the mouth. Benton's glance wavers, searching. Fixes on the upright figure of Voorhees as if to ask some question. Voorhees tries to speak. Chokes, no words coming. The dark eyes of Benton go suddenly wide and staring. The head falls sidelong against the ground.

'He's dead, kid,' Schwab says.

A cry comes back from the fair-haired youth, a savage, wordless, animal noise, midway between a retch and a scream. Voorhees whirls around from them both. Rushes, still yelling, at the thinning numbers of renegades ahead, laughing crazily as the nearest makes to meet him, hefting a clubbed muzzle-load gun.

The young soldier ducks the clumsy blow, stabs low and hard to rip the belly wide open. The first shape goes down howling as he charges on, hacking his rifle-butt against the jaw of the one who follows. Voorhees kills in a red frenzy of hate and loss, barely seeing those who come up against him, feeling them only as a soft-fleshed thump against the point of his bayonet before they fall away.

Last he kills is a young black boy, maybe twelve years old. Kid runs by him through the smoke, howling. Out of his head with the shell-bursts and the stink of death. Voorhees sees him as a flicker of movement coming in from the left. Pivots to drive the bayonet home. This time the high-pitched yelp as the blade guts the child is enough to clear the redness from his eyes. Voorhees stands, looking down on the upturned face of the boy as he whimpers and goes limp. All at once his hands shake so bad he can't hold the rifle no more.

Voorhees sinks to the ground, strength gone out of him like sawdust from a ripped doll. Hands to his face, careless of all about him, he begins to weep.

Gifford swipes with his rifle-butt, and the last figure topples aside. Suddenly there's no-one left to be killed. The ground clear, but for a litter of bodies. The sergeant looks about him, gasping. Peering through the last of the smoke for fresh targets.

We done it, by God, Gifford thinks at last. Still eyeing the twisted forms all around him, he doesn't smile.

Way he figures, it already cost one hell of a lot more'n it was worth.

As they gain the sunlight, he catches a glimpse of the skull tree in the compound, splintered by shellfire, leaning drunkenly to one side. Same time he sees it the tree groans and crashes down, showering white skulls everywhere, the noise of its fall overlain by the howls and shrieks of the old folk and kids who run through the smoke, scared already half to death. Justus grabs tighter on Mary's wrist, searching desperately for a way out. Last of the shells whistling in as he stands, the scream of their fall drowning out all other sounds.

'Down!' the big man yells, pushing her to the ground and lying over her as the compound bucks and shudders beneath the force of the blast. Back of them the long house flies apart in a blossom of flame, smoke palling up and out as the debris rains down. Flat to the earth, Justus flinches as a wood hunk slaps down on his shoulder. Tries not to think of himself back in there, under the shell. Mary's dazed, frightened look answers the question in his eyes. The big man swallows, helping her up with him as he scrambles to his feet, still holding the fresh-loaded pistol.

From here he kin see the blue soljers as they pour in through gaps in the wall, smashing the brush barricades aside, bayonets and gun-butts going in as the last of Shango's fighters reel back under the onslaught. Soldier he sees, and 'Gator Head, struggling to hold them together as more blue-clad figures charge in after the rest. Not a hope now! They lost here, for sure.

Got to git out from here, Justus thinks.

He's turned half around, aiming for the far side of the compound, when Mary screams out from beside him. Justus whirls as the massive black figure of the goddess bulks up in his path, knowing as the thick-bladed gleam of the knife comes hissing towards his head, that he's already too late. For in that brief, hideous span of time, he's seen her broad face pushed close, the bared grin that creases her flesh, smelt the sour stink of her enormous, sweating body. Even as he ducks away, some other shape drives in by him, hard and fast, hitting low for the gut. Mama Odu rocks back, stopped in her tracks, as the leaf-bladed spear ploughs through her below the breasts, the shaft following the iron shank, sinking in to half its length with an ugly, sucking sound. The huge black woman grunts, blood bubbles at her lips in a dark foam. Leans, collapsing. Justus stands back as the huge bulk of her thuds against the ground, still quivering as her mouth puddles blood into the earth.

'The god fail!' Heron gasps. He straightens up, blood running from the blade of his spear, spattering in the dirt, as he pulls it free. Back of him Jewel kneels swiftly, her cane knife hissing down towards the black bulk on the ground. At the second blow the head of Mama Odu rolls loose in a spout of blood, and Mary turns away with her hand over her mouth. Justus stays where he is,

192

fighting to hold back a shudder, sweat pearling him in another skin as he meets the fierce stare of the spearman.

'You took Shango, looks like,' Heron says. His dark stare marks the bigger man with respect, wary for once. 'Could be the god in you, after all. Best you should run now, you hear me?'

Meeting that stare, Justus forces himself to nod in answer, seeing Jewel rise to join her brother, the knife in her hand fouled and thick with blood. Feeling too the glowing hunger of her eyes turned upon him.

'Thanks, Heron,' Justus says at last. 'Like you say, we gonna run—if we can.'

More of the whites pouring in at the stockade as he speaks. Looks like the cavalry they ambushed a while back, this time without their horses. He sees Lawrence, too, heading his dismounted riders, the bunch of them yelling like crazy as they fire into anything that moves. Justus swears once, savagely, then turns to plunge back into the gathering shell-smoke. In that last moment he sees the planter halt in the middle of the compound, level his gun on an old hobbling nigger, and fire. With the crash of the shot the oldster tumbles down.

'Oh, no!' Mary sobbing as she runs with him, coughing in the smoke. 'No—those poor people!'

Justus running, snarling harsh in his throat, rage inside threatening to bust again any time. Ain't it what you expected, white gal? Ain't this the way they use us—*always*? No more to it fer them than a turkey-shoot, ain't that so? Wanting to shout it, but memories crowding up to stifle the words—memories of Shango, and Mama Odu. The rage gutters, seething somewhere in the pit of his belly. He takes hold of Mary's hands. Makes at a run for where daylight shows through a gap smashed in the far wall of the stockade.

Others running with them into the smoke, away from the blue death of thrusts and clubbing blows. Heron and Jewel, and the rest of those who still live and can run.

Not many of them, all the same. Shango's people lost heavy from the first, and now the soljers are inside, ain't nothin' gonna be left.

*

Inside the stockade, the fire slackens, only the occasional gunshot blasting amid the sparse scatter of arrows in flight. Maitland comes in through a breach in the wall, kicking down a charred stake in his path that showers him with blackened fragments. In front of him, the compound seethes in turmoil, panic-stricken figures fleeing in all directions as the infantry push on over the broken barricades. Smoke drifts from the holes formed by the shells, screening the running shapes from sight before it lifts again. The captain leaps the rubble in the opening. Stands in the cleared space, drawing breath. Back of him come Elliott and the Cherokee tracker, holding his bloody knife, then the men of his troop. Over to the right, Lawrence and Whiteside head another rush through the broken wall.

An arrow sings viciously past his head, thudding in the wall beyond. Maitland turns to bring up the gun in his hand. Across from him a few of the renegades are regrouping for what looks like a last stand. Two oldsters head the bunch, a stooped-over black with a shotgun, and a white-haired Indian. Both of them look way too old for the job. Even as he sees them, the group gets off a ragged volley, the noise echoing sullenly back from the walls. To the right of him a trooper clutches at a feathered shaft sunk in his chest, falls backward without a sound. Further over, the old buck's shotgun blasts out, sending one of Lawrence's riders spinning to earth. Maitland yells in answer, sets running forward, taking aim as he does so on the hump-shouldered figure behind the shotgun.

The old man is hurrying to reload, jamming his loads into the breach. Up close, his skin has a greyish tinge. In the moment before he fires, the renegade lifts his head, and Maitland is met by the hostile glare of a single eye, green and strange in the darkness of the face. He pulls the trigger, the gun kicking back at his palm. Soldier hunches, flung back and around by the force of the slug. Drops the long gun as a shot from Elliott smashes his shoulder. Tight-lipped, Maitland fires a third time. Watches as the grey head dissolves to a blur of red. Soldier pitches away to the ground, thin arms outflung as if to clutch at the earth beneath him. At once the group of renegades wavers, breaking apart.

'Nigra bastards!' Whiteside's high-pitched whoop brings his

head around. The fat man's own shotgun lifts, blasting with both barrels into the midst of the savages who are left. The main force of the charge hits 'Gator Head, blowing him to ruin at the waist. The old Indian goes down, his upper body leaning raggedly askew from the blast. Back of him a young Choctaw buck rolls in the dirt screaming and clawing at his shattered legs. Whiteside yells again, grinning. Breaks open the gun to reload in haste. In front of them those renegades still standing throw down their weapons and start to run.

'Kill 'em! Kill every last one of the black, murderin' scum!' Lawrence stands, his lean-lipped face harsh and merciless. Maitland doesn't care overmuch for the mad-dog glare in his eyes. The planter brings up his pistol, aiming at a shape that hobbles uncertainly through the smoke. With the boom of the shot the man flops over, face-down to the earth. Back of Lawrence the rest are storming in, yelling like madmen as they look for targets. Jared he sees, and Hooker, and Clayt Green. Anything that moves is fair game to them, it seems. Maitland sees Hooker gun down an unarmed black woman who stands in the compound looking dazedly about her, making no attempt to move until the shot slams her over. The hammer of gunfire tears down most of the running hostiles, men and women alike. Lawrence and the others pour more shots into the bodies as they writhe on the ground. Somewhere at the edge of vision the figure of a child emerges through the smoke, wobbling uncertainly on its feet, hands up as it howls. Green levels on it with a barrage of shots, emptying his gun. Throwing the small shape down like a rag doll, thudding loosely to earth.

'My God!' Maitland breathes. All at once, he feels sick at what he sees.

'Mister Lawrence!' At his shout the planter turns, lowering his smoking gun.

Something in the younger man's voice warns him, the hatred giving way to a wary, questioning look. Seeing the half-crazed faces of the men beyond him, Maitland fights to keep back the sickening pulse of anger in his gut.

'Mister Lawrence, that's enough! Your men will hold their fire! This force is not at war with noncombatants. Am I understood?'

The dark man meets his gaze sullenly, his eyes narrow and harder than before. Back of him, Whiteside and the rest deliberately reload their guns.

'These here are savages we're dealin' with, Capten,' Lawrence says, lips drawing back to show his teeth. 'Young 'uns grow jes' the same, I reckon . . . You ain't forgettin' the plantations they hit before, are you, sir?'

At his back the troop have ceased firing. Now they look to him, waiting for the word. Maitland feels his hands clench hard at his sides. For a moment he struggles against the urge to grab Lawrence and throttle the life out of him with those same bare hands.

'While on this expedition, you are under *my* orders, Mister Lawrence.' The voice of the captain grates harshly, his eyes as pale and chill as ice. 'You would do well to carry out such instructions as I choose to give . . .'

'And if we don't?' Lawrence glares back into his face, pushing as hard as he dares.

Maitland glances to the sergeant. Elliott nods, stony-faced. His own pistol is up and levelled on the planter's belly. Beyond him the rest of the troop fan out to either side, their guns lined. Maitland's muzzle fixes on the fat gut of Whiteside. Right now he doesn't trust himself to point it Lawrence's way.

'You have your answer, Mister Lawrence,' the officer says coldly. 'Have your men holster their firearms. Further bloodshed is to be avoided at all costs.'

Recalling his own fierce hatred as he speaks, he feels his face grow hot in sudden shame. Lawrence's thin face twists, the teeth biting hard together. The planter sheathes his gun, the men behind him murmuring sullenly as they follow suit. Whiteside scowls, lets fall his shotgun to the ground. Maitland breathes out, slowly.

'Thank you, sir,' the captain says.

As the words leave him, he catches sight of two running figures in the smoke. A man and a woman, crossing a stretch of open ground between two rows of blazing huts. With a sudden jolt of recognition, Maitland sees that one of them is the big, bush-haired negro who took part in the ambush in which Rose and Craig were killed. Sight of the other sets him frowning harder. From here, it looks like a blonde white woman in a soiled print dress. She and the black running together, hand in hand.

He sees the change in Lawrence's darkening features out of the corner of his eye. The captain dives hurriedly in, claws down the gun before Lawrence pulls the trigger. The shot roars in to the ground, Maitland chopping his own weapon down on the planter's wrist in a blow that unlocks the fingers. The pistol drops, Lawrence nursing his hand as he looks again down the barrel of Elliott's levelled gun.

'Hold your fire!' Maitland calls out to the men behind him. 'He has a white woman with him!'

No sooner are the running pair glimpsed than the smoke swallows them afresh and they vanish as if they had never been. Maitland sighs, holsters his gun.

'Round up the prisoners, Sergeant,' the officer says. 'And see what can be done for the wounded—ours and theirs. It appears that the fighting is over, at least.'

'Sir!' Elliott salutes. Turns, holstering his gun. Some of the other troopers follow him, glancing towards the blue-clad bodies for any signs of life. Taggart he sees, the tall man looking his way for an instant. Meeting his eyes, Maitland reads in them the same sick emptiness that lodges in his gut. After a while, the trooper moves away.

Thank God he's alive at least, Maitland thinks.

He looks out over the compound to where Sergeant Gifford leads his infantry among the bodies that litter the open ground— mostly renegades, with here and there a tell-tale blue uniform splotched with blood. Death everywhere, it seems. Hale's mangled corpse in the gap of the stockade wall. Infantry fallen outside the breach. Men of his own troop, shot down in the last minutes of fighting. Dully, he thinks of Moody in the ditch. Of Pfister, who must have been killed in the rush up the slope. Of his friends killed in that first ambush. Right now, he can't muster too much sympathy for Lawrence and his kind.

A handful of their enemies wait, huddled together in the middle of the compound—less than twenty, from the look of it, most of them young children or women, or wounded. Some of the wounds are horrifying enough. One man lies glaring up at him, holding the flesh closed over a jagged rent in his belly, his mouth already bloody, the dark eyes harsh and without hope, waiting for death. Behind him, the faces of the rest hold the same, dull defiance. All of them gone beyond pity or hope, resigned to death or chains. Empty of feeling.

Maitland shakes his head, checking a sudden surge of grief that threatens at the back of his eyes. He turns from the silent prisoners to the mounds of dead, black and red alike, torn and mangled by bayonets or shell splinters. Somewhere away to the left, Private Voorhees sits weeping helplessly by the young boy he has just killed. Further on Private Schwab, the Iowa farmer, has turned away to vomit on the ground.

So much wasted for nothing, the captain thinks. Then, more bitterly: what the hell are we doing here?

He frowns, peering ahead into the black, drifting smoke, but finds no answer there.

'Reckon we safe now,' Justus says.

Sinks his pole in one last time, the pirogue driving through reeds and water to beach itself in the mud. The big man steps ashore, black mire claiming him ankle-deep as he turns to lift her after him. Mary makes the leap, clings to him a moment, her white arms at his neck, the two of them standing that way for a time; Justus holding her to him with her blonde head rested on his breast.

Two other pirogues knifing through the shallows of the lagoon, headed towards them. Three was all the boats they could find this side of the stockade, away from the soldiers. Those on the near side would have been stove in before the attack. Justus eyes the narrow prows as they cut the surface, the greenish wake spilling away to either side. Heron in the nearest of them, coming upright behind his bloodied spear as the craft beaches. Jewel crouches at his back, and behind her, a tall black lets go the pole. The second boat has two Choctaw youths and a black girl whose hair is covered with a blue headtie. Four men. Two women. Eight with Mary and himself. The only ones to get free from the stockade.

The big man stands watching as Heron and his sister come

198

ashore, the others following. His glance measures the bunch of them thoughtfully, gauging each in turn. All young and fit, all but the black girl holding weapons. Knives and spears, but no guns. Justus sighs inwardly, turns his head to meet the black, questing gaze of Heron.

'We headed fer the brakes,' Heron says, studying the face of the man above him. 'Somehow, we gonna make out . . . All we need someone to give word, you read my meanin'?'

'You tell it, we do like you say,' Jewel puts in from beside him, her eyes on him still, searching.

Justus shakes his head in answer. 'Thanks,' the big man says. 'We got our own trail to keep, I reckon.'

For a while brother and sister stay where they are, the two of them eyeing him in silence. Finally Heron nods.

'Have it your way,' the dark spearman says. Turns, shrugging his thin shoulders. 'Let's go, Jewel.'

He steps away through the reeds, moving with the familiar long-legged, birdlike walk, some of the others going on after him. Jewel stands for a moment, not moving.

'Goodbye, Justus,' the woman says.

His look stays with her as she too turns away, following the path of her brother, waist-deep among the reeds. Before long the group of them are lost to sight.

Over on the island, the sunlight welters in blood beyond the burning stockade. No sounds of shooting now. Only the black, thick-rolling smoke, hiding the place from view across the water, sole monument to the fall of Shango and his kingdom.

Justus eyes the smoke-pall a while, not speaking. Was a prison for him and Mary both, once. Now, he ain't so sure. In his mind, he recalls faces of the dead: Red Wolf, Diamond, Cedar, Crow Feather . . . Yeah, an' Soldier, an' old 'Gator Head. They must be dead, too, he figures. Soldier was somethin' like to a friend, back there. Inwardly he finds himself missing that face with its twisted grin, the one-eyed stare and humped shoulder with its scars.

God damn, Soldier. You wasn't so bad. How come they have to git you a–tall?

Memory of his own killing rouses only hollowness in the pit of his belly. Three men down to him, he knows. Munson, Sims,

199

Shango. Right now it don't grieve him none. He don't hardly feel it. Just somethin' had to be done, he figures. While he ain't over-proud of it, he cain't say he's sorry neither. Sooner them lie dead than him or Mary.

He sees again the lean-fleshed face of Lawrence behind the gun, snarling as his shot tore down the hobbling old man, and feels a sudden spurt of anger like fire through the veins. Yeah, an' the blue-coat soljers with him, blazin' away at anythin' that moved. Men, women or kids. God damn them to hell, the white bastards.

He bites hard on his lip, fists clenched on his rage.

'White folks, I hate 'em all,' Justus says.

Checking himself almost as he speaks. Watching her as she turns towards him. Blue of her eyes brimming wet, the marks of tears already on her freckled cheeks.

'Me too?' Mary asks.

At sight of her, the big man sighs. Shakes his bushy head. Almost wearily, he lifts one dark hand to touch her face gently, feeling the warmth of her tears at his finger-tips. After a time he smiles.

'Let's go, gal,' Justus says. 'Got a ways to travel, I reckon.'

He turns, his hand rested on her shoulder as she moves with him, the two of them stepping away into the tall reedbeds, treading the black mud that squelches underfoot, clinging to them ankle-deep. Presently the reeds close back of them, and there is quiet.

Beyond, the sun sinks westward, bloodying the surface of the lagoon.

EXCERPT FROM REPORT OF CAPTAIN JAMES A. MAITLAND ON THE ACTION AT THE STOCKADE, SEPTEMBER 30th, 1865.

'... OUR FORCES ENCOUNTERED A COSTLY INITIAL SETBACK WHEN MY OWN TROOP AND A PARTY OF CIVILIANS UNDER MR LAWRENCE OF SWEET RIVER AND SHERIFF WHITESIDE WERE TAKEN IN AMBUSH BY THE RENEGADES. THIS SKIRMISH TOOK THE LIVES OF FIVE TROOPERS, AND FOUR OF THE CIVILIANS. THREE HORSES WERE ALSO LOST, TWO OF THEM PROPERTY OF THE ARMY...

... THE RENEGADE STRONGHOLD WAS SUBJECTED TO A BOMBARDMENT BY OUR COMPLEMENT OF TWO NINE-POUNDER GUNS, ABLY SUPERVISED BY SGT RIORDAN. A CROSSING WAS THEN MADE, USING IMPROVISED RAFTS, BY THE MAIN BODY OF THE EXPEDITION. THIS COMPRISING MY DISMOUNTED TROOP UNDER SGT ELLIOTT, THE INFANTRY COMPANY LED BY LT PFISTER, AND MR LAWRENCE'S VIGILANTES. ONE RAFT WAS SUNK BY CATAPULT FIRE CLOSE TO SHORE WITH THE LOSS OF FIVE INFANTRYMEN KILLED. THREE OTHER MEN WERE INJURED IN THE SAME INCIDENT. THE ATTACKING PARTY THEN STORMED THE FORTIFIED STOCKADE. AT THIS POINT LT PFISTER AND AN INFANTRY PRIVATE WERE KILLED BY FIRE FROM A SHARPSHOOTER IN THE TREES ALONG THE SLOPE...

... THE STOCKADE ITSELF HAD BEEN THOROUGHLY DEVASTATED BY ARTILLERY FIRE, BUT IN SPITE OF THE LOSSES ALREADY SUFFERED BY THE RENEGADES, RESISTANCE WAS DETERMINED. IN THE COURSE OF CROSSING A DEFENSIVE DITCH AROUND THE PERIMETER OF THE WALL, FRAGMENTS OF FLESH WERE OBSERVED IN THE WATER. I HAVE TO REPORT THAT WE WERE THAT MOMENT ATTACKED BY A BULL SHARK, A CREATURE WHICH MY INDIAN TRACKER INFORMS ME IS FOUND ALONG THE ATCHAFALAYA RIVER FROM TIME TO TIME. THE FISH KILLED TROOPER MOODY BEFORE WE WERE ABLE TO DESPATCH IT WITH FIRE FROM OUR SIDEARMS...

... ONCE INSIDE THE BREACHES MADE IN THE WALL, THERE WAS FIERCE FIGHTING FOR A TIME. MASTER-SGT HALE AND SEVEN INFANTRYMEN WERE LOST, WITH OTHERS WOUNDED, ONE MAN SUFFERING A SHATTERED ARM WHICH WAS SUBSEQUENTLY

AMPUTATED. SGT GIFFORD PROMPTLY TOOK OVER LEADERSHIP OF THE COMPANY, BREAKING THE HOSTILES IN HIS SECTOR WITH GREAT RESOLUTION. I MYSELF LOST A CAVALRY TROOPER KILLED, AND ANOTHER OF MR LAWRENCE'S CIVILIANS. AT THIS POINT THE RENEGADES WERE BROKEN WITH CONSIDERABLE LOSS OF LIFE. I MYSELF, WITH THE ASSISTANCE OF SGT ELLIOTT, SHOT DOWN ONE OF THEIR LEADERS, A ONE-EYED NEGRO KNOWN TO THEM AS 'SOLDIER', WHO HAD ALREADY BEEN RESPONSIBLE FOR THE DEATHS OF SEVERAL MEMBERS OF THE EXPEDITION. A CHOCTAW BY THE NAME OF 'GATOR HEAD WAS KILLED BY SHERIFF WHITESIDE...

...FROM ACCOUNTS BY SURVIVORS OF THE MASSACRES AT BLACKWATER AND WILLOW BEND, MY OWN ESTIMATE OF ENEMY NUMBERS WOULD BE SOMEWHERE IN THE REGION OF A HUNDRED, OF WHOM POSSIBLY ONE QUARTER WERE NONCOMBATANTS. AS IN MANY CASES WOMEN FOUGHT ALONGSIDE THE MEN WITH GREAT FEROCITY; THE CATEGORIES WERE OFTEN HARD TO DISTINGUISH. THE MEN UNDER MY COMMAND WERE OBLIGED TO DEFEND THEMSELVES AT ALL TIMES. IF AS A RESULT NOT ONLY MALE RENEGADES WERE KILLED, THIS WAS REGRETTABLY UNAVOIDABLE IN THE CIRCUMSTANCES. IN ANY EVENT, ONLY EIGHT HOSTILES WERE SEEN TO ESCAPE, AND SEVENTEEN WERE TAKEN PRISONER. FROM THE BODIES SINCE BURIED, AND THE FRAGMENTS LEFT FROM SHELLFIRE, I WOULD SUPPOSE THAT AT LEAST SEVENTY OF THESE PEOPLE PAID FOR THEIR CRIMES WITH THE ULTIMATE PENALTY. OF THESE, MAYBE HALF DIED AS A RESULT OF THE BOMBARDMENT FROM OUR GUNS. I REGRET TO REPORT THAT A NUMBER OF NONCOMBATANTS WERE KILLED BY MR LAWRENCE AND HIS CIVILIANS ONCE THE PLACE WAS TAKEN, AND AS A RESULT I TOOK IT UPON MYSELF TO DISARM HIM AND HIS FELLOWS. RESPONSIBILITY FOR THIS ACTION IS MINE ALONE, AND I AM MORE THAN WILLING TO ANSWER ANY CHARGE WHICH MAY BE BROUGHT AGAINST ME ON THESE GROUNDS...

...AMONG THE BODIES WE DISCOVERED THE CORPSE OF A NEGRESS KNOWN AS 'THE GODDESS' OR 'MAMA ODU', WHO WAS NAMED AS A LEADER IN THE PLANTATION ATTACKS. THE MAN ANSWERING TO THE NAME OF 'SHANGO' OR 'THE GOD' WAS NOT FOUND, ALTHOUGH PRISONERS INFORMED US THAT HE HAD

BEEN KILLED BY A RIVAL LEADER PRIOR TO OUR ENTRY. IT IS POSSIBLE THAT THE REMNANTS OF HIS BODY WERE SEEN IN THE WATER BEFORE THE SHARK ATTACKED US, AS IT APPEARS THAT SHANGO KEPT THE BEAST IN A SECRET PLACE AND REGULARLY FED IT WITH HUMAN VICTIMS. BEARING THIS IN MIND, ONE CAN FEEL LITTLE SYMPATHY FOR THE MANNER OF THIS CRIMINAL'S END, WHICH SEEMS A FITTING PUNISHMENT. THE MAN ALLEGED TO HAVE KILLED HIM IS THE RENEGADE JUSTUS, WHO TOOK PART IN THE AMBUSH AND WAS SEEN TO MURDER TWO OF MR LAWRENCE'S COMPANIONS. HE FLED THE PLACE AS WE ATTACKED, TAKING WITH HIM A WHITE WOMAN BELIEVED TO BE MRS MARY KIMBALL, KNOWN TO HAVE BEEN ABDUCTED BY THIS DESPERADO SOME MONTHS BEFORE. I REGRET TO SAY THAT THEY AND SIX OTHERS ELUDED OUR EFFORTS AT CAPTURE, AND MUST STILL BE AT LARGE...

...I HAVE DELIVERED THE PRISONERS TO THE AUTHORITIES AS REQUESTED. IN SPITE OF THE CRIMES FOR WHICH THEY WERE IN PART RESPONSIBLE, I MUST ADMIT TO BEING MOVED BY THE PLIGHT OF THESE WRETCHES. MORE THAN HALF ARE WOMEN, SEVERAL ARE WOUNDED, AND ALL WERE IN A PITIFUL STATE WHEN CAPTURED, AFTER PUTTING UP A SPIRITED RESISTANCE. IT IS NO LONGER MY AFFAIR, I KNOW, BUT IT IS TO BE HOPED THAT IN THEIR CASE JUSTICE WILL BE TEMPERED WITH MERCY. FOR ALL WE KNOW, THESE SAVAGES MAY BE AS MUCH SINNED AGAINST AS SINNING...

...I WISH TO COMMEND THE SOLDIERS UNDER MY COMMAND FOR THEIR COURAGE AND SPIRIT IN THIS DIFFICULT ACTION. IN PARTICULAR I WOULD LIKE TO PLACE ON RECORD THE STERLING SERVICE OF SGTS ELLIOTT, RIORDAN AND GIFFORD, EACH OF WHOM WAS A MAINSTAY IN THE SUCCESS OF OUR ATTACK. LT PFISTER LED GALLANTLY IN THE STORMING OF THE STOCKADE, AND IS DESERVING OF INDIVIDUAL MENTION, THOUGH SUCH PRAISE IS SADLY NO SUBSTITUTE FOR THE LOSS OF A GOOD AND RESPECTED OFFICER. OWL MAN, OUR TRACKER, PROVED EMINENTLY USEFUL IN TRACING THE HOSTILES TO THEIR BASE. AS FOR MYSELF, I HOPE I OBEYED THE ORDERS GIVEN ME TO THE LETTER. IF SOME CIVILIANS HAD TO BE RESTRAINED, THE ARMY THANKFULLY NEED NOT TAKE THE BLAME FOR THEIR ACTIONS...

...I HOPE THAT AS AN OFFICER OF FIVE YEARS' STANDING I KNOW MY DUTY. I FEEL BOUND TO STATE THAT IN ALL OF MY WARTIME SERVICE I HAVE NEVER ENCOUNTERED SUCH A DISAGREEABLE AND DISTURBING TASK, NOR ONE THAT HAS COST SO MANY GOOD MENS' LIVES SEEMINGLY TO SO LITTLE PURPOSE. AS A SOLDIER IT IS FOR ME TO OBEY ORDERS, BUT I CANNOT HELP BUT SAY HERE THAT I TRUST AND PRAY SUCH AN EXPEDITION DOES NOT COME MY WAY AGAIN...

JAMES A. MAITLAND
CAPTAIN, UNITED STATES ARMY
SEPT 30th, 1865.

How Justus and Mary fared in the big thicket of Texas, and how he went back to Sweet River to settle with Lawrence, are told in the third volume of this trilogy.

Book Tokens

**Give them
the pleasure of choosing**

Book Tokens can be bought
and exchanged at most
bookshops in Great Britain
and Ireland.

NEL BESTSELLERS

T51277	'THE NUMBER OF THE BEAST'	*Robert Heinlein*	£2.25
T50777	STRANGER IN A STRANGE LAND	*Robert Heinlein*	£1.75
T51382	FAIR WARNING	*Simpson & Burger*	£1.75
T52478	CAPTAIN BLOOD	*Michael Blodgett*	£1.75
T50246	THE TOP OF THE HILL	*Irwin Shaw*	£1.95
T49620	RICH MAN, POOR MAN	*Irwin Shaw*	£1.60
T51609	MAYDAY	*Thomas H. Block*	£1.75
T54071	MATCHING PAIR	*George G. Gilman*	£1.50
T45773	CLAIRE RAYNER'S LIFEGUIDE		£2.50
T53709	PUBLIC MURDERS	*Bill Granger*	£1.75
T53679	THE PREGNANT WOMAN'S BEAUTY BOOK	*Gloria Natale*	£1.25
T49817	MEMORIES OF ANOTHER DAY	*Harold Robbins*	£1.95
T50807	79 PARK AVENUE	*Harold Robbins*	£1.75
T50149	THE INHERITORS	*Harold Robbins*	£1.75
T53231	THE DARK	*James Herbert*	£1.50
T43245	THE FOG	*James Herbert*	£1.50
T53296	THE RATS	*James Herbert*	£1.50
T45528	THE STAND	*Stephen King*	£1.75
T50874	CARRIE	*Stephen King*	£1.50
T51722	DUNE	*Frank Herbert*	£1.75
T52575	THE MIXED BLESSING	*Helen Van Slyke*	£1.75
T38602	THE APOCALYPSE	*Jeffrey Konvitz*	95p

NEL P.O. BOX 11, FALMOUTH TR10 9EN, CORNWALL

Postage Charge:
U.K. Customers 45p for the first book plus 20p for the second book and 14p for each additional book ordered to a maximum charge of £1.63.

B.F.P.O. & EIRE Customers 45p for the first book plus 20p for the second book and 14p for the next 7 books; thereafter 8p per book.

Overseas Customers 75p for the first book and 21p per copy for each additional book.

Please send cheque or postal order (no currency).

Name ....

Address ....

....

Title ....

While every effort is made to keep prices steady, it is sometimes necessary to increase prices at short notice. New English Library reserve the right to show on covers and charge new retail prices which may differ from those advertised in the text or elsewhere.(7)